FOUR FOR THE ROAD

FOUR FOR THE ROAD

K.J. REILLY

 New York   London   Toronto   Sydney   New Delhi

𝒜
atheneum

An imprint of Simon & Schuster Children's Publishing Division

1230 Avenue of the Americas, New York, New York 10020

For information about special discounts for bulk purchases, please contact Simon & Schuster Special Sales at 1-866-506-1949 or business@simonandschuster.com.

The Simon & Schuster Speakers Bureau can bring authors to your live event. For more information or to book an event, contact the Simon & Schuster Speakers Bureau at 1-866-248-3049 or visit our website at www.simonspeakers.com.

Interior design by Karyn Lee

The text for this book was set in Rotis Serif Pro.

Manufactured in the United States of America

First Edition

10 9 8 7 6 5 4 3 2 1

Library of Congress Cataloging-in-Publication Data

Names: Reilly, K. J. (Writer of young adult fiction), author.

Title: Four for the road / K.J. Reilly.

Description: First edition. | New York : Atheneum Books for Young Readers, 2022. | Audience: Ages 14 up. | Audience: Grades 10-12. | Summary: "When seventeen-year-old Asher embarks on a road trip from New Jersey to Graceland to get revenge on the drunk driver who killed his mom, he brings along three new friends from his bereavement groups"— Provided by publisher.

Identifiers: LCCN 2021032650 | ISBN 9781665902281 (hardcover) | ISBN 9781665902304 (paperback) | ISBN 9781665902311 (ebook)

Subjects: CYAC: Grief—Fiction. | Self-help groups—Fiction. | Automobile travel—Fiction. | Forgiveness—Fiction. | Memphis (Tenn.)—Fiction. | LCGFT: Novels.

Classification: LCC PZ7.1.R4553 Fo 2022 | DDC [Fic]—dc23

LC record available at https://lccn.loc.gov/2021032650

For all the dandelions looking for a crack in the concrete;
and for the sweet peas who know to hold on

1

My mom died and everyone says that I'm not handling it well.

I would think that if I *was* handling it well, that would be the time to worry. Like if I was going to parties and having friends over and acting normal, because no one should act normal when things are not normal. I mean that would be like watching TV when the house is burning because you forgot to shut the oven off which I only did once. Not because I wanted to die or didn't care that the house was on fire—it was just that I really didn't notice on account of the fact that my mom died and that made me not notice things. But just about everyone found that hard to believe, especially the firemen because they said that when they found me there was so much smoke in the house that I couldn't see the TV and I was still sitting there staring at it anyway.

Okay, so my mom died twelve months three weeks one day six hours and fourteen minutes ago and some people think that I should be better by now and not burning down the house and maybe I should be smiling sometimes and speaking more and going to parties and because that's not happening I ended up at the Bergen County Hospital Center on Monday night at seven thirty in Room

212 which is on the second floor just turn right past the vending machines and the restrooms on the left.

Inside Room 212 there's a circle of chairs and boxes of tissues and a coffee setup with Styrofoam cups and cookies with swirls of chocolate on them and everyone here is seventy or eighty or a hundred years old except for me so it's weirder than I thought it would be and it makes me really sad to be here, even sadder than I was before I showed up, especially when one of the really old guys named Henry starts to cry when he tells us about his wife of fifty years and probably four weeks three days fourteen minutes and thirty-two seconds or something like that. I look at him—we all look at him—as he gets up to speak and a wisp of cotton for hair hovers like a cloud over his head and his lip quivers. He says her name is Evelyn and she has blue eyes the color of the sky in Montana in winter and then he says that they went on a whale watch in Nova Scotia for their fortieth wedding anniversary and grow sweet peas and tomatoes in their backyard and she saved up sleeping pills and then he helped her mash them up in chocolate pudding so she could go peacefully and on her own terms when she was ready and I'm thinking I'll never come back to Room 212.

When Henry's finished talking, the moderator who has short blond hair and freckles on her cheeks and looks like Peter Pan except without the green tights turns right to me and says, "Do you want to say anything or introduce yourself to the group or tell us who you lost?" And I say, "No." Then she says, "Please," so I say, "I lost my mom."

Then it gets all quiet, last-man-on-Earth, apocalypse quiet, until Peter Pan says, "I'm so sorry. How did she die?" and I say, "Me. I killed her."

That completely sucks the air out of the room and shocks Peter

Pan and now all the old people look even more concave and shriveled than they did before I said it but Henry at least stops crying and everyone looks at me with their sunken old-people eyes like I am a monstrosity of unprecedented proportion or one of the great Horrors of the Western World and then they turn away and stare at their feet because people don't like to look at murderers especially if they killed their mom. For the longest time it just stays all quiet and nobody eats cookies or drinks coffee and Peter Pan doesn't know what to say so she just sits there like the rest of them and I feel even worse than I did before I came into Room 212. I mean I have no idea why I said that I killed my mom because my mom died in a car accident and I wasn't driving or in the car with her or texting her or yelling at her on the phone and I wasn't the drunk driver of the eighteen-wheel tractor trailer that hit her either.

The words

Me.

I.

Killed.

Her.

just came out and now they are sitting there like a disgusting amorphous thing in the middle of the room and I can't take them back or rewind my mouth or cover them up so I just stand up and leave Room 212 and head for the elevator which is left past the vending machines and the restrooms on the right.

Peter Pan–without–the–green–tights runs out after me and finds me punching the down button to the elevator over and over again and says, "Please wait."

I say, "I should probably just leave because I upset everyone, especially Henry who doesn't need to be any more upset than he already is."

Peter Pan says, "Please don't go. I'd really like you to come back inside. We all would."

I smash the down button again and say, "If Henry dies of a heart attack brought on by shock and extreme sadness tonight it will be my fault and I'll have to come back on Wednesday and tell all the other old people that I killed him, too."

"Look," Peter Pan says, "we have a group for teens that meets on Tuesdays and Thursdays that you would probably like better than the Monday-Wednesday group."

"Will you be there?" I ask, and before she can answer I add, "Wait, that doesn't make sense, 'cause kids my age are too young to have lost someone," and she says, "I know you've lost your mom, and I can't imagine how hard that must be, but you're not the only one. And yes, I'll be there."

I look at her pixie hair and freckles and nice smile and she says, "Losing someone you love at a young age happens more than you think," so I say, "Okay, maybe I'll come back tomorrow."

Then Peter Pan tries to give me a hug and I get all awkward and kind of tense up and pull away and then I feel even worse but she says, "Whatever you are feeling is okay, and we will work with you to make it better," and I want to tell her that what I'm feeling *isn't* okay at all because if it was okay it wouldn't feel this bad and my dad wouldn't have had to sign me up for this group, but instead I ask, "How? How will you make me feel better?"

She says, "One step at a time," and smiles.

Her smile is just one of those things that makes you feel better even though you're soaking wet and freezing cold and were just struck by lightning and are probably going to die any minute. So when the elevator door finally pings and slides wide open with a slurpy electronic hiss, I don't step inside because Peter Pan is standing there with this hopeful, expectant look on her face and it's like the sun just peeked out when it's raining.

She's quiet for a minute and then she smiles again and says, "Let's go back inside."

Her voice is soft—mom-talking-to-little-kid soft—and she doesn't have a big bright smile. It's more of a trust-me-on-this-one smile which is just the right amount of smile under the circumstances so I say, "Okay."

So, here I am. Staring at my feet slapping against the shiny, slime-green linoleum on the second floor of the Bergen County Hospital Center as I walk back to Room 212 with Peter Pan walking right next to me. When I steal a glance over at her, she looks happy—like, found-one-of-the-Lost-Boys happy—so at least that's something.

As soon as we sit down we go around the circle again and everyone except for me and Henry introduces themselves and says who they lost and how they're doing—which is not good or they wouldn't be here—and then Henry picks up right where he left off like I never said a thing about me killing my mom. He tells us the whole point of his life was to take care of Evelyn and then it gets so quiet and so uncomfortable again that it sounds and feels like it would if you were standing in a morgue waiting to identify a body. I mean, it's almost as bad as when I said I killed my mom because everyone in Room 212 knows that Henry is going to die any second because he just told us that the whole reason he is living is Evelyn, and Evelyn is gone.

And we all know what that means.

Because if you are living a life that no longer has purpose it tends to end in a hurry.

Then Peter Pan uses her gentle mom voice to get a couple more people to talk and all of them still have reasons to live like book groups and fishing trips and Labrador retrievers and grandchildren and when they're finished talking Peter Pan says, "We're done for tonight," and everyone starts grabbing their things and there are a few coughs and the sound of chairs being pushed back but mostly it's quiet. Two of the really old people who have aluminum walkers for legs and the crooked backs of old bent trees hobble to the snack table and stuff some cookies into their pockets, and then the rest of the group shuffles to the door all gangly and hunched over like their limbs are the branches of the weeping willows in the park at the end of my street. I stand up with a jolt and rush to the elevator trying not to knock anyone over on my way out and trying not to think about me or my mom, or about Henry being dead.

I smash the down button on the elevator and when the doors slide open I step inside and stare at my sneakers grateful that the car is empty because at this point even saying hello to someone would be too hard.

They might smile or say hi and I wouldn't be able to say hi back because what would be the point?

I'm just the weird kid who never smiles 'cause his mom died twelve months three weeks one day seven hours and sixteen minutes ago.

2

Okay, my dad is waiting for me in the parking lot because some people think it might not be a good idea for me to drive even though I got my license right before my mom died. I totally don't want to drive anywhere anyway on account of the fact that there are 18-wheelers and steel signposts everywhere that I might plow into and I don't want to do anything anyway and don't have anywhere to go now except maybe Room 212, and my dad can drive me there.

After I climb into the front seat of my dad's Jeep, he says, "Hey, Asher. You're early. How did it go?" But I don't answer, and I don't tell him that he signed me up for an old people group and I don't tell him that I just told all of them that I killed my mom and I don't tell him that Henry is going to die any minute and that'll be my fault too. "Bohemian Rhapsody" is playing on the radio and I just stare out the window for a while and watch as the drops of rain run together like tears on the glass and the world swirls by in a blur as Freddie Mercury cries his heart out.

Then, as we turn left on Main and the streetlights are reflecting brightly in the puddles on the pavement and the raindrops are still desperately trying to cling to the window glass I announce, "I made a new friend and his name is Henry."

My dad says, "That's great, Asher," but I don't tell him that Henry is a hundred years old and likes the blue sky in Montana in winter and chocolate pudding and whales and sweet peas. I just ask, "Can we pick up pizza because I didn't eat before we left?" and my dad smiles at me and says, "Okay, Asher. Pizza sounds like fun."

He would totally say okay to anything at this point even if I said that I wanted to eat kangaroo. I mean he would figure out a way to get kangaroo, cook kangaroo, and fucking serve kangaroo, even though it's not normally eaten in this country because I'm all he has now because I don't have any brothers or sisters except for Chloe and she's only four and never talks about my mom and never thinks about her probably because Chloe can't remember her because twelve months three weeks one day seven hours and thirty-two minutes is such a long time ago if you are four years old and it's easier to forget than if you are seventeen and knew your mom for sixteen years six months four days and thirty-two minutes which is most of your life. So Chloe plays and is happy and goes to birthday parties with balloons and doesn't burn the house down or write essays about Holden Caulfield that make the English department think they should call the police or at least your dad and a whole committee full of professionals in adolescent psychiatry.

My dad says, "Go ahead and place the order, but get the pizza with no pepperoni." I want to say, *I know Chloe doesn't like meat when it's orange and cut into circles, so you don't have to remind me.* But I don't say anything; I just take out my phone to text the order and when I'm done, I ask, "Can I come back tomorrow and maybe on Thursday too for a different group and on Wednesday again too, to see Henry?" And my dad says, "Sure," and kind of smiles like maybe this is progress, but it's not. I'm just curious to see what other people my age who lost someone important enough to them to go to Room 212 for cookies twice a week look like, and I also want to come back on Wednesday so I can hear more about Evelyn because I only know that she has blue eyes like the sky in Montana in winter and I want to know if Henry still grows sweet peas and tomatoes and I'm thinking that maybe I should tell the old people in Room 212 that I didn't kill my mom, that she was killed by a drunk driver and I don't drink and don't have a license to drive an 18-wheeler with a double cab and a TV in the back that I could have been sleeping in or watching TV in if I did drink and had too much Jack Daniel's from the bottle I keep open in the truck even though it is against the law.

After I stare at my dad for a minute, I turn to face the window again where the raindrops are still quivering as they try to hold on to the glass, and Freddie Mercury declares in a very convincing voice what has become my personal anthem of late. *Nothing really matters to me.*

3

There were exactly 10,262 people killed by drunk drivers last year in the United States and it would have been one less than that if my mom hadn't gone to the mall to pick up new soccer cleats. The Nike Superflys in lime green in men's size eleven and a half that I needed because mine got stolen from the locker room at school and I had a game the next day against Claymont High School, which is four towns over from where we live.

My mom said, "Asher, I don't have time to drive to the mall today, and you should be more careful with your things."

That was the last thing she ever said to me, that I should be more careful with my things.

Then she went to the mall anyway.

And so did Jack Daniels. Well, maybe he didn't go to *the mall* exactly, but he got close enough to kill my mom.

I don't play soccer anymore. I can't play without the Nike Superflys in lime green and I don't have a pair. The new pair got destroyed in the accident and the old pair was stolen from my gym locker. I wonder if kids who do things like that—stupid shit like taking somebody's things—ever think that maybe they're setting off a whole chain reaction that will end up with someone being dead. I mean, if you think about it, our whole lives are chain reactions and everything we do causes other stuff to happen one way or the other, but I don't recommend that you think about that too much because then you won't be able to do anything at all. I mean, once you figure out that everything is connected and everything has consequences, it's really hard to decide if you should have the pancakes or the toasted bagel for breakfast because depending on which one you pick you could cause global warming or a locust infestation in Latin America or maybe make a delivery guy in Bangkok catch on fire. Not that you wanted to, or planned it—it just happens. Trust me, I've thought a lot about this stuff, and it's a whole domino thing.

Jack Daniels didn't die or even get hurt and his truck was fine too and he has two kids named Connor and Grace who still have a mom and he can still drive his big rig because the judge said, *Case dismissed.* He didn't go to jail because the officer on the scene didn't do a Breathalyzer and even though the detectives who came to investigate said it was a 10-51—person is drunk—all the charges were dismissed due to lack of evidence.

There was plenty of evidence because I saw the pictures of the Land Rover and my mom is dead but the judge said, *That's not enough.*

I Google him—the truck driver, not the judge—six or seven times a day, sometimes more, way more, and he's on Facebook and lives in Tennessee at 114 Culvert Street in Memphis and he took his family to Disney World in Orlando three weeks ago to go on the teacup ride and Space Mountain probably because they were upset that he was in an accident twelve months three weeks one day nine hours and fifty-seven minutes ago and could have been killed. But he wasn't.

We went to the Magic Kingdom once but Chloe was only a baby then so she couldn't go on Space Mountain; she just got to go on the baby rides like "it's a small world," but that ride is messed up because, let's face it, the world is not small at all.

It's actually so big that you can easily get lost and never find your way home.

Grace is my age, and Connor is Chloe's age so if you think about it, it's like their family is my family in reverse.

I mean, their mom didn't die and mine did.

My dad didn't drunk drive and theirs did.

They can go to Disney World and we can't.

I could go on but what would be the point? I mean, you get it.

Sometimes I wonder if Connor and Grace ever think about Asher and Chloe because I think about them all the time. But then I think they probably don't think about us ever because Grace has to think about her new boyfriend who's named Sam Hunt just like the singer but who isn't the singer and they have to play soccer and write essays about Holden Caulfield that don't say he should have just killed himself on page one that upset the entire English department at their school and they have to go to parties with balloons and concentrate on not burning down their house when they put a frozen pizza in the oven but forget to take it out of the box first, and then I start to wonder if Connor and Grace have ever been to a room like 212 at the hospital or to a morgue or a cemetery because all kinds of stuff are flammable not just cardboard pizza boxes, but Land Rover SUVs and people's moms, too.

Before the accident I had a girlfriend, but that burst into flames too. The first day I went back to school after my mom died, as soon as I saw Emily I said, "Look, I just can't do this right now."

"Do what?" she asked. She was already crying because we hadn't seen each other since the accident but I had to just get it over with fast so I said, "I can't love anyone right now."

She started to cry even more when she said, "You lost your mom, Asher. But you don't have to lose me. Not like this. Not now."

I slammed my locker closed and said, "I'm dating someone else. She lives in Tennessee," and walked away. I didn't say anything else because WHAT WOULD BE THE POINT? Emily has no idea what it's like when you can't trust the people you love to keep on living.

4

I started to make a list of all the people who killed my mom, and I came up with at least nine:

> *Jack Daniels.*
>
> *The person who stole my Nikes.*
>
> *The man who put up the utility pole on Route 287 West near the 3.7-mile marker.*
>
> *The people who built the mall.*
>
> *Everyone at Nike for making soccer cleats.*
>
> *The governor of New Jersey for allowing people to drive.*
>
> *The owner of the trucking company.*
>
> *Whoever invented tar.*
>
> *David Beckham for making me like soccer.*
>
> *Mia Hamm for making me really like soccer.*
>
> *My gym coach for not catching the kid who stole my cleats.*

That's eleven.

Then there's the big ugly thing sitting in the middle of Room 212 that no one wanted to look at and I can't take back or rewind or cover up with something.

Me.

I.

Killed.

Her.

Which makes twelve.

Because I did.

Kill.

Her.

It's just that a whole bunch of other people helped.

I probably shouldn't tell you this, but sometimes—okay, several times a day—I text Grace and send her Facebook messages.

She doesn't know who I really am and she thinks we're friends.

I had to set up a fake account and use a different name.

I mean, it's pretty easy to stalk someone and then make friends with them. All you need is a fake Facebook page with some real friends.

She thinks I'm Sam Hunt.

Not the singer. Just a normal kid named Sam Hunt who's her fake new friend and sort-of-maybe-fake-new-online boyfriend.

To seal the deal I went on iTunes and gifted her every Ed Sheeran song ever written.

I hate Ed Sheeran.

I mean, you have to hate him. He wrote a bunch of songs for One Direction.

Then I texted her that if we had a song, it would be "Body Like a Back Road" by Sam Hunt.

The singer.

Not the fake me.

She texted, perfect! And I wrote, You mean, Perfect as in the Ed Sheeran song? And she wrote, No. Perfect as in Body Like a Back Road being our song, if we had a song.

And there we were.

I mean, I basically catfished her. The daughter of the man who killed my mom.

And that was the beginning of me and Grace going sixty in a thirty and getting tangled up in the tall grass of pain and lies.

And it kind of explains the me-breaking-up-with-Emily thing too. Because I *am* kind-of-sort-of-but-not-really dating someone else.

5

I don't remember anything about my mom dying except waking up in the hospital after my dad told me what had happened because when he told me about my mom's accident I got so upset that I freaked out and passed out and hit my head so hard on the corner of the coffee table in the living room that the glass shattered and I knocked myself out and almost lost my eyesight and my dad had to call an ambulance to take me to the hospital for a head injury. I didn't wake up for two weeks because I had to be put into a medically induced coma to protect my brain from swelling. Then my dad had to tell me a second time that my mom died because when I woke up again I didn't remember. I didn't remember him telling me about my mom or me freaking out and the coffee table. So it was like my mom died twice in two weeks.

The doctors say I AM VERY LUCKY THAT I CAN STILL SEE OUT OF MY LEFT EYE and they told me that I have something called dissociative amnesia. It happens when THERE IS A TRAUMATIC INCIDENT that you don't want to remember, so you don't. It's like the brain just says, *Nope! Not dealing with this!*

The shrinks told me it's a way to protect myself from something I can't face. So big surprise, I can't face that my mom died.

At first I thought, *Maybe it's like a severe case of denial.* But the shrinks say it's not like I'm *denying* that my mom died, and it's not that I don't *believe* that she died; it's just that the news was so shocking that I can't *remember* anything about that day. Then they pat me on the shoulder and say, "Don't worry, these types of memories usually come back."

I'm thinking, *Why would I want to remember?* but don't say anything because the entire medical community is acting like me remembering will somehow be a good thing.

In case you're wondering, it's been twelve months three weeks one day eleven hours and—hold on—seven minutes, and so far? *Total blank.*

After she died and after the coffee table and the hospital and the coma and me missing the wake and the funeral and the burial and we returned home to pretend nothing is wrong, my dad told me that my mom left me a letter that she was going to give to me when I graduated from high school. He said she wrote it the day I was born, and then he asked if maybe I wanted to read it now.

I asked, "Why? Do you think I won't live long enough to graduate from high school?" and he said, "No, of course not, Asher. I just think it would be nice for you to read it now that you are missing her so much." Then he handed me the letter.

For three weeks I just stared at my name on the front of the powder-blue envelope. The *A* of Asher has a fancy loop at the bottom and the *r* swoops up at the end. I figure it was probably the first time she had written my name anywhere unless they make you write it on a baby's birth certificate. I don't know how that works.

The letters of my name looked so optimistic sitting there on that envelope, like they were dancing across the paper, which, if you think about it, is deeply disturbing based on how things turned out. I mean, it didn't look like the kind of letter that was going to say something of extreme value like DON'T EVER ASK ME TO DRIVE TO THE MALL TO GET YOU NEW SOCCER CLEATS! Which is the kind of thing she should have written if she wanted to be helpful.

Then after three weeks of staring at *A-s-h-e-r* with the fancy loop to the *A* and the *r* that swoops up at the end, I flipped the envelope over. It was a moment of superhuman strength or a kind of personal renaissance for me, maybe like the Enlightenment. A moment where all of a sudden I could do something I could never do before. But it's not like I invented a printing press or discovered that the planets orbited the sun, and it's not like I'm saying I'm Michelangelo or Copernicus or Machiavelli—if you think about it, who the fuck are they and what did they do? I mean, I did something completely *impossible*.

I managed to turn that envelope over and look at the back.

But that's as far as I got.

My mom drew this small, perfect heart on the back of the envelope in the same blue ink as the writing on the front. It's sitting there like a kiss, right where the envelope closes. I knew that when I broke the seal and lifted the flap, it would break that small blue heart. Because that's just how it works.

The irony of that kills me.

I mean, you get it. My heart got broken and hers did too. And mine's been broken a hundred million times since then, and I know that when I lift the flap and take the letter out, my heart will break again.

Sometimes—okay, every day—I take the envelope out and look at it, wondering what she said, but I can't bring myself to open it and find out.

The other day my dad asked me if I've read the letter yet, and I said, "Only the beginning."

He looked worried and asked, "What do you mean?"

I said, "I mean the first word."

He didn't speak for a whole minute, and then he asked, "You mean where it says 'Asher' on the envelope?" and I nodded my head.

I figured he was thinking that I've had the letter for over a year and it's totally weird that I didn't read it yet, and that means that I'm even more messed up than he thought, but I know he only thinks that because he doesn't know about the loopy *A* and the swoopy *r* and the seal on the back with the blue heart that can never be fixed once it's broken. But my dad surprised me and nodded his head slowly and said, "That's good, Asher. It's a start."

I figure he's right and that my mom probably thought the same thing when she started writing the letter to me. I was probably lying there in the hospital next to her in the bassinet all laced up tight like a burrito or a soccer cleat, and she probably wrote 'Asher' on the front of the envelope with the loopy *A* and the swoopy *r* and then thought, *That's a good start.* Plus, what could she possibly say anyway? We'd just met.

I mean, back then we hardly knew each other.

On Tuesday night my dad says, "Hey, Ash, I'll take you to that meeting you wanted to go to at the hospital in five minutes. Mrs. Levitt is coming over to watch Chloe." Then he adds, "How about we pick up pizza on the way home like we did last night?" and in that moment it feels like spring. You know, like a day in May when the grass is dewy and the flowers are blooming and the sun is warm and summer is just around the corner. It's like someone opened a window and the breeze blew in so clean and fresh that you can smell stuff growing.

Chloe says, "Remember no pepperoni," and I roll my eyes.

I mean, I get it. Plus, she won't eat a lot of other stuff besides pepperoni—like bologna, because bologna's just like pepperoni, only bigger and pinker and less spicy—and she won't eat anything green or red except for pizza sauce and watermelon lollipops and Robitussin cherry cough syrup when she's sick, and she won't eat anything but pizza with nothing on it and French toast and plain pasta with no red sauce and chicken as long as it doesn't look like an animal. Like a whole chicken with the legs attached would be totally out. But I say, "Maybe we should get pepperoni on half the pizza," and for those few seconds it's almost like the world is normal. Or better than normal even. Like it's raining and the sun is out at the same time but you aren't wet and freezing cold or being struck by lightning and going to die any minute because this time you are safe inside looking out at the world and it's a world where nobody you love is dead. But that feeling only lasts for a few seconds, so that part sucks.

This time in Room 212, next to the coffee and cookies they have big bottles of soda—Pepsi and orange Crush. I don't take any cookies with chocolate swirls or pour coffee or soda into a Styrofoam cup; I just sit down in one of the chairs in the circle. There are a couple of other kids here already, but I don't look at them and nobody says anything. I mean it's not like we're all in a good mood. Peter Pan's just sitting there across from me as she waits for everyone to show up. She has her head down, and she's flipping through some folders and reading some papers, probably filled with warnings about how messed up we all are. When she finally looks up, I can tell she's surprised to see me. Not tar-pit surprised, just a normal amount, you know, like, *Oh, no! Asher's here.*

Three more kids show up and now there are seven of us in this group and we go around the circle and introduce ourselves, and when it's my turn Peter Pan looks nervous because she's probably worried I'm going to say that I killed my mom, but I say, "Hi, I'm Asher and I'm seventeen. I have a four-year-old sister named Chloe, and my mom died twelve months ago." I leave off the three weeks two days six hours and seventeen minutes part because it would probably sound weird and raise some red flags and then I add, "She died in a car accident," but I leave off the part about the big rig and the Jaws of Life and the downed utility pole and the fire and the Jack Daniel's and how I'm stalking the truck driver and his family on Facebook and pretending to be someone named

Sam Hunt who is in love with his daughter, Grace, because you shouldn't kill someone's mom when you could just watch TV at a truck stop and drink all the Jack Daniel's that you want or not drink Jack Daniel's at all and drive right by Asher and Chloe's mom without crashing into her.

Since there were six other people in the group besides me if you don't count Peter Pan we make up a whole week of tragedy. One day is me with the dead mom in the burned-up SUV and then there's Sloane who is sixteen and lost her dad to non-Hodgkin's lymphoma and then Will who is seventeen and lost his eight-year-old brother to neuroblastoma.

I don't listen to the other four days of the week because they are just too depressing so I block them out and sit there while the room fills with smoke because someone forgot that lots of things are combustible and not just cardboard pizza boxes and Land Rovers and moms, but kids too.

Then Sloane says, "I have two younger sisters named Anna and Claire and they're doing better than I am. Way better. But my mom's a fucking mess. I mean, you don't even want to know."

I look up and say, "At least you have a mom."

Sloane looks at me like, *What?* And then Peter Pan says, "That's a healthy way to look at it, Asher. Thank you. Let's all be grateful for the people we still do have in our lives."

Then Will jumps in and says, "Who would you trade to get your mom back, Asher?"

And Peter Pan says, "This is not going in a healthy direction. Let's give someone else a chance to speak."

Will looks away. He's now hiding behind his mop of shaggy hair. His eyes flick. He's surveying the enemy. *But I see him. I know him.* Know his strategy. It's the strategy of the wounded.

Attack. Retreat. Lick wounds. Reload. Attack again.

Will's just like me. He doesn't want to be.

No one does.

But he *is.*

I look around the room. *They all are. Just. Like. Me.*

No one says anything, so I look over at Will and repeat his question. "Who would I trade to get my mom back?" Then I tell him. "Pretty much everyone. I mean, I would trade all the people north and south of the equator and everyone in my school and—"

Will interrupts. "I would trade *me* to get my brother back."

I think about that for a minute and then ask, "How would that work, because if you were dead and your brother was alive, you still wouldn't be together and he would be the one being really sad instead of you, and since he's only eight years old that would be a pretty big thing to lay on him?"

For a flash, Will looks confused and angry. And then the angry part becomes just soul-crushing sad. I mean, he thought he had a plan and I pretty much just told him that he didn't. I didn't mean to say anything to hurt anyone, but there is no plan to get out of the mess that we're in, and the thing is, nobody wants to tell us that. Everyone wants to pretend that somehow this will all be okay if we just go to therapy and eat cookies and disappear until we're better. Then Peter Pan jumps in to explain how we all have to cycle through the seven stages of grief.

"I'm sure you've all heard the list before," she says. "*Shock and denial. Pain and guilt. Anger and bargaining. Depression, reflection, loneliness.* Then, *the upward turn. Reconstruction and working through.* Followed by *acceptance and hope.*"

I raise my hand and tell her that's way more than seven. Then I say, "And I haven't experienced any of them."

She ignores the *more than seven* comment, then dances around the *I haven't experienced any of them* thing like she's supposed to, because let's face it, I'm a fragile egg and might crack at any moment. Then she looks around the whole group and suggests that some of us might find ourselves stuck in anger and depression and I figure by "some of us" she pretty much means me. So I ask, "When will *some of us* get to experience one of the good ones like the upward turn? Or denial or acceptance?" and she says, "That's what we're working toward here, Asher."

Will just retreats behind his curls again, and some other kid says, "You guys are in the bargaining stage." Then someone else calls out, "Yeah, but they're not supposed to bargain *out loud* like it's real."

Will ignores that kid and peeks out from under his hair and asks, "Would you trade *me* to get your mother back, Asher?" and I'm about to say, *Absolutely*, when Peter Pan jumps in and says, "Stop."

Will ignores her and says, "At least you have a sister, Asher. I have to go through this alone. And I'm scared that when my parents are old, I'll have to take care of them all by myself."

I say, "Yeah, but I'm scared that if my dad dies, I'll have to take care of my sister, too, instead of just taking care of me."

Sloane joins in and says, "But at least you don't have to worry about your mom taking care of three kids alone. Or about her dating."

All the other kids are watching us like this is a ping-pong match between three people who hate each other.

Peter Pan steps in and says, "Each of us is affected differently when a family suffers a loss. But what I am hearing is that every one of you is thinking about it in a very caring way."

"Actually, we're not," I announce. "We're all thinking about this in a selfish way. Will's worried about himself. I'm worried about me. And Sloane's worried about herself, too."

"Asher . . ."

I point at the clock and say, "Meeting's over." Then when I'm about to stand up and head out, Peter Pan says, "We still have a lot more time, Asher." And then she adds, "Look, everybody grieves differently, and we shouldn't judge anyone because that wouldn't be fair." Then she turns back to Sloane and asks, "Would you like to tell us a nice memory that you have about your dad?"

Will jumps back in and asks, "Why are you changing the subject? We had a good conversation going."

And Peter Pan says, "Because my job is to take the conversation in a healthy, positive direction," and Will retreats behind his hair again, and I realize, *It's not a mop; it's a helmet.* Then I look down at my sneakers for a minute and shut up.

I look back up when Sloane says, "No. I don't want to talk about my dad." She sounds pissed off, and she's twisting a tissue between her fingers, but then her face and eyes get bright and she starts to tell a story about her dad anyway. "He liked to ride his motorcycle, and barbecue. He had all sorts of special gadgets for the grill, like a headlamp and a special device with fourteen tools like screwdrivers and thermometers. And one time he was wearing this apron that said *Best Dad in the World* on the front, and it caught on fire so he took it off, and everyone was stomping on it and running around trying to put the fire out."

Sloane has a dazed looked on her face now and a half smile like she's left the room and is somewhere else. It's like she's back in the past when her dad wasn't dead.

"But it wasn't really scary," she continues. "It was just funny because my mom—she poured a whole bottle of white wine on him even though he wasn't wearing the apron anymore and he wasn't even still on fire."

Sloane looks down for a minute lost in the memory, still smiling.

"Then, later that night, my dad asked her if she was trying to kill him because wine is flammable and my mom—she just looked horrified because she didn't think of that."

Sloane swipes at a tear.

"And then they hugged, and my mom said she was sorry she almost flambéed him. Then we made s'mores. My dad loved s'mores."

When she finishes, Sloane looks better, better than before, like telling that story helped her. It's like she just ate a s'more with her dad. But I'm a mess. I mean, it's like her words left footprints on my heart because I'm thinking that her dad could have burned up until nothing was left and nobody should be barbecuing or wearing aprons or pouring wine on people who are on fire because everyone should know that ALCOHOL IS FUCKING FLAMMABLE— blow-up-your-life, flames-licking-the-sky *flammable*—and no one in that story should have been laughing or eating s'mores and I want to say that people need to be more careful because sometimes you lose things that you didn't think you could lose like soccer cleats and moms and dads and little brothers because they get stolen from you or they just burst into flames when it never occurred to you that they could.

I mean, if you think about it, everything can incinerate and disappear. Nobody ever tells us that, and someone should.

7

I have to get up and leave the room because I'm thinking about Sloane's dad burning up and Will comes out after me
and when he catches up with me in the hall, he says, "Hey, are
you okay?" and I realize that nobody at school has ever asked me
that. Not Emily and not my friends (back when I still had them)
and not my teachers. At least not in such an I-mean-it, I-get-it,
I-really-care way. When I came back to school, everyone just
looked at me scared—like deer-in-the-headlights scared—because
they were afraid of what I would say or do because of course *I
wasn't okay* but that's not what they wanted to hear. BUT, since
Will lost his brother, I figure that even though he probably hates
me and we don't even know each other, *he knows what I'm going
through*, so I tell him the truth. I say, "Not really. But I'm working on it and thanks for asking," and then his eyes dart around
a bit before he says, "Sorry about before," and I say, "Me too,"
and then when we walk back into Room 212 together, Will says,
"But I would totally trade you to get my brother back," and I say,
"I know. I would trade you in a second for my mom," and then
when we sit back down, Peter Pan looks up at us, and she has an
expression on her face again like she just found the Lost Boys

she was missing, and this time there are two of us.

My phone pings and I take it out to look at it. It's a text from Grace. She said, Wish you were here! I type, Me too! and put my phone away.

Then Peter Pan without the green tights but with the perfect pixie haircut and pretty face splattered with freckles says she has a writing exercise for us to do that some people find helpful and she hands out paper and pencils and says we should finish the sentence, *I will always remember that* . . .

She leaves us alone for a while and probably goes into the hallway to cry because being around sad people all the time must be hard and then when she comes back, she asks, "Would any of you like to read what you wrote out loud?" and Will storms out of the room.

I run out after him this time and ask, "Hey, are you okay?"

He says, "Not really, but I'm working on it and thanks for asking." Then he hands me his writing exercise that he crinkled up into a ball, and I'm not sure if he wants me to toss it into the trash or shred it or maybe smooth it out and read it to myself or maybe even read it out loud to the group and it's like I'm holding a pipe bomb and if I do or say the wrong thing it might blow up and destroy everything for miles around so I look at him and whisper, "Do you want me to toss it or shred it or read it?"

He says, "I don't know," and it comes out as a big sob.

So I smooth the paper out with my hands as I press it up against the cold green of the hospital wall and say, "How about you don't decide now and I'll just fold it up and put it in my pocket and save it for you and if you want to read it sometime in the future, you can just tell me?"

He nods his head, but he's punching the wall with both fists and crying.

I fold up the thing he will always remember and put it in the pocket of my jeans and then fold up the thing I will always remember and hand it to him and say, "Here's mine and I want you to shred it because it's such an awful thing that I wrote that I never want to see it again."

Then Will stops punching the wall and eats my paper.

He chews it up and I say, "Hey, man, they have cookies inside if you're hungry."

That makes him laugh a little which isn't easy because he's trying to chew up something awful while still crying and then he says, "This way no one can ever read it because no one will find it in the trash by accident."

And I say, "You shouldn't talk with your mouth full," and he laughs again and it's like I have a real friend for the first time in my life.

Not like a normal friend or just a fun kid at school to go to a movie with or shoot the shit with and not like all my old friends who I've been avoiding because I look at them and think *I'm not like you anymore*—but a *real friend*. Someone who's actually being swallowed by the same tar pit that's swallowing me. It's like Will's my best friend in the whole world now even though I hardly know him because he chewed up my bad thoughts without even reading them first because he knew that even though they were choking me, he could get them down okay if he just tried hard enough.

Will is just standing there chewing, so I ask, "Do you want to see something cool?"

He says, "Sure," then swallows.

I take him up three floors in the elevator to see the new babies in the nursery, which I remembered about because it was the first place I ever saw Chloe. On the way up I ask, "Do you ever think about killing anyone?"

He gives me a quick glance, to see if I'm serious, and when he sees that I am, he says, "All the time."

I ask him, "Who would you kill and what stops you?"

He says, "I want to kill everyone, but I don't do it because I'm not cancer."

I don't say anything back but if I did say something it would have been, *I'm not sure, but I might be Jack Daniel's.*

A fucking 18-wheeler barreling down a highway about to hit someone.

8

We stand in front of the nursery window with our hands pressed on the glass watching the babies for a while not saying anything until Will asks, "What do you think they're thinking about?"

I say, "Boobs." Then I ask, "What are you thinking about?"

And he says, "Kierkegaard's philosophy on existential despair."

I look at him like, *What??*

Will shrugs. "He's a Danish philosopher who's the father of existentialism."

"And that's . . . ?"

"The search for the meaning of existence." Then he adds, "Kierkegaard said that everyone suffers from a deep kind of despair over their existence."

I say, "So he knows us, then."

Will laughs and I add, "And existentialism is basically the opposite of boobs," and he says, "Exactly." Then he kind of smiles. Not a real smile, but close enough.

I turn back to the nursery. "I don't think babies think about Kierkegaard."

Will watches them for a minute. "You're probably right; I mean, look at them."

They are all squished up either screaming or sleeping, like for them there are two states of normal—pissed off or out cold—and I know it's a small thing, but for those few minutes me and Will are just normal. Okay, maybe not normal-normal for regular people because it's not normal to stand here looking at strangers' babies for no reason, but normal-normal for us.

Then a nurse in a little white hat and green scrubs comes out from behind the control center down the hall and asks, "Are you two supposed to be somewhere else?" and we just look at her without answering for a beat because neither one of us wants to tell her we belong to the death group downstairs. Then we just turn and walk away and head back down in the elevator to the second floor and step into Room 212 and by the time we get there, the meeting is already ending, so me and Will don't take a seat; we just hang out by the coffee and soda for a minute and then stuff some cookies into our pockets and walk out with Sloane.

The three of us hang in the hallway for a bit and Sloane tells me that she and Will have been going to Room 212 together for months. Then she says, "The meeting tonight totally sucked and just made me feel worse and the only good part was the cookies."

And Will says, "Ouch, that hurt. I thought the good part of the meeting was me."

Sloane says, "Dude, you suck worse than the whole rest of the meeting," and then she asks me, "Did he bring up Kierkegaard yet?"

I say, "You mean the gloom-and-doom existential philosopher who says we are destined to a life of despair?" and Sloane nods. I say, "Yep," and then I tell Will, "Dude, she's right. You do suck."

Will says, "I know," and then he ducks back behind his hair again, and I ask, "Are you guys coming back on Thursday?" and they both say, "Of course."

I say, "Me too," and then we all laugh, mostly because it means Kierkegaard is right.

Life is basically a miserable black hole and we're only here for the cookies.

None of us says anything as we go left past the vending machines and the restrooms on the right and step into the elevator and out of the building and before each of us gets into cars with the people we have left, which is one short of what it should be, which totally sucks in a way that no one else can understand, we exchange numbers, and then I kind of wave at both of them and say, "See you in two days," after I decide that Sloane is the prettiest girl I have ever seen in my entire life even though she is wearing black motorcycle boots with studs in them that look way too big for her, like she's trying to look biker-chick-tough even though she's all shredded inside and would probably tip over if she took the boots off. Then I wonder if she would go out with me or if I would like her if we didn't meet in a death group and then I get sidetracked and start to wonder if Sloane and Will are hooking up or if they stalk cancer doctors online because they blame them for not saving their dad and brother, but then I think, *probably not*—at least to the stalking part—because that would be weird.

I mean, at least the doctors tried hard. It's not like they were drinking Jack Daniel's and drove a big rig into someone who was just picking up soccer cleats at the mall.

When I get home, me and Chloe and my dad eat pizza with no pepperoni and then I go to my room and send Grace a picture of me playing soccer. In it I'm scoring a goal against the Belmont Bulls, a line drive to the upper right corner of the net, and wearing the Nike lime-green Superflys that got stolen from my gym locker.

Grace likes the photo so I send her a picture of Sam Hunt, the singer, not me. She sends me an audio clip of "Body Like a Back Road" and then invites me to her prom.

I freeze, think, Oh, shit! Then she types, It's a week from this Saturday!

So I type, Yes! Definitely! and she sends back a kissy-face emoji and a picture of a prom dress. I don't text her back. I just put my phone down and take my mom's letter out of the drawer where I keep it and stare at the loop of the *A* and the swoop of the *r*. Then I turn the envelope over and carefully slide my finger under the blue heart on the back to break the seal and split that heart wide open.

I half expect to see blood spill out all over the paper, but nothing happens at all except the flap pops open like it has springs.

I stand there for a long time, but I can't bring myself to lift the letter out.

I'm just not strong enough.

9

The next night I go back to Room 212 for the Wednesday old people group and Peter Pan looks surprised to see me again, probably because I was just here yesterday for the teen group. I say, "Don't worry, I won't talk, but maybe I can sit here and listen and the cookies are pretty good—what kind are they?"

She says, "The Pepperidge Farm party pack," then hands me a book.

I look down at it. It's small and white. On the cover there's a child's crayon drawing of a little blond kid standing on a barren planet staring up at the sky.

I say, "I'm not a little kid."

She says, "I know that. But I think this book might help you. It helped me."

"When?" I ask.

She seems to contemplate that. I mean, the *when* part. Then she says, "Every day."

I say, "Shit," and she smiles.

I stuff the book into my jacket pocket, then ask, "Is Henry coming?"

"I think so," she says. "He hasn't missed a meeting yet." And then as if on cue, Henry walks in and sits down and when everyone else arrives and the meeting starts Henry tells us that he and Evelyn have two children, a son and a daughter who are both grown up and middle-aged now, and he's glad he has them to help get through the Evelyn-dying-and-his-world-ending thing. But then he says that sometimes his kids just want to hear that he's okay even when he isn't okay, so he lies and tells them that he's growing tomatoes and sweet peas just like he and Evelyn used to, but he really isn't growing anything; he's just sitting in the dark with the curtains drawn and the lights out feeling lost.

Even though I said I wasn't going to talk, I stand up and say, "I'll buy you some sweet pea seeds and you don't have to plant them but you can if you feel like it. Or maybe I could come over this Saturday and plant them with you if it's not too weird." And then I add, "I mean, I never planted seeds before, but still."

I don't know why I said that but somehow it just seemed like the right thing to do. When I stop talking it gets all uncomfortable and everyone's quiet and it's like my words created a vacuum and we're all holding our breath waiting for the air to rush back into the room because no one can breathe. Peter Pan looks nervous, like maybe I crossed a line, and all the old people are probably thinking, *Why would Henry want to plant sweet peas with the kid who killed his mom?* But then Henry lights up and he looks like an old Christmas tree left over on the next Halloween. It's like there's nothing left but a spindly trunk with a bunch of bare branches and dead twigs and a handful of dry needles that have a few stray strands of tinsel still hanging off them. But then he says, "Asher, you can come over to plant seeds, and then we'll bring some sweet peas to the meeting here in Room 212," and his words are like tiny, bright flashing lights.

All of a sudden I feel good and bad at the same time because on the one hand Henry seems happy but on the other hand it seems like growing sweet peas from seeds will take a long time and that means that this is a room that maybe you don't graduate from.

Later that night my phone bleeps and it's a text from Will. The clock says it's 3:21 a.m. and I have to squint at the bright screen to read the message. It says, Do you want to hang out on Saturday?

So I write, I can't. I have to plant sweet peas with my friend Henry.

He doesn't say anything else for a while but then he types, My brother's name is Michael Hudson Lee.

I text him back, My mom's name is Evelyn Caitlin Hunting.

Then there's nothing back for seventeen minutes so I text Will again and say, My mom will take care of Michael Hudson Lee. She'll find him in heaven and keep him safe. I'm sure of it.

I don't know why I said that because I have no idea if it's true.

Okay, fuck it. I know it isn't true because I don't even believe in God or heaven but sometimes you have to say stuff to make people feel better. I do it all the time with Chloe.

Here are some of the things I told her in the last week that are totally not true:

> *Dad can't die because he has special powers.*
> *I can't die because I got the special powers from Dad.*
> *Mrs. Levitt can't die because she lives next door to us.*
> And *Hamilton the preschool guinea pig with half a white face and half a brown face did not die. He moved to another town that is better for guinea pigs, and your teacher is a liar.*

After Will doesn't text me back, I text Sloane and ask, What's your dad's name?

She writes back, Henry Abbott Willis.

I write, I know a Henry and he's the coolest guy I know.

She sends me back a smiley-face emoji with a tear.

So here's the thing:

My mom's name is Evelyn.

Henry's wife's name is Evelyn.

Sloane's dad's name is Henry.

Henry's name is Henry.

Will's brother's name is Michael.

My dad's name is Michael.

We have two dead Evelyns. One dead Henry. One live Henry. One dead Michael. One live Michael.

It's hard to keep track.

So I stop thinking about it and send Grace a flirty Facebook message and then like all her pictures on Instagram. There are 1,342 of them. It takes a really long time.

I hate all of them.

Then she types, I'm afraid for my dad to meet you!

I think, *Oh, shit! The prom's in ten days!* And then I text back, I'm afraid for him to meet me too.

Then when I can't get back to sleep, I read a whole bunch of stuff online about Kierkegaard and then try reading the book that Peter Pan gave me. It's called *The Little Prince*, and it was written by some French guy a long time ago.

I only get to page two where it says, "Grown-ups never understand anything by themselves, and it is exhausting for children to have to provide explanations over and over again."

The narrator comes to this observation after he draws a picture that all the adults think looks like a hat, but it's really a picture of a boa constrictor that swallowed an elephant.

I figure the reason Peter Pan wanted me to read this book and the reason it helped her so much is that she can relate to that message because she works with kids and she was a kid and she knows that when the bad stuff swallows you like a boa constrictor AND YOU DRAW A FUCKING PICTURE OF IT all the grown-ups *should* look at it and say, HOLY FUCKING SHIT, ASHER WAS JUST SWALLOWED BY A BOA CONSTRICTOR! AND HE DREW A PICTURE TO SHOW US! WE SHOULD DO SOMETHING TO SAVE HIM, DON'T YOU THINK? But they don't. They just look at the picture and think, *How lovely, a hat.*

So my takeaway is that my mom dying is a boa constrictor and I'm an elephant and to everyone but me the whole mess just looks like a hat. Then I draw a mental picture in my head of me swallowed by a boa constrictor and even though I'm not as big as an elephant the picture in my head bears a striking resemblance to the picture in the book. When I think of me standing straight up, it looks more like a pointy wizard's hat, maybe like the Hogwarts Sorting Hat, and if I think of me lying down, it resembles something closer to a French beret—that is, if you are the type of person who tends to see an ordinary thing when that thing sitting right in front of you isn't ordinary at all.

But I decide not to read the rest of the book because it's four in the morning and I already get it, and besides, I remind myself, I have to get some sleep because tomorrow I have to rent a tux and figure out how to get from Bergen County, New Jersey, to Memphis, Tennessee, a week from Saturday to take Grace to the prom. Then I think, *Hold on! Maybe Peter Pan is trying to tell me that she can see the boa constrictor that ate the elephant when most other people just see a hat.* So I decide that maybe I *will* read the book. Maybe even read it slowly. Just not right now because it's late and I have a lot going on.

10

Ever since the accident I get called out of class once a week on a rotating basis to go see the school psychologist, Dr. WhoKnowsNothingAtAll, like it's just another special, no different from music or gym. It's the same drill every week and that's not his real name, but you probably figured that out already. I mostly don't talk, but sometimes I do. I figure it's, like, fifty-fifty. The school describes it as "almost never." The thing is, my dad wants me to talk more, so on Thursday morning when Dr. WhoKnowsNothingAtAll asks, "How are you doing this week, Asher?" I figure it's the second-to-last session of the year, so why not give it a shot.

I say, "I have this dream sometimes. Not the car crash dream, a different one," and he takes out his yellow pad and gets ready to write stuff down.

"This one feels short," I continue, "you know, like just a flash, and then I'm awake. It's one of those moments where you could tip either way. I'm at this precipice—a fork in the road. And it's life or death. There's a cliff and certain death on one side, safety on the other. But I'm blindfolded, and I can't tell which way is which. And there's no time. I have to decide, left or right? Death or safety?"

Dr. WhoKnowsNothingAtAll looks interested and asks, "Is that it?"

"Shit, no," I say. "Then I'm falling. I don't know which direction I chose, and because of the blindfold, I can't see, so I'm scared to death, sweating and shaking. And of course, because I was blind-folded *before I jumped*, me choosing was just a gamble. There was no way for me to know which direction was better."

Dr. WhoKnowsNothingAtAll picks up his pencil. Starts tapping it on the yellow pad he has on his desk like he does whenever he gets nervous or annoyed. Then he asks, "Do you think that you're worried about making a bad decision? That maybe you don't trust yourself?"

I give him the death stare, thinking, *Shit! This is why I don't talk. He doesn't get it.*

"No," I say, clearly annoyed. "You missed the point. This isn't about me making an *informed decision*. I'm *forced to guess* without enough information to guess *well*. So if I were a shrink, I'd say I'm worried about me not having any control."

Tap, tap, tap goes his pencil. "Usually in life, Asher, we aren't blindfolded. There are ways to make better decisions than just ran-domly jumping and relying on fate."

I look him over. He has beady eyes and really small ears. *I won-der if that's why he doesn't hear me.* Therapists should have ears like an elephant. Big floppy things that can hear a mouse sneeze from a mile away.

"You must live in a different world than I do," I snap.

"Why do you say that?"

"In my world," I tell him, "bad shit just happens and I have no way of controlling it. My life *is* that dream. A fucking free fall off a cliff I had no part in choosing."

He's tapping his pencil and watching me. I'm pissed off. Then I say, "You didn't ask me what happens at the end."

"What happens at the end?"

"I die."

He keeps tapping. "Have you ever thought about writing your dreams down in a journal?"

I shuffle my feet around. Look at the clock. *Twenty minutes to go.* Note to Dad: *The whole talking-more thing didn't work out that well.* "You mean, like, my dreams for the future?" I ask.

He shuffles some papers on his desk. I notice that he's moved the little cat figures that he keeps on the windowsill around since last time I was here. I wonder if he has names for them.

"No. Your dreams at night. Like the one you just told me about."

I keep looking at him. I forgot how short he is. He's this little tiny person. With little tiny ears. AND A TINY SHRIVELED HEART. And a little tiny brain full of REALLY TINY THOUGHTS. *How could he possibly help me?* "So basically you're asking if I keep a *nightmare* diary?"

"That's not exactly what I meant, Asher." He reaches over and moves the bright orange cat statue into the sun. "You must have *some* good dreams."

I try to remember the last good dream I had and come up blank. "Not really."

He seems to think about that.

"Even if I did have good dreams, why would I want to write them down?" I ask.

"Sometimes people who are trying to reconcile difficult emotions find it helpful to keep a dream journal."

"So you want me to buy a notebook and write down, *May ninth. Woke up trembling in a cold sweat again. I was dragging my mom's body from the fiery car crash just like I do every night. . . .*"

"Asher . . ."

"*Smoke was pouring from the engine. It's about to explode. . . .*"

He picks up the orange cat again. Moves it to his desk. "Take a breath, Asher."

I clench my fists. Look away. *Inhale, then exhale to the count of four.*

"Now take another breath. Nice and slow, just like we practiced."

My eyes snap back to him. "Let me get this straight. You want me to keep a dream journal so I'm absolutely certain to never forget the trembling night terrors I've been having for the last year?"

"No, Asher. I think that maybe if you chronicle your dreams, we might be able to see some progression."

"Progression? Like, look! Year three! This time my mom lived! Or I know, this time her head didn't come off as I tried to pull her from the car? That kind of progression?"

"That's not what I intended."

I stand up. "A dream journal is for normal kids. Not for me."

"Asher . . ."

"Let's be clear," I continue. "Every. Single. Night. I get a vehicular bloodbath. Carnage and decapitation. So, no thanks to the whole *write-this-down* thing."

Dr. WhoKnowsNothingAtAll doesn't say anything. He just pets the orange cat. But he has this *look*—like he wants to kill me. Maybe strangle me with his tie. Or keep me duct-taped to a chair in his basement where he'd feed me rat poison and gasoline and Brussels sprouts. I stand up and say, "I'm going to the bookstore to buy a notebook." His face transforms. He gets this blank look of vacant, hopeless fear—like he's a zookeeper who just realized that he forgot to lock the lion cage.

And I'm the lion.

"Asher."

"That way I can write my nightmares down so I can be absolutely certain to feel this bad all the time." Then I turn, head for the door, storm out of his office, thinking, *I'm so lost that I don't know where I am anymore, and I'm so lost that I'm going nowhere except spiraling down*, which is what I heard Coach Melvin say when I left his office after the gym locker incident with the baseball bat.

Asher is spiraling down.

The hallway is empty. My sneakers are untied. My shirt untucked. My face beaded with sweat.

"Asher," Dr. WhoKnowsNothingAtAll calls after me from the doorway as I head down C wing.

I ignore him as I storm past some kid in my English class kissing a freshman girl by the lockers. Then I hurry past a bright red poster advertising the pep rally last Friday. I hear band practice in the distance.

The bass pounds.

A sax cries.

It sounds heartbreakingly sad.

Then I hear a basketball slamming the floor in the gym. *Boom, boom, boom.* Then a whistle, loud and shrill. The coach calls, "Triples—crossover, through the legs, behind your back."

A siren screams in the distance. I start to jog.

The coach yells, "Front V-dribble—left hand. Move!"

I have to get out.

I tell myself, *Avoid the quad—too many people you don't want to see.*

I turn left, head toward the doors that open onto the back playing fields.

Mrs. Ellison from the front office scurries by and asks if I have a hall pass.

I don't answer. I just keep going. I have to get outside. Get some air. Some *space*.

I don't fit here anymore.

Not just at school. *I don't fit anywhere.*

It's like no one gets it. *This changed me.*

I need to talk to someone who understands. Someone who is not in my school. *Someone like me.*

I take out my phone. Text Sloane. What are you doing? My heart is racing.

She writes back immediately. Hiding in the girls bathroom.

I take a breath. *I'm not alone.*

I type, How long have you been in there? as I slam through the exit and step outside. I lean against the building and take big gulps of cool spring air. My hands are shaking as I look down at my phone.

No response.

I ask again, How long have you been hiding in the girls bathroom?

Three dots dance on the screen. *She's typing.*

Sloane writes, Ever since my dad died.

11

At the teen group on Thursday night Peter Pan says we're going to talk about forgiveness and then asks, "Does anyone have unresolved anger over their loss?" and when she says it, she's looking right at me.

Will announces, "Mostly I'm mad at God and the universe, and I haven't forgiven them yet because my brother was only eight years old when he died and there's no way that's fair."

Then Sloane says the same thing. She says, "Me too. I'm mad at the cosmic injustice of early death too, because taking my dad wasn't fair."

Peter Pan cautiously asks, "And God?"

Sloane says, "Whole other story." And it's like she slammed a door. I mean, I almost jump when she says it because the words *whole other story* come out of her with *force*.

I say, "It's much easier to be mad at God and the universe than a specific person because you can't really do much about God," but then I bite my tongue because I might have just let the cat out of the bag about Jack Daniels.

I mean, I haven't told any of them that he killed my mom. I just said it was a car crash, so they're probably wondering who the specific person is that I might want to direct my anger at.

Then Peter Pan says, "Asher, do you want to tell us more about what happened to your mom or how you are feeling?" and from her tone I can tell that she handpicked those words carefully.

I say, "No. My mom was just driving along on a perfectly good day and then she drove into a tree for no reason so I can't be mad at her or the tree or anybody really. Just God. I mean, if God's real, that's who I'd be mad at, basically."

I don't think Peter Pan believes me. I have a history of not telling the truth but she probably figures that I can grieve any way that I want to, so if I want to make stuff up, that's okay. But I'm worried that it really isn't okay and that I should probably stop doing it but that doesn't last because next up she asks how my sister is doing and I say, "I don't have any siblings. I'm an only child, and my dad is dead too."

Nobody moves or breathes or says anything so Peter Pan breaks us into two groups for what she says is a healing exercise. She hands everyone a giant clear plastic cup and then takes a couple of big bags of M&M's out of the supply closet. "I'm going to pass these bags of candy around and you can each take as many as you want. Just pour some candy into your cups."

Some kid in the other group yells, "Oh, I thought we were supposed to pee in the cup."

Then someone else in his group asks, "Why would you think that?" and adds, "I want to join the other group," but Peter Pan just ignores both of them.

Sloane and Will are in my group and Sloane pours a few M&M's into her cup and then Will and me fill ours to the brim.

"Everyone, listen up," Peter Pan continues after everyone takes all the candy they want and the bags are returned to her. "The way this works is that you have to tell your fellow group members one thing about yourself for each of the M&M's you put in your cup. So start counting them now."

Will and I look at our cups, do some quick math, and then look at each other like, *Oh, shit!*

Will calls out, "I can't count that high."

Peter Pan doesn't respond directly to him, but she says, "So obviously those of you who took a lot of candy will have to do a lot of talking."

I raise my hand and ask, "Can I give some of mine back?" as Will is pounding his—literally pouring M&M's down his throat—to get rid of them. Peter Pan says, "No. But you can eat them as long as you share."

Will smiles as he holds up his empty cup and says, "Oops," as Sloane slowly counts her M&M's. "I have ten," she announces. "So here goes."

Will sweeps the hair off his face and rolls his eyes and he looks ridiculous because his lips are stained red and blue like a little kid's and I know he's about to claim that he shouldn't have to share because he didn't take any candy.

"*One*. Yellow was my dad's favorite color," Sloane begins. "*Two*. When he was a kid, he had a dog named Buster. *Three*. My mom doesn't know it, but I've been paying a scary dude I found on Craigslist to teach me how to drive my dad's motorcycle when she's at work. *Four*. The day my dad died, I went to a friend's house instead of going to see him. *Five*. Me and my dad had a fight the day he found out he had cancer. *Six*. After he died, I kept my dad's cell phone, and I make my mom pay the bill just so I can listen to his away message. *Seven*. He hated peanut butter. *Eight*. Sometimes I'm so sad that I can't get out of bed, so I cut school. *Nine*. Every night I sneak into my sisters' rooms to check if they are breathing.

And *ten*, I'm never going to get married because I have no one to walk me down the aisle."

I say, "No one hates peanut butter, and I will."

"You will what?" Will asks.

"Walk Sloane down the aisle."

Will looks at me like, *Dude, that's so inappropriate.*

"What?" I challenge. "I can fucking walk, so why not?"

"Okay," Sloane says.

"Okay, *what*?" Will asks.

"Okay, Asher can walk me down the aisle *if* I get married."

So then Will asks the next logical question, which is "What if you marry Asher? Then the plan won't work."

Sloane follows up with "Why would I marry Asher?"

And I ask, "Why *wouldn't* you marry me?"

Then before Sloane can answer, Peter Pan comes over and asks, "How's it going?"

I say, "Not well. Will ate all of his M&M's and didn't tell us anything and Sloane won't marry me."

Peter Pan just stares at me for so long that I have to think of something to do so I count all of her freckles.

She has forty-two. Seventeen on her left cheek. Twenty-one on her right cheek and four on her nose.

I figure she hasn't said anything because there's nothing she *can* say so just to knock the floor out from under a really awkward moment I blurt out, "You have forty-two freckles, give or take."

She says, "Don't change the subject," then lifts her fingers to her face like she might be able to feel the freckles or maybe because she's completely unaware that she *has* freckles or maybe it's just a reflex because she's surprised that I can count.

Then Will says, "I need a ride home."

So I say, "My dad can drive you."

Sloane looks at me and says, "Asher, you just told us your dad was dead *and* that you're an only child."

I say, "That might not have been true."

Sloane asks, "Which part?"

I say, "The whole thing."

Peter Pan is staring at me and Sloane and Will, looking like she's going to throw up or rip up her therapist license and then she turns to the whole group and says, "Okay. Session's over."

I pour all my M&M's into my jacket pocket and then correct her by saying, "No, it's not. We still have ten minutes left."

Peter Pan looks at my empty cup and says, "No, we don't. That clock is wrong," and we all know that she's lying.

Probably because she wants to go sit in a dark closet and count backward from a hundred while breathing into a paper bag.

Or take a horse sedative.

Or move to another city to look for another job.

One that doesn't involve dealing with dead people and the messes they leave behind.

12

After the meeting we drop Will off and eat pizza with no pepperoni and then I ask Chloe if she wants to play a game and she says, "Yes," and then she asks, "Can I have chocolate pudding first?" and I say, "No. Never. Not even when you are a hundred." Then her bottom lip trembles and she gets mad but that only lasts for a minute because I offer to play bear picnic which involves sitting in tiny chairs and pretending to feed stuffed animals fake plastic food and me being bossed around by Chloe.

Later that night my dad sticks his head into my room and asks, "Why is Chloe wearing a bike helmet and life jacket?" He doesn't sound annoyed or overly alarmed, just defeated. Like, *here we go again.*

I figure there are a thousand things I could say in response to that question. I mean, I could tell him that we were just playing a game and that the whole thing was Chloe's idea and I tried to talk her out of it. I could even provide details and tell him that she wanted to pretend we were out to sea riding giant water tricycles and were being chased by sea monsters and jellyfish. Or I could go in a more serious direction and tell him that Chloe's afraid of dying and that I'm afraid of dying—her dying, me dying, *you dying, Dad*—but I don't. Instead, I go with the first solid, respectable, irrefutable-at-the-moment lie that pops into my head. One that will shift the blame to someone not currently under our roof. I say, "Mrs. Levitt thought it would be a good idea."

My dad clearly isn't expecting a response that is so outrageously and obviously ridiculous, so he says, "What?" but it comes out as *WHAT?????* And I take this as an opportunity to deflect. *I tell him that I fired her.*

"You fired Mrs. Levitt?" he repeats.

I nod.

"Again?" he asks. "You fired her again? We talked about this, Ash."

My dad looks awful. Beaten down. Worse than usual for a Thursday night. He takes out his phone and types something.

I feel bad but shrug to confirm. I guess I'm like one of those drowning victims who panics and pulls anybody who comes to rescue them under the water.

"You know that I always *un-fire* her, and I just un-fired her," he states.

I don't react. It's just a game we play. I fire Mrs. Levitt, and my dad tells her I'm a fucking mess and he's sorry and she's rehired.

"Look, Asher. I know you're just trying to keep Chloe safe, but sleeping in a bike helmet and a life jacket isn't making her any safer from—"

I stop him right there. "Do you know what the number one killer of children under age five is?"

He just stares at me blankly. He looks spent—like he's not up for a whole debate probably because he has a job and two kids and bills to pay and HIS WIFE DIED and I keep firing our babysitter. He has bags under his eyes—no, not bags, actual *shopping carts*, big, puffy, cloudlike shopping carts overflowing with exhaustion and worry. He shakes his head.

"Motor vehicle crashes," I report. "Followed by firearm-related injury, malignant neoplasm, suffocation, AND DROWNING. Drowning in swimming pools."

"Asher, we don't have a pool," he says, to which I respond, *"So?"*

"So, if we don't have a pool, then it would be difficult for Chloe to actually drown tonight, unless—"

"Toilets," I interject.

"Toilets?" He sounds genuinely baffled.

"Not *just* toilets," I say. "Dog bowls and cleaning buckets, too."

"Asher, we don't have a dog, and a dog bowl would have to be massive for a child Chloe's age to actually—"

I state the obvious. "We do have three toilets, and they're all full of water."

"I see your point. But don't you think Chloe is a little big to drown in a . . . ?" He's about to say "toilet," and he's holding his hands up to signify the relatively small amount of water they hold, but I jump in front of that by shaking my head. Then I briefly consider reminding him that we both thought MOM WOULDN'T DIE DRIVING TO THE MALL TO BUY SOCCER CLEATS AND THAT HAPPENED and WHERE DID THAT THINKING GET US? But I don't say that. I just sit there.

And my dad just stands there. It's like he's in over his head. I mean, *with me.*

And.

This.

Whole.

Thing.

My dad stares at me for a while, not talking, and then I hear his phone ping. I look away because I know it's the link I just sent him to a website that discusses little kids drowning in toilets and pet bowls. He glances down at his phone, and then he looks at the floor for a minute and then at me again before he asks, "And the aluminum foil mittens on her hands? That's to protect her from what, exactly?"

It comes out as a whisper. A sad, defeated whisper. "Extremely low frequency electromagnetic radiation."

He nods his head slowly and then walks away.

After he leaves, I whisper, *I'm sorry, Dad. I can't help it.*

Then I text Sloane, Are Claire and Anna breathing? Did you check?

She writes back. Yes, I checked. And yes, they are breathing. Then she types, I'm glad someone understands, and then she sends back a red heart emoji and a smile with a tear.

I type, Check again and add a skull and crossbones emoji, three toilets, and a dog bowl. Then I send her a picture of Chloe splayed out on her bed surrounded by an ocean of stuffed animals and picture books. Her bike helmet is strapped to her head. Her soft blond hair is peeking out from underneath the bright pink plastic of the helmet. Her lips form a perfect pink heart. Her Peppa Pig life jacket is tightly buckled on top of her Little Mermaid pajamas. It looks like she is floating in the blankets and sheets that swirl all around her. Her aluminum foil hands are hidden beneath the waves.

Sloane texts back, She looks safe.

I write, Safe enough?

Sloane takes a minute to respond, but then she types, I don't know.

I signed up for another group.

Technically I shouldn't be allowed to attend because it's a group for people who haven't lost anyone yet but will soon. So it's like they're getting ready to be even sadder than they are now. When I ask my dad to drive me, he says, "Are you sure, Ash? It's Friday. Maybe you should go to a movie or hang out with friends." I tell him all my friends are pretty much the people in Room 212 at the hospital now, and he says, "Okay, then."

Tomorrow is Saturday and I have to plant sweet peas with Henry so on the way to group I ask my dad if we can stop real quick at the hardware store. He says yes, and after we park in front, he asks what I need to get and I say, "Nothing," then race inside.

It turns out that sweet peas are not peas you eat; they're flowers. I'm looking for vegetable seeds, like edible-podded peas, maybe English peas or snow peas, but find no sweet pea seeds that are food, just flower seed packets with names like Heirloom Cupid Sweet Pea and Queen of the Night Sweet Pea and Strawberry Sundae Sweet Pea with rosy bicolor and white blooms and Henry Eckford Sweet Pea with bold-orange-to-soft-salmon flowers with a strong, favorable scent, which were introduced in 1904.

I realize that I don't know Henry's last name, but I wonder if it's Eckford.

I have to hurry because my dad is waiting in the car and group is going to start and when I can't decide which seeds to buy because I thought sweet peas would just be sweet peas, not a whole complicated thing, I buy all the sweet peas. One packet of each kind they have, which is fourteen packets, because you don't want to show up at someone's house with the wrong sweet peas when sweet peas are all they have left.

When I get back to the car, my dad asks what I bought, and I say, "Nothing," and he says, "Okay," and then we both look at the brown paper bag, feeling weird. Then we just drive to Room 212 without talking.

I totally get that they don't like to mix in people like me who already lost someone with people who are waiting to lose someone but when I show up, Peter Pan doesn't tell me I'm not allowed to be here or I'm here on the wrong day; she just smiles and says, "Asher, come on in." Deep inside I figure she's probably thinking, *Oh, shit! Not Asher again*, because she's worried that I'd blurt out something awful like *I killed my mom* or invite myself over to someone's house to plant sweet peas, but she doesn't say that, probably because she doesn't want to hurt my feelings. So, I just sit down and it's all awkward because no one else is here and there's nothing to say, so we both just try not to breathe or make noise or look at each other and then just when I'm thinking, *Shit, this is too weird*, my phone pings and it's a text from Grace. She sent a picture of her with her friends. They're crammed into a booth at a restaurant and laughing. I type, Can't wait to meet them and hit send, and then Peter Pan looks over at me and asks, "Asher, did you read the book I gave you?"

I lie and say, "No."

I know what she wanted me to say. That I read the book, devoured it in an hour and then read it again and again and I understood not only the part about the picture of the hat and the boa constrictor but also the part about the picture of the crate and that when she gave me the book it was like she'd drawn me a picture of a crate and what I needed was inside. I didn't want to admit any of that because when she gave me the book I wanted to see *an empty crate*. Just a fucking crate with nothing in it. Not a crate full of possibility. I'm not saying I don't want help, and I'm not saying the book isn't full of metaphors for everything wrong with me; I'm just saying that I'm not ready to admit when something might be helping, I mean, if that makes any sense, which it probably doesn't because you're probably normal and I'm spiraling down.

Then Peter Pan tells me that the part of the book she likes the best is when the Little Prince explains that he lives in a place that is so small that if you move your chair a few feet you can see the sun set on the other side of the planet.

I want to tell her that I liked all of it the best, but mostly the part about the flower with thorns, and I hope she knows that I am basically like a rose and that I don't mean to hurt anyone; it's just that I need the thorns for protection because I am vulnerable and weak. But of course I can't tell her that because I DIDN'T READ THE BOOK, so I just say, "In July, Henry and I will bring you sweet peas and they will be as beautiful as the sunset and I looked it up—sweet peas don't have thorns, just in case you were wondering." Then I tell her that she won't have to move her chair at all to see the sweet peas because Room 212 is so small that she'll be able to see them from everywhere.

She gets this surprised and kind of confused look on her face like I am a crate FULL OF LIES and she can't decide if she wants to know more about what's inside or if that is the worst idea ever and she should just cover her eyes or look the other way because Asher is a crate you do not want to peek inside of under any circumstances. But then luckily all the people who are about to lose someone start showing up and basically change the subject.

I try not to say anything that will upset anyone but they say all sorts of things that upset me because it never occurred to me before the Friday night group that some people know ahead of time that they are going to lose someone so it's like pain in slow motion instead of having no warning at all and getting blindsided by an 18-wheeler in the middle of the day.

The people in the Friday night group mostly have family members who are dying of cancer because that's something that happens slowly, or at least more slowly than a car crash, and they all say that it's so hard to see their family members in pain and suffering and scared about dying. The way I see it is that the people in the slow-motion group get to prepare and say goodbye and that means they can be more careful and plan on not getting their soccer cleats stolen so their mom might not go to the mall and die and then she will live to be eighty or a hundred, and maybe they will get to prepare something nice to say instead of maybe hanging up on her when she says they should be more careful with their things because they were mad that they were going to miss the soccer game with the team from four towns over and now they can't even say they are sorry, they didn't mean it, and they can't call her back and not hang up or plan something nice to say when she is as old as Henry and they are mixing the sleeping pills she saved up to put in chocolate pudding so she can go peacefully and on her terms right after they say, "I love you more than anything in the whole world and I will take care of everything, especially Chloe so don't worry."

Basically there is no one in the Friday night group as good as Henry or Sloane or Will so it's pretty much a bust. But when I head out of Room 212, I start to think about how I am going to go about killing Jack Daniels, so the meeting isn't a complete waste of time. I mean, I start to wonder whether it should be the *slow way* so his family can say goodbye or the *fast way* so they can feel bad that they didn't get a chance to say goodbye and then I start to think more about Connor and Grace and their mom and everything they'll feel if I kill Jack Daniels either the slow way or the fast way and that's fucked up so I decide that maybe I should just drive to 114 Culvert Street in Memphis and stop by, knock on the door, tell them who I am, break up with Grace, and see Jack Daniels for myself, but not kill him.

I'm on the way out of the hospital when I'm thinking, *Which way would be better, the slow way or the fast way or no way at all?* I decide that if I have to pick, it'd be pretty hard to choose between cancer and a car crash, or between being a murderer and killing a murderer. Then I throw up in the men's room because I realize that *being a murderer* and *killing a murderer* are pretty much the same thing and when I look at my face in the restroom mirror and see how pale and drawn it looks, I pretty much figure that I have cancer that is eating away at my insides. Maybe brain cancer and stomach cancer and heart cancer, if there is such a thing, and all that cancer is making me crazy and then I decide that I should try to think about something else once in a while besides the soccer cleats and the Jaws of Life and the utility pole that fell on my mom's car and crushed her. Then maybe everyone wouldn't be so worried about me, and I wouldn't have to drive sixteen hours and fifty-one minutes to 114 Culvert Street in Memphis to maybe or maybe not kill Jack Daniels.

14

On Saturday morning I go to Henry's house to plant sweet peas and when my dad drives me over he's upbeat. Okay, practically singing-in-the-shower-waltzing-on-the-moon upbeat because he's probably thinking that things are looking up because I'm doing something normal like visiting a friend on a Saturday, but then he sinks into a tar pit when he sees Henry's old person house and the junk car in the driveway with the tire missing and the bushes that need trimming and the peeling paint. Then the tar pit swallows him whole when he sees Henry at the door with his aluminum walker legs because I told my dad that I was going to hang out with a friend from the bereavement group, the new friend I told him about named Henry, but he probably didn't think that Henry would be someone who has peeling paint and rickety gutters and is a hundred years old and I'm thinking that I'm sorry but things in life just surprise you sometimes.

Like, totally fucking kick you in the stomach and make you bleed.

I think Henry is surprised to see me even though I told him on Wednesday night that I would come over at eleven o'clock on this coming Saturday to plant sweet peas. Maybe he's not as surprised as my dad and not tar-pit surprised; it's more like happy surprised, like he's being swallowed by something bright and shiny, which makes no sense at all since I am the least bright and shiny thing in the whole universe. Before I get out of the car, my dad asks, "Have you thought about calling Emily?"

I say, "I told you we broke up a year ago, so don't keep asking me about her." Then I add, "Besides, I told you I have a new girlfriend I met online." He gives me a skeptical look and I tell myself to stop talking.

My dad looks worried and he scrunches up his face as if he's in pain, like maybe I just stepped on his foot or told him I lost Chloe at the mall but after he winces and sighs he drops that line of questioning and asks, "What's in the bag, Asher?" and I tell him this time.

"Sweet peas."

Now my dad looks like he's going to cry and then Henry lifts his hand from his walker and waves at us and smiles an old-person smile and my dad looks over at him and asks, "Do you have your phone?" and I nod and he adds, "Call me when you want to be picked up." I get out of the car and he drives away and for a minute I worry that he will drive at high speed into a tree or get hit by an 18-wheel tractor trailer truck driven by a guy named Jack Daniels and then I'll have to take care of Chloe all by myself and that scares me because she doesn't like pepperoni on pizza because orange meat cut in circles makes no sense and tastes weird and if you order it by mistake because you forget, then it needs to be picked off or she won't be able to eat, and then she would starve to death and I would have no one at all.

Henry is still waving at me as my dad pulls out and I walk up the path to his house. His skin looks pale and almost transparent in the sunlight. I should have noticed this before but didn't and when I get close I try not to stare at his forearms and forehead but when he's out in the sunlight standing on his front stoop he looks like one of those white jellyfish that you can see through. Henry's talking but I'm not listening; instead I'm tracing the thick blue veins that run like a tangle of roads to and from his heart and worrying that my dad might burn up in a fiery car crash.

When Henry brings me inside his house it's all dark and closed up and smells like old people and Evelyn is all over the place even though she's gone. She's in the teacups and the pictures and the curtains and the pillows on the couch and there's so much Evelyn that it makes sense when Henry says, "I could never move away from here and I hate to leave the house even for a few minutes because when I'm here it's like Evelyn's hugging me everywhere I go."

He takes me to the back of the house and we sit down in the kitchen and I hand him the sweet pea packets I bought and he shows me how to nick the seeds with my fingernail so they'll grow faster and after that we soak the seeds on wet towels for an hour to soften them and then he pulls out some big paper maps and shows me some of the places he and Evelyn never got to see. Then we go out back and I dig a trench only an inch deep and we bury the seeds in the dirt in Henry's backyard. Henry sprinkles them with water and then shows me how to hang long rows of string for them to climb on because even though the plants will be tall, the stems will be wispy and the flowers will be tiny and when they come up, they might need help standing.

It takes us a couple of hours to plant the sweet peas because I'm not a farmer and Henry's no good with a shovel. When we're finished, Henry says, "You can come back anytime you want to, but in July there will be so many flowers in so many colors that it will be like Evelyn isn't even gone." Henry is standing on the back steps looking as lanky and wispy as a sweet pea. I'm worrying that the wind will blow and knock him to the ground and then just as I'm about to hop up to steady him he secures his hold on his walker and looks over at me and says, "Evelyn is Eve and I am Adam."

I ask, "You mean like in the Bible?" and then I just sit there in the dirt as he stares straight ahead and adds, "Evelyn is the garden at the headwaters of four rivers." He's holding a bunch of empty sweet pea seed packets in his hands and clutching his walker and he's now looking up at the sky as his hands shake and his lips tremble like he's praying or going to cry and I'm not worried about him falling anymore; I'm worried that he's having a stroke or this is the onset of dementia or Alzheimer's or some other old person brain disease that I don't know about so I nervously ask, "What does that mean?" and Henry says, "Everything. It means everything." Then Henry looks at me and says, "You wouldn't understand, Asher."

I say, "That's not true. I had everything once too," and Henry looks at me hard, then nods and steps inside the house and as the screen door bangs against the wood I just keep sitting there on the ground looking up at the twine thinking about the fact that it makes no sense that something as fragile as a sweet pea could just spring from the dirt and figure out all by itself that it has to reach out for something to hold on to.

But then I decide that Henrys and Ashers and Wills and Sloanes are no different from raindrops on window glass or sweet peas. We're all just trying really hard to cling to something we're not entirely sure can hold us up.

I don't call my dad to pick me up. Instead I walk home from Henry's and on the way I get a text from Grace saying, I can't wait for prom, and she adds a thousand exclamation points and emojis of a prom dress and a champagne bottle and I think, *Oh, shit, that's a week from today.*

Then I decide that I'll just have to ask my dad if I can drive again and he'll probably say, "Sure, here are the keys!" because even though he'll be scared and thinking that it's a bad idea for me to drive a car because I might get hit by an 18-wheeler or stomp on the accelerator and drive into a stone bridge abutment for no reason at all, he's probably running low on what he has to say no with because his wife got killed and won't ever be coming home again. I figure he'll probably be thinking that I'll just drive around or visit a friend—hopefully not Henry because that's just weird—but he'll never think that I might be driving to 114 Culvert Street in Memphis, Tennessee, because that's where Jack Daniels lives.

Then I text Grace back, Me too! Can't wait! and add a tuxedo emoji and six hearts, and then decide that maybe I'll ask Sloane and Will if they want to come to Memphis with me because it'll work out perfectly since school ends this Thursday. Next I decide that maybe I could ask Henry to come along with us too because he's good with maps. I know that because when he took out that big map of the world before we planted the sweet peas and he showed me all the places he and Evelyn wanted to go visit but didn't get a chance to because life got in the way, he looked like he knew his way around the world—at least if that world was condensed down to a tangled mess of lines on paper.

I figure we might need Henry because my dad's car is old and doesn't have GPS and we might have to use a map if we have to turn our phones off if my dad figures out that we're gone and decides to call the police, because the police will be able to find us if our phones are turned on. Henry won't have to turn his phone off because I saw it and it's not a smartphone. It was just for calling Evelyn when they were in the house and he couldn't find her and she isn't here anymore and then it was just for calling the police and his children after Evelyn ate the chocolate pudding and died but that already happened so now his phone never rings and he never calls anyone. It's just a giant plastic thing with big numbers that old people can see and it doesn't really matter if it is on or off if all the people you know are already dead and the ones who aren't don't want to hear from you.

When I get in the house I go to my room and call Father and Son Formal Wear and order a tuxedo in size thirty-eight regular for pickup next Thursday. Then I send Henry a postcard. I have no choice because he doesn't have a real cell phone that I can send a text to or an email address, either, and calling him would just be too weird because he might be sleeping and I wouldn't know what to say and he can't hear that well and I don't know his number anyway, so I find an old postcard in my desk that I saved from Disney World and write:

DEAR HENRY—
YOU WANTED TO GO TO GRACELAND WITH
EVELYN TO SEE THE KING'S HOUSE AND THE
MEDITATION GARDEN AND ELVIS'S CUSTOM JET
AND YOU DIDN'T GET TO GO WITH HER SO I WAS
THINKING MAYBE YOU WANT TO GO WITH ME.
YOU CAN TELL ME YES AT THE GROUP MEETING
IN ROOM 212 OR SEND ME A POSTCARD—
EITHER WAY—BUT IT WILL TAKE 16 HOURS AND
51 MINUTES TO DRIVE TO MEMPHIS, AND I CAN
PICK YOU UP AND TAKE YOU THERE AND WE
WILL BE BACK IN TIME TO SEE THE SWEET PEAS
BLOOM AND MAYBE IT WOULD BE COOL TO GO ON
A TRIP LIKE THAT.

By the time I put the postcard in the mailbox, my head hurts and my feet feel like I have concrete in my shoes, but the postcard is as light as air. Almost like it has wings and feathers and can fly to Henry's house all by itself.

16

On Monday in homeroom I ask to go to the nurse basically because I don't want to be here. Mr. Killjoy just looks at me like, *Not this again.* Or *Oh, shit, it's Asher.* But he says, "Fine. Go."

The nurse says, "Hi, Asher, what's wrong today?" And I just look at her like, *What do you think?* but just say, "The usual," and she says, "Okay, go ahead and lie down," and then she has to take my temperature because that's what they do when you go to the nurse. She announces, "It's ninety-eight point six, which is normal," and then she looks at me with that *we all know you are faking it* face, so I say, "We both know that I'm burning up and your stupid thermometer is broken," so she lets her shoulders drop and kind of sighs, and then she says, "Would you like some apple juice?" and I say, "Yes, please. That sounds nice."

It's pretty much the same every time I go to the nurse. Grave disappointment and massive skepticism on the part of Nurse Ratched followed by a dose of sympathy and resignation. When she brings me the apple juice in a little paper cup, she always asks, "How's Chloe?" and I always say, "She's as good as you can be if your mom burns up in a car accident and you'll never see her again." Then unless there's some emergency, like EMS is en route because some kid had an asthma attack and can't breathe or someone is having hallucinations and seizures or is totally psychotic from doing rails of Adderall with Kenny Silbert in the bathroom, she'll pretty much say, "Asher, do you want to play Go Fish?" and I say, "Yes." But this time she calls my dad and I get to leave early.

When we get home, I ask my dad if I can take the car for a week to drive to Memphis with Henry to see Graceland. He looks like he's in pain when he says no, which really surprises me—not the pain part, the "no" part. That's when I decide to just take the car anyway.

You know, like *steal it*. This Friday.

In four days.

I figure my dad won't do anything about me stealing the car because looking at the truth is like staring into the sun on a hot day and nobody wants to do that because it hurts so much that it can burn out your eyes and explode your heart.

So I figure that I'm the sun on a hot day that nobody wants to look at.

Nobody wants to look at Asher spiraling out of control because there's no way to stop him.

Even to me it's obvious that the weasels are closing in.

17

On Monday night in Room 212 Peter Pan tells me and Henry and all the old people about a boy named Zachary.

She says that when he was three years old, his dad was killed by a substance-impaired driver. That means someone who took drugs, either the illegal kind or the prescription kind you get at the doctor that says *use caution when driving a motor vehicle or operating heavy equipment* right on the bottle. Then she tells us that when he was nine, Zachary's mom died from cancer and then when he was fifteen, he was riding his bike and Zachary was killed by an impaired driver using drugs. She says that the drugged driver who hit Zachary only went to jail for one month because the judge said the accident was Zachary's fault. He was riding his bike where he wasn't supposed to be riding it. I was thinking, *What the fuck*, but it was more like WHAT THE FUCK!!!!!! and I figure the moral I was supposed to take away from this story was how lucky I am that Jack Daniels only killed my mom. But that pretty much doesn't take root. Maybe I have concrete for brains, but I immediately start thinking that me and Chloe and my dad might—read, PROBABLY WILL—die any minute. Then I start to think about the fact that Zachary would have had to go to grieving groups on every day of the week to cover all his situations except he can't go to any of them because he got killed too and they don't have grieving groups for people who are dead because they can't show up.

When I get home I go straight to the garage and take the wheels off Chloe's bike. Not just the training wheels but the real wheels too. Then I hit the bike with a hammer and smash it into a thousand little pieces because there is no way that I can be sure that Chloe won't ride her bike on the wrong part of the road or on the wrong road or right down the double yellow line on the center of some highway with her eyes closed. When my dad hears all the noise in the garage he sticks his head in and looks around and when I look up at him he looks really tired and worn down and his hair is kind of sticking out all over the place and then I hear him sigh right before he asks, "What happened to Chloe's bike?"

I just stand there and say, "It looks like someone broke into the garage and took the wheels off and smashed it." Then I put the hammer down and we both stare at it.

The hammer, not the bike.

Next, I tell him what happened to Zachary and he says he never heard that story and I say I'm surprised because it should be a really famous story like the moon landing or Pearl Harbor or 9/11 and I tell him that Zachary was probably wishing that someone smashed his bike with a hammer, so Chloe's actually lucky. My dad just looks at me like he wants to say something like *Everything will be okay.* Or *Do you want to try another shrink?* Or *Why can't you just be normal?* Or *What do you think about getting Chloe a new bike because she is going to cry when she sees this one?* But I figure that he probably figures that maybe he shouldn't say anything at all on account of the fact that whatever he says won't help or else if it does help it would be because whatever he says is a lie because nothing will be okay if it's your fault when a truck runs you over and you're just a kid on your bike or a mom in your car and the truck driver is Jack Daniels or Meth Amphetamines or if one dead person isn't all you get in life. I mean, if your dad dies and then your mom dies and then you die, what's the point of anything?

Then I start thinking about how many grieving groups they would need to have just for the 10,262 people killed last year by drunk drivers and how there just aren't enough days in the week to take care of that many people with dead family members so I just sit down on the garage steps and think about hammers and baseball bats and then my dad sits down next to me.

I'm thinking about the fact that I only have three days left of school, and only four days left before I leave to go to 114 Culvert Street in Memphis so I text Will and Sloane to see if they want to go with me on a savage journey to the heart of my American nightmare, meaning a road trip to Memphis but without any drugs or ether or a quart of tequila.

I tell them that my friend Henry who is a hundred years old and whose wife died wants to go to see Elvis's house and we should take him.

They both say yes right away, like going to Graceland with some old guy and the new kid they just met in Room 212 is exactly the thing they've been waiting for.

My dad asks me who I'm texting and I say, "My new friends Sloane and Will," and I feel like maybe I lifted some of the weight off his back. But that's only because he doesn't know what's coming and how heavy a weight he'd have to carry if he had to walk around knowing that I'm planning to kill someone.

In the car on the way to the hospital on Tuesday night I send a text to Grace and my dad glances over and asks who I'm texting. I say, "It's the girl I told you about who I met online," and he smiles, like, really smiles, and it breaks my heart to see how eager he is for me to have friends again and be normal when I know that I am so far from normal that normal's like a country on the other side of the world that I may never get to visit again in my whole life.

Then after I take the elevator to the second floor and walk right past the vending machines and the restrooms on the left and take a seat in the circle of chairs in Room 212, Peter Pan starts the meeting by asking if anyone has anything that they want to talk about, and nobody does. When no one volunteers or speaks up, she says, "For a healing exercise today, I want all of you to think about the things people said to you after your loved one died. Things that they thought would help but might not have."

A few people shuffle their feet and pretty much everyone looks uncomfortable. When no one volunteers anything, I shoot Will a glance, like *This is a bust*, but Peter Pan keeps talking. "Maybe there's something someone said that was meant to make you feel better, but it really hurt." She looks around, but still no one says anything because basically no one wants to climb on *that* bus. But she pushes harder. "Come on, everyone. We have to do the heavy lifting if we want to get better." She keeps looking around the room, and we're all watching, hoping that her eyes don't land on us. And then her eyes land on me.

"Asher?"

I flinch. *Finger-on-the-pin-of-a-hand-grenade* flinch.

Then, I don't know why exactly, but something inside me fires and explodes. *Anxiety. Panic. Anger.* I want to flee. Or lash out. And I know that I can't do either. So I retreat. Look down. Find a safe haven in my sneakers. No one is saying anything and I start counting back from a hundred like Dr. WhoKnowsNothingAtAll suggested I do in situations of extreme stress. Before I get to ninety, Peter Pan says, "Come on, Asher."

I look up from my feet and glance around the room and it's clear that we're all, to one degree or another, *broken*. Like Room 212 is a fix-it shop full of people all hoping to be put back together again and now everyone in the group is waiting for me to respond like I have a way to fix them. Like my words can raise the dead or heal a broken heart in a broken person when I can't even heal myself.

I don't. Won't. *Can't* say anything.

Sloane drops her eyes to stare at her feet.

Will slips back behind his hair.

"Anyone else want to volunteer?" Peter Pan asks, all hopeful as her eyes leave me and she glances around the room again.

Then some girl calls out so softly that I can barely hear her. She says, "The worst thing anyone said to me was when I overheard my best friend say, 'Come on, Andrea should have snapped out of it by now.'"

Will blurts out, "The thing that bothered me the most was when people said, 'Michael's with God now.'"

A couple of people shuffle their feet again and nod to agree with him. We all heard that one in one form or another. *Your mom's in a better place, Asher.*

With the room still spinning and my heart thumping hard and my thoughts running on a hot rampage in my head, Peter Pan asks Will, "How did that make you feel?"

He says, "Like I wanted to say, 'Tell God to give him the fuck back.'"

Then one of the kids calls out, "At least she didn't suffer." And that one hits me hard because *everyone* said that to me, and each time I heard it, I wanted to scream, *BUT I'M SUFFERING! MY DAD IS SUFFERING! CHLOE IS SUFFERING!*

I'm listening to everything and I'm still shaky with my adrenaline pumping like I've got an IV dispensing Red Bull directly into my veins but I feel the panic start to wane a bit because for some reason it feels good to hear everyone else talk. It's like finding out that *I'm not completely alone in my head with this monster.*

Peter Pan asks the group, "And did it help? The tough-love-get-over-it message?"

I want to yell, *No, if it helped, we wouldn't be here and be such a big fucking collective mess,* but I don't say that and no one else answers her either, so she says, "I'm guessing no, it didn't help. I'm guessing it just made you feel angry and alone." Then she looks right at me again.

I still don't talk, but I don't look away, either. *I'm listening to her.* And I'm thinking, *Yeah, I heard those things. All of them and more. And yes, I feel angry and alone. Maybe not as alone as I did a few minutes ago, but SO ALONE.*

"But I want you to remember this," she continues. "No one means to hurt us when they say those things. *They are trying to help.*"

I look back down at my shoes. They're not the Nike Superflys in lime green in men's size eleven and a half. They're red canvas Converse high-tops in a size twelve. And they are the wrong shoes. *Every single thing about them is wrong.*

I can't see Peter Pan's face because I'm staring at my feet, but I hear her voice as she says, "When they say, 'She's in a better place now,' or 'He's with God,' or 'Why aren't you better yet?' they aren't trying to hurt us. The truth is, we don't know how to grieve, and our friends and family don't know how to help us. So we're all a little lost." Then she adds, "Here's what I want you to understand. What happened to everyone in this room is the biggest loss a human being can experience. It is horrifically and unfathomably sad. And losing someone you love isn't just a heartbreak; it can be bone-chilling scary. And it can bring up emotions you didn't even know that you had. So, right now, right here, I'm going to give you permission to ignore all your well-meaning but clueless friends and family members who tell you to suck it up. Or who tell you that you're grieving wrong. I'm going to tell you to go ahead and be as sad as you want, for as long as you want, in any way you want, but with one caveat."

I look up.

She looks so sincere. Everyone is looking at her. It's like we're desperate to hear what she has to say. *We need to know how to feel better.*

"Just don't be so sad that it destroys you. Land just short of that. Because if you are *that* sad, so sad that it destroys your life, that means the cancer or the accident or the heart attack that took your loved one, took you, too."

She pauses so that can sink in, then adds, "I want all of you to say to yourselves, 'I can ignore the well-wishers who get frustrated that I'm not getting back to normal fast enough for them and who say things that hurt, because I know they are just *trying* to help, and they don't know *how* to help. And I can be sad. *I should be sad if sad feels right*—even massively sad—for a long time if that's *what I feel*. Just not *self-destruct sad*. Never self-destruct sad."

She stops talking, and the room becomes so quiet that it's deafening.

And then a girl starts to cry.

Sloane gets up to comfort the girl, and her motorcycle boots make loud clomps as she shuffles and stomps across the room.

No one else moves, but I want to *bolt*. Run out the door, go left past the vending machines and the restrooms on the right, skip the elevator and take the stairs two at a time. Not because the meeting is over, but because it's too intense. And not because what happened is bad, but because it helped. No one has ever said something like that to me. No one has ever said that it's *normal* to be this sad. I was always *too sad* or *the wrong kind of sad*. Or *more sad* than people think I should be.

I want to run, but I'm still sitting here looking at my red canvas Converse sneakers when I call out in the deafening quiet of the room, "The worst thing anyone ever said to me was that it's okay to drink and drive, even if you kill someone."

My voice is loud enough and strong enough that it gets everyone's attention—but I'm guessing that it surprises the hell out of me the most. I didn't mean to talk. The words just *erupt*.

I look up and Peter Pan's mouth is open. The room is standing still. The girl has stopped crying. I catch Sloane's eye as she turns toward me. I immediately wish I could claw back the words that just flew from my mouth with such force THAT I COULDN'T STOP THEM, because when I see Sloane and Peter Pan and the other kids looking at me, it's evident that I just knocked the Earth off its axis and we're all tumbling into oblivion.

I look back down at my sneakers again.

Peter Pan says, "Asher, I'm sure no one actually said that. Maybe . . ." Her voice is little-kid-mom soft, but I know she's just like all the other people who say shit and mean well but DON'T FUCKING GET IT and I can't listen to that now, so I say, "Yes. Someone. Did. My mom was killed by the drunk driver of an eighteen-wheel tractor trailer and the judge said, 'Not guilty.' He said that my dead mom wasn't enough evidence to convict. She was decapitated when her car was forced off the road and smashed at high speed into a utility pole that came down and crushed her while the car was upside down and she was strapped into the front seat. Then the gas tank ignited and her body burned. And the guy who did it was drunk and he got away with it because the cop on the scene didn't do a Breathalyzer. As in, *nothing whatsoever happened to the truck driver.* So the worst thing anyone ever said to me after my mom died was that it's okay to drink and drive even if it means that you kill someone."

I'm in a staring contest with Peter Pan that is so intense and laser focused that it's like there's all this energy shooting out of our eyes, but I'm still aware of everyone else in the room. Sloane's holding on to the girl she was hugging. Will is staring at me with his mouth open and eyes wide and then he ducks back behind his steel helmet of hair.

No one wants to hear what I just said, and no one wants to process it now that I've said it. It's just another ugly thing that's sitting there on the floor of Room 212 that I wish I could take back but can't. I can't take it back, but Peter Pan can't just *leave it there*. She has to say or do *something* because it's such a hideous, amorphous, consuming thing and it's just FUCKING SITTING THERE.

I expect her to say, *Leave now, Asher! Just go home or go away! You're too messed up to be here! I can't help you!* Or *That's not true!* Or *Meeting's over!* Because the truth, my truth, is just too raw and hideous to speak out loud, and it's too raw and hideous for a human being to hear, let alone try to live with. Then I want to tell all of them about the 10,262 people who were killed in drunk driving accidents last year, but that seems too fucking cruel, so I just sit there with my mouth shut.

Because of the size and shape of the God-awful thing I just said, it takes Peter Pan a minute to figure out how to respond. She eventually says, "My God, Asher, that's horrible and a travesty of justice, and I am so, so, very, very sorry." And then she comes over and sits down next to me and hugs me. It's not awkward this time, and I don't pull away because it's just the right kind of hug—a big, warm, arms-wrapped-tight, mom-hugging-a-hurt-child hug—so I sink into it and hug her back.

Then I say, "I want to kill the guy who did this to my family."

She says, "I would feel exactly the same way. But feelings are just feelings, and we don't have to act on them."

I don't tell her about the fact that my mom was just trying to pick up soccer cleats at the mall because some low-life hurtbag stole mine even though they were in my locker because I WAS BEING CAREFUL WITH MY THINGS and I don't tell her how I blame the kid who took them and Mia Hamm for making me love soccer and whoever invented tar and the people who built the mall and the governor of New Jersey for allowing people to drive. And I don't tell her about Grace and Connor and the prom. I just cry and think about what everyone in this room just said—that I have to suffer through hearing, *Asher, you've been sad long enough.* Or *Asher's no fun anymore*, and deal with the people who think they are helping me by pointing out the fact that I should be okay when I'm a fucking mess. Then I think, *It's like they're trying to make me feel worse when all I need to hear is that it sucks.* And that I should be sad. *Profoundly sad* because someone I don't know decided to drink Jack Daniel's and drive a big rig into my mom.

Then I whisper, "I don't know how to get better from this kind of hurt."

And Peter Pan says, "Nobody does, Asher. But we will all take the journey with you."

19

On Wednesday in the old people group nothing much happens except Henry tells me that he'll come to Memphis to go to the King's house and I tell him I'll pick him up on Friday morning at ten and then on Thursday in my weekly session with Dr. WhoKnowsNothingAtAll he's not talking and I'm not talking so I start humming this song Chloe sings from this kids' cartoon called *Daniel Tiger's Neighborhood.*

Then I look around the office and see this poster of the planet Earth as seen from outer space and the Earth has this ethereal rim of amber and fiery gold around it like it's emitting this magical and beautiful energy and that makes me think about a film I saw once with Denzel Washington about the end of the world. I'm trying to remember who the costar of that movie is when Dr. WhoKnowsNothingAtAll suddenly decides to speak, probably because he figures he's not doing his job if we have a whole shrink session with me humming the theme song from a kids' cartoon and him looking at his cat statues without either one of us talking. He opens the conversation with a real zinger, too. He's not like, *How was your week, Asher?* Or *Is there anything you want to talk about?* Or *What are your summer plans?* He says, "Let's discuss what happened with the baseball bat."

I'm thinking, *Shit, no!* Then he says, "You did a lot of damage in the locker room that day, and we never really discussed it." I figure he's just trying to tie up some of the loose ends in my file before summer vacation, so I just start humming louder. He starts tapping his pencil on his yellow pad like he can't wait to write down one final damning and discouraging note in my official record, but I'm thinking that the incident with the baseball bat happened over a year ago, so why would I want to talk about it now—or why would anyone want to talk about it *ever*? And that's when I decide that I NEED A DISTRACTION DEVICE, so I launch into a whole thing about end-of-the-world movies.

"You know how after the opening shots in all the postapocalyptic films they always cut to this *one guy*—a survivor rummaging through the remains of some city overrun with vegetation and there are vines wrapping around the vacant buildings and mangy dogs and . . ."

Dr. WhoKnowsNothingAtAll follows my gaze to the poster of the Earth and then looks back at me disappointed, like he would way rather talk about why I smashed the gym lockers with the baseball bat that I took from the wood-and-glass display case outside the athletic office than talk about the end of the world. Then he jots something down on his shrink pad like, *ASKED IMPORTANT QUESTION AND STUDENT EMPLOYED AVOIDANCE STRATEGY,* but I'm thinking, *I made the right decision to try to change the subject because I don't want to talk about the time I smashed seventeen lockers with the Omaha 519 Louisville Slugger that Timmy Ingram used when he hit his home run in the 2017 league championship.* So I keep talking. "After the camera continues to survey the landscape, we cut back to that guy again, and he's scavenging through an abandoned house or a trash can looking for anything he can use, like a pair of shoes or, you know, a rubber band or antibiotics or maybe a few batteries, and he's stuffing that shit into the giant pockets of his army-style cargo coat."

Dr. WhoKnowsNothingAtAll nods his head slightly, like he's going along with me for the moment but he's probably thinking, *Jesus, does Asher feel like he's scavenging through the debris after an apocalypse?* Or maybe it's more like, *WTF? Does Asher think the world is coming to an end?*

"Anyway," I continue, "this scene establishes that at some point whoever was left on Earth got up, scavenged through the scraps of their life, then headed out to scavenge through the scraps of the planet, and somehow figured out a way to get back to living."

That's when Dr. WhoKnowsNothingAtAll seizes the moment, leans forward, and says, "What do you think the message of that is?"

I wasn't really thinking about a message; I was just thinking about how pissed off Denzel Washington must be that the world ended and now the only option he has is to dumpster-dive through the shit left behind as he tries to patch together a life out of what remains. But I don't say that. I give him what he wants. "The message is that human beings are like dandelions that are so desperate to survive that even if they are covered in concrete, they'll find a way to poke their heads out of the cracks in the sidewalk or die trying."

I think I lose him here with the flower analogy, but I keep going.

"I mean, we're supposed to have that kind of resilience. Like, even if the meteor strikes or they pour wet concrete on top of us, we're supposed to find a crack to climb through. Those dandelions might have spent some time thinking, 'This sucks—who put concrete here?' But like the guys in those movies, the ones who survive have to shift their whole mindset and start thinking, 'I woke up today, and there's concrete where there used to be grass, so where's a fucking crack I can climb through?'"

"Language, Asher."

"*Or* the dandelions are thinking, 'Shit! There is no crack! So how can I make one?'"

"Language. Second warning."

"Because if that fucking dandelion doesn't find that crack—a walk-around to a lights-out, game-over personal apocalypse—it will die."

"So," Dr. WhoKnowsNothingAtAll says, ignoring the f-bomb, "what you're saying is that those survivors have to pick through the scraps they were left and deal with what is a painful new now."

"Exactly," I say, "except here's the thing. . . ."

This is where I'm about to explain the thing that's really bugging me. But he gets this condescending look. It's like he's thinking, *Here it comes. This is where Asher falls off the logic wagon and spirals into crazy town.* But I don't care. I keep talking like sane and rational went out of style when the bell rang for fourth period today. "The key difference is that in *those* movies, in *those* scenarios, the apocalypse happens to *everyone*. *Everyone* is either dead or a victim."

"So your point is?"

"That in the case of the dandelions and the new sidewalk—the apocalypse only hit some of us."

He looks startled and jumps all over me like one of his emergency shrink buttons was just pushed. "You said *us*. The apocalypse only hit some of *us*."

I flinch. He keeps talking.

"So you see yourself as a dandelion. And your point is that there are dandelions that did not get concrete poured on them, but you did?"

I don't say yes or no. I just sit there, thinking, *Basically? Yes.*

He jots something down. Probably, *What is this shit about dandelions?* Or *Thank God this is our last session—Asher is off the rails.* But I just keep talking like my mouth is driving the rest of me straight toward a steel signpost at high speed. "So basically we feel royally pissed off that we have to deal with the world ending and everyone else doesn't."

"*We* being the dandelions?" he asks, now frantically scribbling on his shrink notepad at high speed.

"The dandelions and the people in Room 212," I clarify.

He looks up. "Room 212?"

"At the hospital. The bereavement groups meet in Room 212."

"I see. So you go to a bereavement group?"

"Three."

He raises his eyebrows. They move about eight inches north and almost slide over the top of his forehead and slip down his back. "You go to three bereavement groups?"

"Three so far. Old people. Teens. And Not-Dead-Yet."

"How often do they meet?"

"Every day. Old people, Monday/Wednesday. Teens, Tuesday/ Thursday. Not-Dead-Yet, Friday. We get weekends off."

He looks worried.

"Except I just kind of quit the Friday, Not-Dead-Yet group."

"But you go to an old people group?"

I nod. "Because of Henry."

"Henry?"

I nod. "And Evelyn."

He writes that down. "That's a lot of groups. Are they helping?"

"I've met a lot of other dandelions who got concrete poured on them, if that's what you mean."

He sits back. "Is that how you feel? Angry that you have to deal with a loss that others didn't experience?"

I turn toward the window that looks out over the courtyard, which is teeming with kids who are on their phones and drinking coffee and laughing and making out and horsing around in the sunlight while I'm stuck in here in the dark trying to find that crack in the concrete I can crawl through.

"For *them*," I say, pointing toward the courtyard, "the world kept going just like it was going, and I got hit by an apocalypse."

"So, you're saying that it's like they're the dandelions on the lawn a few feet away from you that didn't get concreted over. And that makes you mad."

It's not a question, and if it were, I wouldn't answer. I just keep staring out the window at the life I used to have. "It's not like they're *better dandelions* or they did something to deserve not getting covered in concrete. It's just because what happens is *arbitrary*. And I can't deal with it. Because of duality."

"Duality?"

I turn to look at him. "What do you know about existentialism?"

He sighs. "Very little."

"Here it is in a nutshell," I say. "Stuff happens randomly. Animals don't try to figure shit out. They don't care about *why*. But *people* do. That's the core of our existential struggle."

He puts his pencil down. I keep talking.

"The world dishes out stuff arbitrarily, but humans want explanations for everything. And there are none. It's a paradox. Because we are *rational animals*, we're essentially looking for an explanation for things that are . . . you know, *unexplainable*."

He sits back. Probably thinking it would be way easier if I just told him that I hate everybody and I'm pissed off so I smashed some lockers with a baseball bat.

"So you're reading about existentialism?"

"Kierkegaard mostly."

His eyebrows rise again.

"It's basically my new religion."

"Trying to find meaning for things that have no meaning?"

I nod. *Why is he making me feel stupid?*

"So you think the universe isn't fair and you got a raw deal?"

"Isn't that pretty fucking obvious?"

He doesn't say, *Language, Asher. Last warning.* But I know that he wants to.

Then Dr. WhoKnowsNothingAtAll surprises me. He says, "The universe isn't fair, and you did get a raw deal, Asher. You didn't deserve what happened to you. And it will probably never make sense. But it will be easier to handle things if you accept that the world isn't fair. It never promised to be. And it never will be."

"So you get it."

"Get what?"

"My existential struggle."

He slumps in his chair. *He's in over his head.*

I turn and stare out the window at the dandelions who didn't get covered in concrete. But I don't tell him the really bad part of the dandelion story.

For me, the really bad part of the dandelion story is that for some of those dandelions, while I was getting cemented over, while my mom was being carried to the morgue, their world got *better.* Good stuff happened for them—like Emily got the lead in the school play and Brian got a new car. I was mad that their lives got better and mine got worse. *That they got to stay where they were, and I got sent somewhere else.*

Then he asks me if I've remembered anything about the day of the accident and when my dad told me about my mom dying. I shake my head no. He jots that down. And then I realize the absolute worst part of my entire story about the dandelions and the concrete, but I don't tell him that part either.

Most dandelions that are covered in concrete don't ever find a crack to climb through.

They don't make it.

When the bell rings, I don't go to my next class; I just walk straight to the nurse's office and say, "I'm burning up with a fever." Nurse Ratched looks me up and down like she's doing a threat assessment, but she must see what a mess I am because she doesn't even take out her broken insta-read thermometer to try to prove that I'm not in the least bit sick; she jumps right to asking, "How's Chloe?" and I say, "She's as good as you can be if your mom burns up in a car accident and you'll never see her again." And then she hands me a Dixie cup full of apple juice and asks, "Do you want to play Go Fish?" and I say, "Yes." Then I ask, "Did the shrink call and tell you that I told him some messed-up thing about an apocalypse and wet concrete and dandelions?" Nurse Ratched says, "No. Why would he do that?" And I say, "No clue. Your turn. Go Fish."

20

On Friday I steal the car.

I have to.

Grace's prom is tomorrow night, and before I invited Henry and Will and Sloane, I GPS-ed it a hundred times and it takes sixteen hours and fifty-one minutes to drive to her house from here. So first thing in the morning, when my dad's in the shower, I put the tuxedo and tuxedo shirt and cummerbund and bow tie that I picked up yesterday at Father and Son Formal Wear into the trunk of his car.

I'm going to wear the tux with my old soccer cleats from two years ago because my normal cleats got stolen from my gym locker and stuffed into a trash bin by a low-life hurtbag looking for a laugh, and the new ones got burned up in the accident with my mom. I find the cleats stuffed in a bin in the garage, toss them into the trunk, and then quickly head back upstairs and pack regular clothes and some random stuff I need into my backpack, then freeze when I hear Chloe singing as she walks past my room. When I hear her head down the stairs, I zip up my backpack and take my mom's letter out of my desk drawer.

It feels heavy like a brick.

I never got a real letter from anyone before—only Post-it notes in my lunch box when I was little—*Be nice at recess! I gave you enough cookies to share! I love you!* And text messages when I got older: Clean your room before practice, please! Don't eat all of Chloe's Popsicles! If you don't give the gerbil water, he will die! Remember tonight is movie and a pizza!

I couldn't bring myself to do it before, but this time I manage to lift the flap and gently take the letter out of the envelope.

It's a single piece of paper folded in three.

I don't want to sound ungrateful, but I expected more. Like perfume and confetti and reams of pages with thousands and thousands of tiny, neat, IMPORTANT words.

You'd think that if you were writing a letter to someone who knows nothing at all, you would need to write a lot.

Especially if you were going to die way before that person expected.

I know that whatever my mom said in this letter is going to be the last thing she ever says to me, and she said it way before we even knew each other.

I mean, we'd just met on the day she wrote it.

Which means that when she wrote it, we were practically strangers.

But it still bothers me that everything she had to say fit on one page.

So it's probably not that hard to figure out why I can't bring myself to read it.

I just stare at the neatly folded powder-blue paper and then slide it back into the envelope and put it into my backpack, then I pull my dad's baseball bat out from under my bed. It was his when he was a kid, and I don't play, so we don't need it. I hang in my room until I hear my dad in the kitchen with Chloe putting raisins in the shape of a smiley face on a pancake, then quickly send Will and Sloane a text saying, Be there in fifteen, turn my phone off, carry the backpack and the bat down the stairs, swipe the car keys from the table in the front hall, walk out the door, put the backpack in the trunk of the Jeep and the bat on the floor of the back seat, and drive away.

21

When I pull up in front of Henry's house, he's already standing outside on the front steps leaning on his walker waiting for me. There's a red plaid suitcase with thick leather straps sitting at his feet and a cardboard box planted right next to it. I hop out of the car and run across the lawn and carry his suitcase to the car, and then go back for the box, which Henry warns me is VERY SPECIAL AND VERY FRAGILE. I carry the box for him as Henry slowly walkers his way to the car, with him warning me the whole time not to jostle the box too much. I'm nervous that this is taking so long because I keep thinking that maybe my dad is going to show up and say, *What are you doing and why did you take my car?* which makes no sense at all since he has no way to get here BECAUSE I TOOK HIS CAR AND MY MOM'S LAND ROVER WAS TOTALED IN THE ACCIDENT AND I SMASHED UP CHLOE'S BIKE WITH A HAMMER. Plus, he has no idea where I am anyway. But still, Henry is going so slowly, it's stressing me out. Then when we finally get him and all his stuff to the car and I'm standing next to the trunk holding the box, he says, "We can put the suitcase and the walker in the back, but the box has to ride up front with me."

When I ask him *why* the box has to ride up front, he says it's on account of the fact that Evelyn is inside.

I'm thinking, *Oh, shit!* but it's more like *OH, SHIT!* because a whole bunch of possibilities are running through my head AND NOT JUST THE FACT THAT MY DAD COULD GET HERE BY UBER. Now there's the whole EVELYN IS IN THE BOX THING.

I stare at the box and then slowly bend down and gently place it on the lawn and pull the flaps open.

There's an urn inside.

I look back up when Henry says, "It's the premium, one-hundred-percent brass, Love Lasts for Eternity model from Heavenly Creations."

I try to collect myself, then manage to say, "Okay, but maybe we don't have to tell anyone that," and Henry asks, "Tell anyone what?" and I whisper, "That Evelyn's inside the box."

"Urn. She's inside the urn."

"Got it."

And then he asks, "Who's anyone?" so I say, "My two friends Will and Sloane from my Tuesday night bereavement group at the hospital."

Henry peers in through the windows like he's checking to see if Will and Sloane are sitting in the car and somehow he didn't notice, and then he seems to forget about them entirely and he looks back at me with an expression of surprise and asks, "You go to more than one group?"

I say, "Yes," and that makes him look sadder than usual. Like, basset-hound sad. Or EVELYN-DIED-AGAIN SAD. I'm still on the lawn kneeling down next to the urn-box, so I whisper, "Hi, Evelyn" and "It's nice to meet you," making sure I say it loud enough for Henry to hear, and he must not be too deaf because he instantly lights up and now he looks happy—like old-guy-doing-cartwheels happy, or maybe even EVELYN-ISN'T-REALLY-THAT-DEAD happy.

Next, I get Henry and Evelyn settled in the front seat, and then we head over to pick up Sloane at the designated spot a block from her house since she told her mom that her friend Mallory's gerbil died while birthing a litter of pups and she's going to stay with her to spend a few days, maybe even more, feeding the baby gerbils around the clock with doll bottles on account of the fact that she can't tell her mom that she's driving to Tennessee with three guys, even if one of them is really old and one of them will walk her down the aisle when she gets married.

When me and Henry pull up to the designated pickup corner, Sloane's standing there wearing a short yellow skirt and bright red knee socks and the same motorcycle boots she always wears. Even though it's summer, over her tank top she's wearing a huge leather jacket that I haven't seen her wear before. She looks put out and pissed off, which is pretty much one of the only two facial expressions she has. Sloane either looks mad at the world or completely toppled by it. She's either *ferocious predator* or *vulnerable prey*— and I get it, because that's how I feel most of the time. Vulnerable and weak might be my hometown, but pissed off is a safe harbor to hang out in after your life gets ripped apart—it's so nice that, as Dr. WhoKnowsNothingAtAll pointed out to me more than once, some of us (he meant me) move in and take up permanent residence.

I hop out of the car and try to get Sloane to smile by saying, "Your boots and jacket are way too big," but she snaps back with, "They're not too big. They fit perfectly." Then she goes from really pissed off to totally devastated and mumbles, "They were my dad's."

I think, *Oh, shit!* and whisper, "Okay. Got it. The boots and jacket are perfect." Then she gives me a half smile, like she's saying it's okay that I hurt her feelings, but it gets weird and awkward between us for a minute and I'm afraid she'll change her mind about coming to Memphis. Then she glances in through the car window at Henry in the front seat and turns to me and makes a funny face and says, "Jesus. Will looks like shit," and I just smirk and she hands me a couple of magazines she was holding and wheels her suitcase around to the back of the car. I toss her suitcase into the trunk and then introduce her to Henry.

Before Sloane gets in the car, I look down at the magazines, then back up at her, and she gets all defensive and hostile and says, *"What?"*

I smile and say, "Nothing," then hand her back the copies of *Easyriders* and *Biker World* with motorcycles and half-naked girls on the front that she asked me to hold.

After Sloane gets in, we pick up Will. When he gets into the back seat with Sloane, he announces that he told his parents that he was going to tag along when I drive my grandpa back home to Atlanta because he came north for a memorial service we had for my mom. He says that when he told them that, they both took out their phones and Venmo-ed him cash for the trip and said what a good friend he was and cried a little. Then he told us that he felt bad for lying, but only for a minute. After he settles in, he says hi to Henry and then asks, "What's the baseball bat for, Asher?"

I don't want to tell him it's for killing Jack Daniels, so I say, "For hitting fly balls," and then Henry changes the subject when he says, "No hanky-panky, you two," and at first I think he means me and Will, but then I realize that he means Will and Sloane, and everyone kind of laughs and I'm thinking this is already weird so it's a good thing that I left off the part about killing Jack Daniels and the part about Evelyn being in the urn in the box at Henry's feet.

I mean, Will and Sloane probably wouldn't have wanted to come along if I had said, *Hey, I'm going to murder some guy, and this is Henry, and he brought his wife, Evelyn, with him, but in case you're wondering why you can't see her, it's because she's dead.*

Right when I'm cruising up the on-ramp to the highway, Henry says, "Asher, don't drive over forty miles per hour."

I turn to him and ask, "Even on the highway?" and he says, "Yes. Evelyn doesn't like going fast." I put my flashers on and drive as close to thirty-nine miles per hour as I can, petrified that Will or Sloane will ask, *Who's Evelyn? Or Where's Evelyn?* but Henry distracts everyone when he looks right at me and asks, "Is Sloane your sweetheart?"

I feel really embarrassed but manage to say, "No. We hardly know each other," and then I think that maybe that was the wrong thing to say, but it's too late. I console myself by thinking that in the cosmic scheme of things, that wasn't *that bad*; I mean, at least I didn't say, *I killed my mom* or *Maybe I can come over to your house and plant sweet peas.*

When I check in the rearview mirror, Sloane's looking out the window trying not to smile, so I try to put a Band-Aid on the comment by saying, "It's just that Sloane lost her dad and I lost my mom, so we have a lot in common and we're friends."

Henry smiles, and then he asks Will, "Is Sloane *your* sweetheart?" and Will gets embarrassed and says, "No," and I say, "I think Sloane may like girls, Henry," and Sloane says, "That's not true. I bought them for the hogs." That seems to fly over Henry's head, but when I glance back in the mirror, Will is looking at me like, *WTF is going on*, and then Sloane holds up one of the motorcycle magazines for Will to see, and he says, "Oh, I get it now. Hogs as in *motorcycles*, not farm animals." Then Henry announces that his sweetheart,

Evelyn, prefers Applebee's to TGI Fridays, so everyone looks confused because Henry just pretty much blew the Evelyn thing wide open. When he adds, "So we have to eat at Applebee's," I just run head-on into the mess and say, "Applebee's it is, then," thinking I'm really glad the door's still open for Sloane to like me.

I figure Sloane and Will are probably now thinking, *Who the hell is Evelyn? And when are we going to pick her up?* And then they're probably wondering, *Shit, where will Evelyn sit because the car is already full?* And while they're thinking that, I'm wondering if Henry is going to bring dead Evelyn into the restaurant, being that Applebee's is her favorite place to eat, but luckily nobody asks any of those questions out loud.

Basically they all fall asleep and I drive. Which means I have a whole lot of time to think.

Which is not good.

Then everyone wakes up, and the whole Evelyn thing comes to a head when we stop for dinner and Henry asks me to carry the box with Evelyn in it into Applebee's.

No one says anything, but I think, *Oh, shit!* but it's more like, *OH, SHIT!!*

And then Henry has me sit Evelyn down on the chair across from him and orders her pancakes with strawberries even though it isn't breakfast. Still nobody says anything, but I'm pretty sure Will and Sloane have figured out what's in the urn Henry keeps in the box based on the fact that he's been talking to Evelyn the whole time like she's really here. Plus, he ordered her food. Plus, they both peeked in the box when Henry went to the restroom, and I pretended not to notice by humming the Daniel Tiger song while I read all about the Applebee's Dollarmama Bahama Mama drink made with Malibu coconut rum that's advertised on the triangular menu card sitting in the middle of the table.

It then gets even more awkward when Evelyn's meal arrives and the waitress sets it down in front of the box, what with the fact that there's a whole stack of pancakes and no one in the chair. Then Henry makes the whole thing even worse when he says, "Evelyn, dear, would you like some tea?" When the box doesn't answer and Henry says, "She would. A cup of Earl Grey, please," the waitress gets this *and I'd thought I'd seen everything* look on her face, probably not sure if she's getting Punk'd or if he's fucking serious. But Sloane jumps in and smiles a really cute *Aren't I adorable?* smile that falls under the umbrella of her vulnerable look and tries to change the subject by saying, "Tell me about your mom, Asher," and the waitress walks away, presumably to retrieve a cup of Earl Grey.

I say, "She was tall like me and had matching scars on her knees because she was always falling out of trees when she was a kid, and her dad used to call her his orangutan, and she always helped at my school and baked cookies on Fridays ever since I can remember because she said that Fridays were for parties, even if we had to make up a silly reason to have one." Then I say, "Tell me more about your dad because he sounds funny." We're both smiling when the HIGHLY SKEPTICAL AND ENTIRELY FREAKED-OUT WAITRESS brings tea for Evelyn, and Sloane acts like it's perfectly normal, and then she leans over and pours some milk into Evelyn's tea and tells us how her dad got them a puppy for a surprise one Christmas and took them rafting in Colorado even though he was afraid of the water because he couldn't swim. Then Henry tells us that Evelyn makes a mean chicken pot pie, and Will says he had promised to take his brother, Michael, to see a New Jersey Devils hockey game, but Michael didn't live until winter, so this year he went to the first game of the season alone and pretended that Michael was with him, and then Henry says Evelyn is going to make her famous peach pie on the Fourth of July. He explains that the recipe card says *This is Henry's favorite* in Evelyn's handwriting and we should all come over to try it and he'll help Evelyn make it because she could use the extra set of hands.

I'm thinking, *I'll bet.*

But when we're done eating, everyone is in a good mood and I pay for everything, all the food and gas, too, because when I took my dad's car, I took his credit card, figuring, *Why the hell not?* I mean, what's stealing a credit card if you steal a car and are planning to kill someone? I figure if I pay for everything, Will can keep his cash, which he might need if I kill Jack Daniels and the three of them have to take a bus home because I have to drive to Ecuador to hide out.

Every country sends murderers back to the US except places like Iran and maybe North Korea, and I can't drive there and don't want to learn Farsi or Korean and get a visa, so I figure I'll just drive to Ecuador and wait there until a SWAT team of federal agents shows up to collect me. I picked Ecuador because it looks nice in the pictures. I mean, there are waterfalls and cool-looking beaches and mountains and palm trees, and the people look happy and play soccer and basically, I like empanadas.

As we leave the restaurant, Henry calls, "Shotgun!" and that cracks Will up and no one fights him for it. After I carry Evelyn back to the car, I put Henry's walker in the trunk and take out my mom's letter. I don't lift the flap or take the letter out. I just hold the envelope in my hands for a few minutes, looking at the optimistic loop of the *A* and the swoop of the *r*, and then flip it over and look at the broken heart on the back, and then I look up and watch as Sloane shuffles to the car in her dad's giant motorcycle boots and jacket that fit her small frame so perfectly.

When Sloane gets to the car, she looks over at me holding the envelope and asks, "What's that?" and I say, "Nothing," and she says, "It doesn't look like nothing; it looks like a letter," and I put the envelope back in my bag and slam the trunk closed like the loud bang and all that steel of the car is a metaphor for *end of conversation.*

But she asks, "Who's it from?"

I say, "A dead person," and she looks away. I mean, I get it. She's trying to be normal—we're all just trying to be normal—and I can tell that if we *were normal*, she would have been able to ask, *What's that?* and I would have been able to say, *A letter from a dead person*, and she could then make a joke and say, *A dead person like George Washington or a dead person like Biggie Smalls?* And I'd smile and say, *Biggie. How'd you know?* And she'd look at me all smug, and I'd tell her, *He writes to me all the time.*

But she knows it's from my mom, so her mouth says nothing but her face says, *Oh, shit!* and she just climbs into the back seat.

Then we wait for what feels like an entire lifetime for Henry to get settled in the front with Evelyn tucked in on the floor near his feet, and I'm thinking, *I'm actually feeling better already. Like leaving town suits me.* Then I'm thinking, *It doesn't matter how long Henry takes,* because he has a look on his face that says he's feeling really good because he just took his sweetheart to her favorite restaurant for pancakes. Then I wonder what Peter Pan would think about the BIG lie Henry is telling himself, and I decide that she'd think it's okay—because she was the one who told us that we can grieve any way that we want to.

22

Before I turn the engine on and before we leave the Applebee's parking lot, everyone but Henry starts checking their phones, so I turn mine back on to see how many times my dad's called and texted me.

It's basically way too many to count. He texted stuff like, Asher, where are you? Did you take my car? I'm worried! Please call.

Followed by Okay, I know you took the car! Call NOW!

And Please don't make me call the police. I need to know that you are okay.

There are, like, fifty more.

I feel really bad because I don't want him to worry, but I had to do this, so I text him back and say, I had to go somewhere and I'm with friends and don't worry and please don't call the police or order pizza with pepperoni or buy Chloe a new bike.

He types, Thank God you're all right! and it comes out as a sigh even though it's a text message.

Will puts his phone away and says, "Come on, Asher, let's hit the road," and I tell him to hold on as I text my dad.

I write back and say, Promise you won't send the police or leave the toilet lids up or let Chloe eat chocolate pudding, and he writes,

Asher, I promise. No police. Lids down. No pudding. Just tell me you're okay and promise you will come home safe.

I write, I'm okay and I will, and he types When? I write, Soon, but it's one of those times when I'm pretty sure none of what I'm saying is actually true. I'm thinking, *At least one good thing happened.* Since my dad promised that he wouldn't call the police, now I can let everyone keep their phones.

Then he writes, Asher, the doctors are worried that you taking off like this will be too much for you. You have to come home now.

I know by "doctors," he means shrinks. And not just Dr. Who-KnowsNothingAtAll but the whole Team Asher Shrink Crew I've had since the accident, but I write, I can't come home. I have to do this.

He types, I'm worried something will happen. If I call, will you pick up so we can talk about this instead of texting?

I say, I can't talk. I can't hear your voice. And I have to do this.

He asks, Why can't we talk?

I say, I don't want you to convince me to change my mind.

Change your mind about what?

Nothing. Just this.

He doesn't type anything for a while. I stare at my phone waiting, and then he writes, Chloe misses you.

I swipe at a tear and type, I miss her too and I'll be back. My fingers and heart burn when I type that because I'm not sure that it's true—the *I'll be back* part. I'm not sure of anything anymore, so I write, There's extra aluminum foil for her hands under my bed.

I wait but my dad doesn't type anything after that. He's probably thinking, *How colossally messed up is Asher if he keeps aluminum foil under his bed to protect Chloe from radiation while she sleeps and what's wrong with chocolate pudding?*

So I type, Dad????

I'm here.

Just promise about the aluminum foil.

There's a long pause, so I add, And the pudding.

Then he types, I promise.

I type, Sorry about the car.

And he types, I know.

I check my other messages, and there are none except for one from Grace. She sent me a picture of her prom dress. She's holding it up, and she has such a big smile on her face.

It's purple.

The dress, not her face.

I hate it.

It is the ugliest dress in the history of ugly dresses.

Sloane, who's sitting right behind me in the back seat, leans forward and says, "What's that a picture of, Asher?" So I say, "Nothing," and then I stare at the dress for a minute and type, WOW! and hit send.

I'm thinking, *Grace is probably feeling really good right now.* Just like my mom did when she bought the new soccer cleats and was driving home from the mall.

Then Sloane taps me on the shoulder and asks, "Who are you texting?"

I can't say, *This girl I catfished who I'm now kind of going out with and who thinks my name is Sam Hunt, but don't worry, I'm not a sociopath. I'm only doing it because her father killed my mom and I basically lied to all of you about this whole trip and we're driving to Memphis so I can kill him.* But I have to say something, so I look at her in the rearview mirror and say, "Elvis Presley."

She smirks.

Henry smiles.

Then Sloane asks, "You're helping Elvis Presley pick out a dress?" and Will looks up from his phone.

It stays eerily quiet for, like, a second, and then Sloane kind of smirks again and then she lunges over the seat and tries to grab my phone. That starts a whole thing and Will reaches for my phone and takes it from me and he's tucked against the window in the back seat staring at the screen and scrolling and I'm afraid he'll see my texts to Grace or from my dad and I practically have to climb into the back to try to retrieve the phone. It eventually falls to the floor in the scuffle and I manage to grab it, then climb back up front and stash the phone in my sweatshirt pocket, turn the engine on, and put the car into reverse. As I'm looking over my shoulder backing out of the parking space, Sloane has this impish smile and that makes me smile and then she asks the next obvious question.

"So, what'd you say to Elvis?"

I look right at her, smile, and say, "Purple's not your color."

Then I turn back around and glance out the front windshield for a minute. Sloane asks, "What else did you tell him?"

I look at her in the rearview mirror and say, "I told him, 'We'll see you soon.'"

Then I put the car into drive and we crawl back toward the highway.

23

It's just after ten on Friday night when we get to Roanoke, Virginia, so I say, "Remember, I have a credit card. Let's stop at a hotel." Then I ask Henry, "Which hotel does Evelyn like best?" but before he can answer, Will says he slept all day and he can drive through the night so I can sleep in the back and that way we'll get to Memphis before school starts in September. We switch seats and I get in the back next to Sloane, and Henry turns around and in a serious voice says, "Remember, you two, no hanky-panky back there." Then he turns to Will and says, "You need a barrette for your hair so you can see."

Sloane laughs and says, "I think I have one you can borrow," and she starts digging around in her pockets, but Will gives her the evil eye in the rearview mirror and Sloane sticks out her tongue, and then Will puts his baseball cap on backward to keep the hair out of his eyes.

Henry looks at him with approval and says, "Don't go over forty, and keep the flashers on." Then he asks, "Does anyone like opera?" Sloane raises her hand with that funny smirk on her face, but Will looks like he's going to cry. Henry finds a radio station he likes and tells us it's "The Music of the Night" from *Phantom of the Opera* and then goes to sleep.

Me and Sloane both start dozing off, and when I wake up a couple of hours later, there's still operatic music playing softly in the background. Sloane's out cold, slumped so far over that she's leaning on my shoulder, and I'm afraid to move because I don't want to wake her up because when someone important in your life dies, the only time that you're not suffering is either when you're asleep or in that little place right after you wake up before you remember the bad stuff. Those are the only two safe spaces from the truth in your whole day, so I know that if I wake her, there'll be this moment of not remembering when she opens her eyes and looks around and thinks, *Where am I and what is happening in my life?* And then she'll think, *Oh, maybe this is a good day and everything is coming up sweet peas* before the bad stuff plows into her like an eighteen-wheel tractor trailer driven by a guy like Jack Daniels. She'll remember that her dad's dead, and it'll be like slamming into a bridge abutment at high speed and rolling over three times and landing with the roof of your car caved in and your neck broken and flames licking the gas tank, which is about to explode any minute. And that moment will hurt so much that it'll be like her dad just died again, and that same scenario will play out every single day of her life over and over again until she dies, and I know that because that's what happens to me. And if you think that means that waking up is the worst part of the day because that's when you remember, you'd be wrong. As horrific as that moment is, it's basically downhill from there.

Which is why I sometimes think that it would be better if I didn't wake up at all. Waking up just starts the whole pain cycle again. But then when that thought sets down roots in my head, I usually get to thinking about Chloe and my dad and how I don't want them to wake up every day and remember that *two* people are dead instead of just one because one is so bad, two must be impossible to survive. Which generally leads me to think about Zachary again. I mean, before he got run over and died because he rode his bike the wrong way on a street, he woke up every day, and the only happy moments he had were probably the twenty-six seconds of not remembering that his mom and dad were dead.

I timed it once when I was looking at the stopwatch on my phone. I left myself a Post-it note the night before that said, *When you wake up, start your stopwatch and time how long it takes before you to want to kill yourself.* When I woke up the next morning, I thought it was so weird that I wrote that and thought, *What is wrong with me?* but I set the stopwatch anyway, and then I remembered that my mom burned up in a car accident, and then I decided that note was not weird at all under the circumstances.

It took twenty-six seconds.

Twenty-six seconds before all the bad stuff rushed in to fill up my head.

That's it. That's all I got.

Get. That's all I *get.*

But in the car headed for Memphis, when I'm trying hard not to move and not to wake up Sloane, I fall back asleep thinking how nice it is to have her cheek resting on my arm, and then I ruin the whole thing when I wake up about an hour later screaming.

I sit bolt upright and lean forward as I let out a cry that sounds like a baby deer being eaten by a pack of coyotes, or maybe it's more like a triceratops being devoured by a T. rex because I scream so loud that I startle Will and he swerves the car and says, "Jesus, Asher!" The whole thing wakes up Sloane but not Henry, and she reaches over and pats my back and tells me, "It's okay."

I'm disoriented and confused and say, "I'm not in the hospital," and Sloane says, "You're in the back of your dad's car. Will's driving. It's just a nightmare."

I'm still confused and disoriented and shaking, but she's looking at me so cutely that I don't want her to stop, so I say, "Who's Will?" And Sloane smirks and says, "A Kierkegaard scholar," and then Henry snorts so loudly that Will swerves the car again and almost hits the guardrail, which gives me a heart attack.

I put my hands up against the window, and it's raining and the drops are there again, shimmering and glistening on the glass, clinging for their life because it's like they know that if they can't hold on, they will hit the pavement at thirty-nine miles per hour and that will be it.

It's basically the same nightmare that I have at home. I mean, sometimes the details are slightly different and usually there is no rain, but the ending is always the same. And trust me, it's not good.

So sometimes when I wake up, I don't even get the good twenty-six seconds of not remembering. I just go directly to the car burning up and the flames licking flesh.

It's always the same black Land Rover.

The same mom.

The same eighteen-wheel tractor trailer.

The same Jack Daniels driving.

I can see his face.

In the nightmare Lil Durk is always blasting on the radio, and most of the time my mom is driving, but sometimes I'm driving and sometimes my dad is driving and sometime Chloe is driving and my mom is sitting in the back seat.

Then there's always a bright white light. So bright that I have to cover my eyes. Then there's the cry of tires screeching as we crash, always in s-l-o-w motion. The song ends, always in the same spot with Lil Durk rapping, "Dis ain't what you want. Dis ain't what you want. . . ."

Then the airbags explode in a loud face-slamming *Pfffffttttt! Baaaammmm!*

The back of my head hits the backrest. *Hard.*

I hear glass shattering.

My head's always spinning—no, *we're always spinning*—the whole car is spinning. Then it's rolling over and over . . . and then I realize, *No, the song didn't end. It's just that I can't hear it anymore because of the screams. My screams.*

And then I realize that there are no mom screams.

Then there's the revelation that she can't scream because . . . *Oh God!*

Then the world goes dark.

There's nothing at all.

Just black vacant silence for a long time.

And then the sirens in the distance.

At this point my foot's usually slammed down hard on the imaginary brake pedal, or I'm trying to pull my mom out through the window of the imaginary car but her head isn't connected to her body, or it is connected to her body but when I pull on her arms, her head comes off, just falls and rolls like it isn't attached. That's usually when I wake up, and that's when the real horror begins because *I remember she's gone.*

Sloane is still slowly rubbing my back when Will asks if I'm okay, and now Henry's awake and he turns to face me. He looks like the grim reaper. Death himself in the front passenger seat reaching back with gnarly old-person hands to pat my leg. His transparent skin, his blue veins, tracing their way to his heart. *Thump thump. Thump thump.*

I realize it's my *pulse that I hear throbbing in my head. Not his.*
I want to pull away from Henry, from Sloane—from the car, from everyone and everything. From *me* even.
From me most of all.
But there's no room. No room in the back seat of the moving car. No room in my head. No room in my life. I'm trapped with nowhere to run.
Henry says, "Asher, it's just a bad dream."
I look at Henry and think, *It's not just a bad dream. It's my bad life*, but I don't say anything because there are still flames devouring my mother's face and her head is still detached from her body and it's an image that I can't shake.
When I told my last therapist about the nightmares—not Dr. WhoKnowsNothingAtAll, another one my dad took me to who's not from school—he said, "Maybe you're having that nightmare because you think that if you had been there, then you could have saved your mom." And then he asked, "What do you think about that, Asher?"
I told him that he'd have to be a dumb fuck therapist to ask that question.
I mean, seriously? The guy asked me if I wished that I was in the car so I could have saved my mom—like maybe I could have said, *Hey, Mom, there's a truck coming. Maybe you should pull over and get in the next lane.* Or maybe after we were hit, I could have pulled her out before her head detached from her body and she burned up in the fire.
The therapist didn't say anything about my "dumb fuck" comment; he just wrote something down on his pad and popped a wintergreen Life Saver in his mouth, like that would be a good time to freshen his breath.

I didn't see that therapist again.

I told my dad that he had really bad breath and I couldn't go back again without a gas mask, but my dad said he talked to him on the phone that day and the shrink said that he'd fired *me*. My dad didn't say "fired," exactly; he said something about how the doctor thought he wasn't a good fit for me or something like that, but my dad sounded mad, so I'm pretty sure it had something to do with the fact that I called the shrink a dumb fuck.

I had to defend myself, so I told my dad that I called him a dumb fuck because he is a dumb fuck, but my dad just asked, "Who said you called him a dumb fuck? He didn't tell me that." I was thinking, *Oops*, and then there was a long pause—you know, the kind where someone is putting things together and figuring out that one of the players in this equation is about to tell a whole pack of lies—and then my dad said, "Asher," and just shook his head.

But Sloane finds my hand and holds it up and whispers, "Try this." Then she spreads my fingers and says, "Start with your thumb, and with the pointer finger on your other hand, slowly trace up the side of each finger as you inhale, then exhale slowly as you trace down the other side." Then she holds on to my wrist as I breathe in and out slowly as I trace each finger. When I get to my pinkie, she whispers, "Five-finger breathing. It calms me down." I look at her and she looks at me, and then she starts tracing my fingers with her finger, and Will looks back in the rearview mirror and smiles and says, "No hanky-panky, you two." Then he starts singing an Elvis Presley song I don't know. One about a boy meeting a girl.

Then Henry joins in singing, and I pick up Sloane's hand and start slowly tracing her fingers with mine.

24

After the nightmare incident Will pulls into a rest stop to use the bathroom and we all go in, and I buy three packages of peanut butter cups, the ones that come two to a pack, and eat all six of them one after another. Then I buy four toothbrushes and four little tubes of toothpaste and give one of each to everyone. After me and Will brush our teeth, he looks in the bathroom mirror and asks, "Do you think I should cut my hair?" and I say, "Absolutely not," but I don't tell him it's not because it looks good long; it's because I don't want him going around without a helmet to hide behind when he so clearly needs one. He drops the hair thing and says, "Hey, Asher, we hardly made any progress, what with the whole going-under-forty-miles-per-hour thing. Do you think you could talk to Henry?"

I say, "It's Evelyn's rule. I'd have to talk to Evelyn."

Will just looks at me, asks what my address is, and then he pulls up a travel calculator on his phone and shows me that it would have taken sixteen hours and fifty-one minutes to get to Memphis from my house if we were driving sixty-five miles per hour, but it'll take twenty-eight hours and eighteen minutes if we continue going thirty-nine. Then Henry walkers over to us and says, "Asher, I don't have teeth, so I don't need a toothbrush."

I say, "Henry, I'm sorry," meaning, *I'm sorry you don't have teeth* and "No," to Will, meaning, *No, I will not talk to Henry or Evelyn, and we have to keep going thirty-nine*, and then right in the men's room at the rest stop Henry takes his teeth out to show us what hundred-year-old gums look like. When he smiles, he looks so funny that I think it must have made Evelyn laugh. Will is laughing too, and then some little kid comes over with his dad, and Henry makes funny, gummy, no-teeth faces at him and the kid cracks up, and then Henry says, "This is what happens if you don't brush," and he gives the kid the toothbrush and toothpaste I'd given him.

After we exit the bathroom, Will and Henry are still laughing when I spot Sloane leaning against the wall practically swallowed by the too-big boots and dad-sized motorcycle jacket she has draped herself in as her eyes burn holes through something or someone on the other side of the rest stop lobby. It looks like without the wall there to support her, she would be splayed out on the floor like a puddle. Will heads to the parking lot with Henry, and I hurry over to Sloane and follow her gaze back across the room, and my eyes land on a tall guy around forty with brown hair and glasses who is holding the hands of two little girls with bows in their hair wearing matching yellow sweaters. Even though Sloane doesn't say anything, I know exactly what happened because it's happened to me a thousand times.

I'd hear a voice or see a coat or a flash of hair, someone in a crowd, or maybe just a silhouette in the distance, and for a split second it would be *my mom*—not *sound like her* or *look like her* but *be her*. I'd be *that* certain. And then I'd remember she's gone and it *can't* be my mom, and it would be a steel blade to the heart.

I put my arm around Sloane's shoulder and whisper, "It's okay."

She says, "That guy . . . with the little girls . . . He looks like my . . ."

I say, "I know," and then I take her hand and hold it up and, starting with her thumb, I trace up the side of each of her fingers slowly with the pointer finger on my other hand as we both inhale; then I slowly trace down the other side of each finger as we exhale. When I get to her pinkie, I whisper, "Five-finger breathing. It calms me down."

She smiles, and then I hug her.

She's frailer than I thought she would be, and there's more motorcycle jacket and leather boots than actual girl, but she fits perfectly in my arms. It feels like we are the last two pieces needed to finish a jigsaw puzzle. And not the corners or edges or the obvious pieces either. Me and Sloane are the plain pieces in the middle of the puzzle that are a solid color like the sky, two of the pieces you tossed off to the side and never thought would fit anywhere.

25

Me and Sloane catch up with Will and Henry at the car, and Henry's putting his teeth in a little Tupperware tub he's filled with green liquid that he has in a bottle in his suitcase. We pile in with Will driving and Henry back in shotgun and me and Sloane in the back. Will drives for the rest of the night, creeping along the highway, half in the low-speed lane and half in breakdown lane. I watch out the window as all the other cars whiz by us as we lumber along, under the speed limit, limping toward Graceland. I doze on and off, tossing and turning, trying not to have another nightmare and trying not to disturb Sloane, who's now asleep on her side of the car with her head against the window. Henry wakes up every once in a while and either checks on Evelyn or hacks up something disgusting from his throat or mumbles something that makes no sense to anyone who can breathe and think clearly. Sometime in the middle of the night I put my headphones on and listen to the Paul Simon song "Graceland" over and over again as Henry snores in the front seat and Will goes twenty-five miles per hour below the speed limit and the lights on the highway stream by as Paul Simon sings, "And my traveling companions are ghosts and empty sockets. . . ."

Then when she's sleeping, I find Sloane's hand under the sweaters and jackets piled up between us on the back seat, and hold it.

When she wakes up, she gives my hand a squeeze. I pull my headphones off and whisper, "Is this okay?" and she smiles and says, "Yes." Then I lean in close and tell her that sea otters hold hands when they're sleeping so they won't drift apart, and her lips turn up in that half smile.

26

When the sun comes up on Saturday morning, we stop for coffee and donuts on Merchant Drive in Knoxville, Tennessee, and Henry puts his teeth back in right there in the parking lot. Then when we pull out, Will tries to leave his window open, but Henry tells him we can't drive with open windows because if her top comes loose, Evelyn might blow away. Nobody talks, but Will quickly rolls his window up, and Sloane hands Henry her pink sweater without saying anything. Henry drapes the sweater on top of Evelyn's box, and then we drive with the AC on high until we stop for an early lunch at an Applebee's in some random town west of the city. The four of us order the food we want, and then Henry orders the grilled chicken Caesar salad for Evelyn, who's sitting in her box in the seat across from him. The waitress looks around the table, counts to four, and then confirms, "So that's five entrées?"

I nod.

And then it gets worse.

Henry asks, "Asher, what would your mom like to order?"

The waitress is standing there chewing gum and tapping her pencil on her pad, glancing around the table again, confused, probably trying to figure out why we're ordering so much food and which of these people is my mother.

I don't want to hurt Henry's feelings, so I look over the menu carefully and then say, "She'll have the grilled chicken Caesar salad, just like Evelyn."

The waitress says, "Should I be writing this down?"

I nod.

"So that's the four meals you originally ordered, plus two grilled chicken Caesar salads?"

I say, "Yes."

She looks at me with her eyebrows arching up, questioning WHO THE FUCK THE CHICKEN CAESAR SALADS ARE FOR, and I confirm, "That will be two grilled chicken Caesar salads for the two Evelyns." Henry smiles, like my mom Evelyn and his Evelyn are best friends who order the same thing in restaurants and finish each other's sentences.

Then Sloane looks up at the waitress and says, "Me and both Evelyns would like a cup of Earl Grey, and my dad will definitely have the Bourbon Street steak and garlic mashed potatoes." And then Will jumps on board the crazy bus and says, "Michael will have a Coke, for sure a Coke, and the chicken mac and cheese from the kids' menu." The waitress looks at me and I nod my head like, *Go ahead, write that down*, and then Will says, "Michael will be sneaking French fries from my dad's plate, and my dad will say, 'Michael, you have your own fries,' but he'll be smiling, and then Michael will ask, 'Can I get dessert?'" and the waitress asks, "Will that be all?"

I smile and say, "For now."

At this point I'm thinking this is no different from playing bear picnic with Chloe, but the waitress is probably thinking, *What The*

Fuck is going on at table twelve? But me and Will and Sloane and Henry are thinking about being with our whole families and being eight years old and how in a few minutes we'll get to look at the dessert menu, and it's like the sun has come out and is shining on our hell, and for these few precious minutes before it slips back behind the black cloud that's hovering over our lives—which, by the way, is way fucking bigger than the black cloud of this waitress—we're happy. So I decide that next time we should just ask for a bigger booth.

One that's big enough for eight people.

That need becomes pretty clear after the waitress puts the first four entrées on the table and then asks, "Where would you like the others?" There's a busboy standing behind her with another big tray of food.

We manage to make room—but just barely—and then we have ourselves a feast.

After we finish eating, we show the waitress pictures of my mom and Evelyn and Michael and Sloane's dad, Henry, and she's looking around the restaurant wondering when they're going to show up and how we're going to explain why we ate their food, so I try to distract her by ordering a Triple Chocolate Meltdown for everyone.

"Eight of them," the waitress confirms, and I nod my head and say, "Yes, that will be eight Triple Chocolate Meltdowns." I do this mainly because Will is missing Michael and I'm missing my mom and Sloane's missing her dad and Henry's missing Evelyn, but not really, because just for a few minutes today they're here with us.

After we all eat as much as we can, Sloane has hot fudge sauce on her face, and I smile at her and tell her she should clean it up because it doesn't align with the whole tough-girl, biker-chick look she's trying to pull off, and she smiles back but doesn't make a move to clean it up. The waitress practically has her back arched and her ears twitching as she keeps her suspicious cat eyes on us the whole time. Then when she comes over to see if we want anything else, it gets even a little more weird. I mean, with the eight half-empty bowls and the four people and the urn, it could seem *off* to Margaret.

That's the waitress's name. Margaret. *Margaret with a happy face.* That's what it says on her name tag. Like her last name is an emoji.

Margaret looks at Sloane, with her giant leather biker jacket and sad eyes and hot fudge face, and then she turns to Henry, who has hot fudge around his lips too, and stuck in his white whiskers that are poking out in all directions like his face isn't really a face at all but an unkempt, patchy, and parched lawn during a seasonal drought, and then she glances over at Evelyn, who's just sitting there in the urn nestled in the box with her dessert half eaten. As she takes in Evelyn, Margaret gets this look that says she feels sorry for us. Not in a mean way, but in the same way that you might look at a butterfly with a broken wing or something else that was beautiful once but now can't be fixed. It's an expression that just happens because you don't want to tell the broken thing that it is broken in a way that can't be fixed, but you can't help looking at it like it makes you sad. Margaret starts tapping her pencil on her order pad like she's waiting for Evelyn—Urn Evelyn—to magically appear or say something like, *I'll have a spot more tea*, and for a minute it looks like she might say something to us like, *Should I call someone to come get you? Or Who's in charge here?* But then she comes to the same conclusion that everyone else who has ever had that look on their face before does—*shut up and walk away because the only hope here is that the broken thing has no idea that its options have run out.* But after she gets a few steps away, Margaret turns back around and says, "The dessert is on the house."

She says it in such a nice way, but even still, it takes a really long time to swallow food after that. I mean, it's hard to eat thinking about broken things like butterflies with broken wings. Especially if that broken thing is you. And especially if you just ate enough food for yourself plus a dead person.

We basically all had to do that because ordering food for yourself plus a dead person and then leaving it there untouched would be too weird. So I go back to thinking about the 10,262 people killed by drunk drivers last year and all the families with dead loved ones and all the waitresses that must be tapping pencils with sad looks on their faces.

Then I look up, and Sloane is taking pictures of Will and Henry with her phone, and the waitress is whispering to the busboys and the cook, who are peeking out from behind the swinging kitchen doors looking at us. I want to say, *Don't look at us like you feel sorry for us; look at us like you're fucking impressed. Like we found a place that maybe makes no sense at all to you, but for us it's a different story because we're in a bad place headed to a worse place, and just for a few minutes we found a good place to hang out.*

It's like maybe today, this booth in Applebee's is a mirage in the desert, even if it's one that not everyone can see.

When we leave the restaurant, I smile at Margaret and say, "Thanks for the Triple Chocolate Meltdowns," as I carry Evelyn to the car because Henry has his walker. Then I have an argument with Will over who is going to drive. He says he wants to, and I say, "But you drove all night and didn't sleep," and he tells me he's fine. I basically don't believe him, but I want to sit next to Sloane in the back, so I say, "Okay."

When you set out on a road trip to murder someone, you don't expect to fall in love along the way. But I did.

It took twenty-six hours and thirty-seven minutes for the eight of us to get to the Applebee's a couple of hours west of Knoxville, Tennessee.

En route I fell in love with a car full of strangers.

And half of them were dead.

27

"Oh, no!" Sloane calls out when Will's driving and I'm drifting off to sleep as we're cruising along in the slow-speed lane. I open my eyes, squint in the bright light, and see that Sloane's finally looking at her phone that's been pinging all day, just leaning forward staring at the screen with her mouth open and her eyes big.

"What?" I ask, still slumped sideways with my head against the window.

"Where are we?" she calls out, a little frantic.

"I-40 West. Headed out of Knoxville toward Memphis," Will answers.

"My mom found out about the hamsters."

I sit bolt upright. "I thought they were gerbils."

Sloane rolls her eyes at me, and Will looks at us in the rearview mirror and asks, "Is this hamster-gerbil thing some kind of code?"

"No!" Sloane says, and she's upset. *Really* upset. "I told my mom I'm staying with one of my friends to take care of a litter of hamsters." She looks at me and corrects, "Gerbils. A litter of gerbils. I told her I was taking care of gerbils."

"I'm assuming there are no gerbil-hamsters," Will states, and Sloane rolls her eyes again.

I ask, "What did your mom say, exactly?"

"'Call right now! I know you're not at Mallory's.' And it was in all caps and with a lot of exclamation points and a rodent emoji."

I say, "Uh-oh."

Will eyes us in the mirror again. "Jesus, Sloane! You have to call!"

"Jesus, Will!" Sloane almost yells at him. "I know I have to call! But what do I *say*?"

"Tell her . . ." I can't finish the sentence. *Tell her what?*

Henry's awake now. His eyes are closed, but he's listening. "The truth," he calls out. "Just tell your mom the truth."

Sloane starts laughing. Then she asks, "Which is *what* exactly?"

Henry opens his eyes for a minute, looks dazed, and says nothing.

I say, "Tell her to calm down. Double down on the lie and add details. The more ridiculous the better. Tell her that the baby gerbils died and you're . . ."

Will says, "Jesus, Asher, what's wrong with you?"

"Planning the gerbil funeral . . ."

"Don't listen to him, Sloane," Will adds. "Henry's right. Just talk to her. Tell her the truth."

Sloane sighs, then says, "I'm going with the grandpa story. The one Will told."

I give Will a look that says, *See? You lied too!*

Sloane's already dialing the phone. "Everyone, just be quiet unless I ask you something!"

Her mom picks up.

"Mom, it's me," Sloane says. Then there's a big pause when Sloane's not talking and her mom is yelling. So loud that Sloane has to hold the phone away from her ear and we can all hear her mom screaming.

"Mom, slow down." Then Sloane manages to squeeze in, "Let me talk!" and it gets quiet for a minute. "First of all," she begins, "I'm okay. And I had to lie about the gerbil-hamsters because I knew you would never let me go if I told you the truth. . . . Yes, I told you, I'm fine. . . . I'm with my friend Asher."

Sloane looks over at me and then pulls the phone away from her ear when we all hear her mom yell, "Who the hell is Asher?"

"He's . . . He's . . ." Sloane keeps looking right at me. I shrug.

"I can't explain now," she says, "but he's in my bereavement group, and we're taking his grandpa to Graceland. . . . Yes, in Tennessee! Yes, I know how far that is!"

More silence, then Sloane says, "No! I'm not making this up." Sloane's quiet for another minute as she listens, and then she says, "Look, Mom, Asher lost his mother. And it's not just his grandpa. His grandma's here too."

She glances at me, then at Henry. I flinch; Henry smiles.

Sloane shrugs and whispers, "Her name is Evelyn." Then a pause, followed by "No! You can't talk to her!"

Sloane's mom yells, "Why not?"

Sloane whispers, "It's complicated."

I wonder what Henry thinks.

"Yes, Graceland. . . . No. It's not weird. . . . Yes, it is too true."

Then there's a big pause as Sloane gets another lashing. She lowers the phone as her mom yells, and Sloane starts scrolling through her pictures. Then she puts the phone back to her ear. "Mom, I just sent you a picture of Asher's grandpa. Yes, I'm eating! Look at the picture! We just ate at Applebee's. I had two meals and two desserts. No! I'm not gaining weight! Jesus, Mom! And you know Will? From the Tuesday night group? He's here too. Yes, *that Will*. . . .

"MOM! He's no more messed up than me!"

Will glances back at her in the mirror.

I pick up Sloane's free hand and start slowly tracing her fingers, and Will catches my eye in the rearview mirror and says, "Is that some kind of weird sex game?" and Sloane kicks his seat. I say, "Yes," and then Sloane yells, "NO! I don't want to FaceTime you, Mom! And NO! I will not come home!" Sloane pulls her hand away and covers the phone. "Jesus! My mom wants a picture of Henry holding up today's newspaper. She said the picture I sent could be an old picture or a picture of some random old guy I'm not with."

Will says, "Tell her they don't print newspapers anymore and this isn't a kidnapping; you came along voluntarily."

I ask, "Why would you have pictures of random old guys on your phone?"

Sloane says, "Stop! Neither one of you is helping!" Then she yells into the phone, "Mom, YOU STOP TOO! I'm not having S-E-X with Henry! Or Asher. Or Will!" Then she steals a sideways glance at me.

I start making faces at her. Funny faces like I make at Chloe when she gets upset. Goldfish face, bunny rabbit nose wiggling, deer antlers . . . I have a whole routine. Sloane's been trying not to cry, and now she's trying not to laugh. The conversation goes on for a few more minutes, and then when Sloane hangs up, I ask, "Is everything okay?" and she has that completely broken, *the world just toppled me* look, but she says, "Sort of. She's not going to call the cops and report me missing, if that's what you mean. I told her I'll be home in a few days. She sort of said okay."

Then Henry asks where my grandpa is, and I actually contemplate telling him he's right here with the rest of us, but in deference to Will, I resist that instinct and tell Henry the truth. It's the first true thing I've said in a long time. I say, "Both of my grandpas are dead."

Then Henry asks, "Dead-dead?" and startles everyone.

I don't know how to answer, so I say nothing.

Then Henry asks, "Which one is coming with us to Graceland?"

I swear to God, that's what he says. So I run with it. I tell him, "It's my grandpa Frank, on my mom's side. He loves the King and has all his albums."

Henry starts humming the Elvis song "If I Can Dream" and introduces Evelyn to Grandpa Frank. Then Will joins in singing the lyrics, and it's like they're all right there in the car with us. Not just my mom and Will's brother and Sloane's dad and Evelyn, but my grandpa Frank and the King.

I know it sounds weird, but it's not.

It's actually kind of nice.

28

Two hours later we pull off the highway to make a pit
stop at another one of those giant twenty-four-hour rest stops
with snacks and fast food and pinball machines and kids running
around. After I help Henry out of the car, my phone starts ringing
and it's Grace, so I hit decline.

When we get inside, Sloane stops in front of a ball pit to watch
some kids about Chloe's age playing. I ask, "Do you know how
many kids die every year on playgrounds?" and she immediately
says, "Fifteen." I do a double take, but she just shrugs and walks off.

I catch up with her a few minutes later in the potato chip aisle of
the mini-mart, and she defensively says, "What? I looked it up." Her
phone pings, and she reads the message, rolls her eyes, and shoves
the phone back into her jacket pocket.

"What's wrong?" I ask, as if it isn't obvious.

"My mom's still giving me a hard time." Then she turns to watch
as some guy with a long ponytail who's carrying a motorcycle
helmet and is covered in tattoos pulls a six-pack of Budweiser out
of the fridge and then kisses the girl who's with him on the mouth.

"When you look at me, what do you see?" Sloane asks with her
eyes riveted on the couple.

I want to say, *I see the most beautiful girl I have ever seen in my entire life*, but I know that would be like saying *I see a hat*. And if I say *I see a hat*, she'll know that I don't see her at all.

So I study her face. Look past the outline of boots and jacket and the silky hair and sad dark eyes and those lips of hers that always look like they will either turn up in a sneer or quiver and bring her to tears. I look past broken and pretty and fragile and vulnerable and search for what's underneath and inside and trailing in her wake and hovering in a self-defining way all about her.

I whisper, "I see a girl who was swallowed by love," and as soon as I say it, I know it was the wrong thing to say because that's not *all I see*. That's the wrong love—it's sad love that swallowed her—and I know that's not all of her, and I instantly know that it's going to backfire and ruin everything, and it does.

Sloane swipes at a tear, and I tell myself that it was going to happen anyway, no matter what I said—that she was packed and loaded and primed to cry—and then I tell myself I should NEVER BE HONEST, or maybe it's that I should BE MORE HONEST, BRUTALLY HONEST EVEN, or maybe I should just LEARN MORE WORDS or just learn *BETTER WORDS* or MAYBE JUST LEARN TO SHUT UP AND NOT TALK AT ALL because that isn't what I see at all. I don't see a girl *swallowed by sad love*; I see a girl who *is* love, *fiery and fierce and strong love*. So much fiery love that losing her dad could topple her to pieces. So much fierce love that she watches her sisters sleep to make sure that they are breathing. So much strong love that she's fighting back and rising from the ashes, and I should have said that.

She says, "Look at me! I'm just . . . *stuck!*"

So I kiss her. Right there in the middle of the day in the potato chip aisle of the rest stop mini-mart. Risky move, I know, but I do it anyway. And I'm not talking adoring, sweet best-friend kiss like the meatball-and-spaghetti kiss in *Lady and the Tramp*. I go in BIG. Hand swooped under the small of her back, full-on open-mouth, sweep-her-off-her-feet, knock-the-Fritos-off-the-shelf, passionate, you-are-infinitely-lovable, movie-kiss BIG. And don't think sweet and romantic, like when Jasmine kisses Aladdin, either. It's far more epic and more passionate—it's Jack kissing Rose in *Titanic*. Or the Katniss-and-Peeta kiss in *Catching Fire*. *JUST BIGGER AND BETTER*. It's some kiss from some future movie that hasn't been written yet with equally tragic characters who are romantically doomed but forever tied together, who have to save their world from crashing down in a tragic end or sinking to the bottom of the ocean.

It's a kiss to melt the big screen.

When it's over, I open my eyes and pull back a few inches. Sloane keeps her eyes closed for a few seconds more, and then she slowly opens them. She's now looking at me kind of shocked and kind of confused, but good shocked and good confused. She's not talking and I'm not talking, and her phone is still pinging, but she's ignoring it, and then she breaks eye contact and looks away and stands up and straightens her dad's motorcycle jacket. I sense someone else near us, and I think, *Oh, shit! What if it's Will or Henry? What if they saw?* But I glance over and it's not either of them. It's this lady I saw earlier who has a whole bunch of little kids who are now running up and down the aisles. She says, "I hate to interrupt, but you two are blocking the salty snacks." Her cheeks are puffy and red and she's annoyed. The kids flitter and flick like fireflies around the store, but we don't move. Not Sloane. Not the lady. And not me.

Sloane ignores her and smirks and says, "You better not have enjoyed that."

I lie and say, "I didn't. Not one little bit. That kiss was just to, you know . . ."

She looks at me like, *No, I don't know.*

I shrug and say, "You know, to . . ."

She raises her eyebrows.

"To unstick you."

I wanted to tell her that *I was wrong.*

That I don't see a girl swallowed by sad love.

And I wanted to say that *she is wrong.*

You are not stuck; you're surviving. And that's halfway to somewhere.

But I couldn't say any of that. Not to Sloane. Not here. Not in a rest-stop mini-mart. So I just smile and step out of the way so the lady with all the kids can buy potato chips. Then she gets this look—Sloane, not the potato-chip lady—and her lips turn up into the sort of smile that's more of a smirk, an adorable smirk. "To unstick me?" she asks.

"Yeah," I say. "To unstick you."

"Like your kiss has superpowers?"

"It does," I tell her, smirking back at her.

Now she's full-on smiling and I'm full-on smiling, and I don't break eye contact with her as I take a step back, almost crashing into the neatly lined-up cans of soup on the shelf behind me.

I can't explain it, but Sloane has this *look* on her face, like she *sees me.* It's like I could draw her a picture that *looks exactly like a hat* and she'd *know* that it's not a hat and never was a hat—*couldn't possibly ever be a hat.*

It's like she'd know immediately and without thinking that what I drew her is a boa constrictor that ate an elephant.

Back in the car, after a half hour of me and Will and Sloane playing *What's the best movie kiss ever?*—a game Will suggested and a development that makes me wonder if he *did* see us in the snack aisle at the mini-mart after all—Henry wakes up and announces that it's Grace Kelly and Cary Grant in *To Catch a Thief*.

"Sorry," Sloane says. "Haven't seen that movie."

"Me neither," I say, and Will adds, "Better make that three."

Meanwhile, I've been arguing for *Lady and the Tramp* but not getting anywhere because Will keeps insisting that "poodle-smooching doesn't count."

I insist, "They're not poodles," but Sloane says, "Sorry, Asher. No four-footers and definitely no tail-bearing creatures in the kissing contest."

I say, "Not fair!" but everyone ignores me.

Sloane's been arguing that "it's absolutely, no questions asked, Bella and Edward in *Twilight*," so I finally ask, "Which *Twilight*?" and she looks all soft and dreamy and says, "All of them."

I take out my phone and pull *Twilight* clips up on YouTube and have to agree that she has a point, and then I ask, "Seriously, Sloane. Which one?"

She smiles and says, "The first kiss in Bella's bedroom when Edward tells her that he's been climbing in through her window to watch her sleep."

I pull that clip up, mainly to get some kissing tips, and I'm not disappointed.

Henry asks, "What's *Twilight* about?" and Sloane says, "It's a love story between a girl and a vampire," and Will says, "It's more like hot-stalker, creepy vampire porn."

Sloane yells, "Don't ruin it for me!" and then she hands Henry my phone to watch the clip. I object, then make a last-ditch pitch for *Lady and the Tramp*, mostly because it's Chloe's favorite movie. I basically argue that if vampires are allowed, then dogs should be too, but Will and Sloane overrule me.

Sloane tells Will that he didn't vote yet, and he says, "Fine. The best kiss, hands down, goes to the Ferris wheel kiss between Simon and Bram in *Love, Simon.*"

Sloane says, "Defend your position."

He says, "MTV said so."

Sloane counters with "MTV also voted best kiss for *Twilight*," and Henry asks, "What's MTV?" And Sloane says, "It's a cable channel," and Will says, "No, it isn't. It's like NPR had a baby with *Rolling Stone* and TikTok and Carson Daly and a gossip magazine—"

Then Henry interrupts him and says, "Simon and Bram sound like two boys."

Will says, "They *are* two boys," and then he's looking at Henry, trying to read his reaction, and the car starts drifting out of our lane, and my heart starts racing and my hands get sweaty and I yell, "Jesus, Will! If you're gonna drive, keep your eyes on the road!"

Will tells me to calm down, but then he must remember about

how my mom died so he catches my eye in the rearview and adds, "Sorry, Asher. My eyes are on the road!" And Henry tells us that maybe Cary Grant should have been kissing Clark Gable or Rock Hudson, not Grace Kelly, because lots of people think they were gay just like Simon and Bram, and Will smiles at him. Then Henry adds that kissing girls and kissing boys and kissing dogs are okay with him, but there shouldn't be movies where there are vampires kissing anyone, so I count that as one uptick for *Lady and the Tramp*. Then Henry tells Sloane that she really has to watch *To Catch a Thief* because it's a great love story, just like his and Evelyn's.

Sloane says, "The Henry and Evelyn story should be made into a romantic unlimited series for Netflix," and Will says, "I think you mean *limited series*," and Sloane says, "No. UNLIMITED. That's the point. It never ends. There could be thousands of episodes that go on forever and ever." Sloane then tells Henry that she'll watch *To Catch a Thief* if he'll watch *Twilight* and *Love, Simon*, and Henry says, "Yes to *Love, Simon* but no to vampires." He's smiling at Sloane, probably because of what she just said about the Henry and Evelyn never-ending love story. I'm smiling at Sloane right now too, and it's a big, confident smile. I'm figuring that the kiss we just had in the potato chip aisle was at least as epic as the one between Bella and Edward in *The Twilight Saga: Breaking Dawn—Part 2*, so I announce, "I can kiss just like Edward, better, even, because my kiss doesn't require that the person on the receiving end slip over and sell her soul."

"Are you sure about that, Asher?" Sloane asks with this smirky grin. "I mean, I get the impression that you might have a dark side."

"As dark as Edward's?" I ask.

Will chimes in with "Darker."

I don't respond, but I'm thinking, *They don't know the half of it.* But Sloane's looking at me like Bella looks at Edward, so I search for her hand and find it tucked under the sweatshirts and jackets and all the other shit that's sitting here piled up between us.

30

I've been holding Sloane's hand for one hour, twenty-seven minutes, and not enough seconds when she sits bolt upright, drops my hand, and starts pointing to her right as she calls out, "Pull in there!"

We're off the highway now and driving by mattress stores and body shops, and Will asks, "Where?"

"There. Over there," she says, making it seem like there's some pending emergency. She's pointing at a run-down strip mall on the right side of the road, barely ahead of us. Will checks the mirrors, sees an opening in the oncoming traffic, and then yanks the steering wheel hard to the right, and we careen across two lanes of traffic, then swerve into the parking lot. It's a bit of a stunt-driver maneuver, and I almost have another heart attack. Then I decide that we're lucky that Henry's asleep because if Evelyn doesn't like going over forty miles per hour, then that move Will just pulled would not have gone over well.

"Here?" Will asks, and Sloane nods.

As I look around at the stores trying to figure out what Sloane saw that seemed so appealing, I come up dry. "The gun store or the liquor store?" I ask sarcastically as I continue to scan the shops and Will pulls nose-first into a parking spot. Some of the stores have bars on the windows, and the rest either look shuttered up or sketchy. Next to the gun shop there's a dilapidated thrift store with an old typewriter and a naked mannequin in the window. There's a sign that says WE BUY THE TITLE TO YOUR CAR FOR CASH. I point at it and ask, "What do you think that's about?"

Will glances over, and I realize that I didn't specify if I meant the mannequin or the typewriter or the sign, but then when he says, "Extreme poverty and gambling," I realize that his answer covers all three.

"Gambling?" I ask.

"Casinos near here. People need cash," he says.

"How do you know that?"

"I've been here before."

"Here, here?" I ask surprised. "Like, in this shopping center?"

Will doesn't answer, but he says, "This doesn't look safe. Go with her, Asher." Then a police car drives by slowly and the cop eyes us. Henry wakes up in time to wave at him, which doesn't help. Sloane takes everyone's drink order—Red Bull for Will, peach iced tea for Evelyn, and water for me and Henry—then opens the door and says, "Wait here." She gets out of the car and heads for a sleazy-looking convenience store that's tucked back in the corner.

I tell Will not to let Henry out of the car, and trail after her.

She's through the door like she's on a mission and goes straight to the register and asks the clerk a question.

I hang back by the door as he points, then eyes me, probably figuring that we're going to shoplift or full-on rob the place at gunpoint, probably with an assault weapon I just purchased in the shop next door with the cash I received for handing over the title to my dad's car, so I wave at him and smile to try to put him at ease, but he just scowls back.

Sloane walks over to where the clerk is pointing, and I watch as she picks up what looks like it might be candy, then goes to the fridge for the drinks. She grabs two motorcycle magazines, then heads to the counter to pay for all of it. I take out my phone to send Grace a text because I never called her back, and I'm starting to get nervous that I'm going to be late to pick her up for the prom tonight. I don't know what to say, so I send her a message, which is basically all emojis, no words—cars and hearts and party hats and streamers—but then write, Almost in Memphis! Can't wait to meet you IRL! before I stuff the phone back into my pocket.

"That was your emergency?" I ask Sloane after she makes her way over to me by the exit. "Candy? And . . ." I grab one of the magazines she bought to eye the cover, ". . . *Motorcycle Mojo?*"

She pushes past me, opens the door, looks over her shoulder, smiles back at me, and says, "Yes."

I trail after her back to the car, but she doesn't get in. Instead she knocks on the driver's-side window, tells Will and Henry to get out, and then hands out the drinks and gives a bag of M&M's to each of us. Then she announces, "We played the game wrong."

Henry says, "I like games," but I'm pretty sure he's not only on another page, he's reading from a different playbook.

Sloane tells us all to open the bags and take out one M&M.

Will says, "Not this again," then chugs down his Red Bull and complains that it's so hot, his sneakers are melting and his feet are on fire.

Sloane says, "Stop whining and just do it."

Henry complies, but his hands shake and his candy spills all over the pavement, so I give him a few of mine. Will flatly refuses to play. He won't even open the bag. Sloane ignores them both.

Sloane and I are now each holding a single piece of candy. Both of our M&M's are melting in the heat. And Will's right. It is *hot*.

Muggy, sticky tar, melt your shoes, *Southern hot*. I eat the M&M and then tell Henry to go back and crack a window so Evelyn can breathe because he left her in the car. He smiles like that's a good idea.

"Now," Sloane starts, "tell me one thing about yourself, Asher."

"Jesus," Will complains. "We're standing in a hundred-degree parking lot for this?"

"Just shut up and let Asher do it," Sloane snaps, and then she turns back to me. "Go ahead. Tell me something."

I don't say anything except, "I'm thinking."

Sloane says, "You go, then, Will."

Will looks pissed off. Still refuses to take out a candy. But Sloane's not gonna let up. She looks at Henry, who's returned from opening the car window, and tells him how the game works. I hand him one blue M&M and shrug. Henry eats the candy and then tells us that Evelyn likes to knit, but I'm not sure if he's actually playing or just making a random comment.

Sloane says, "No. Something else. Something not about Evelyn."

Henry looks lost. I can't tell if it's just normal-Henry-old-person lost, or if it's because there is no Henry without Evelyn.

Will says, "He wasn't even there."

Henry just looks more confused.

Will adds, "Sloane, stop."

"I can't stop," she says, "because *I get it now*. And it's important."

"You get *what*? Some stupid therapy game? So what?" Will's angry and I don't know why. Maybe it's too much time in the car. Maybe it's not sleeping and the heat. Maybe it's something else.

I try to de-escalate the situation by offering something raw and personal. I say, "Okay, my turn." I eat an M&M and take a deep breath. "My dad cries at night." I look down at the tar. My voice shakes. "I can hear him through the walls." Then I eat another M&M as warm tears spring into my eyes.

"No," Sloane says. "Something else." She sounds firm—harsh, even.

"Sloane, you're being mean," Will accuses.

"What do you want?" I ask her. "I don't get what you want, then."

"Here. I'll show you," she says as she holds up two pieces of candy, then pops them into her mouth. "I read the last paragraph of every book before I read the first one. And I love horses. Buttery, cream-colored palominos with white manes and tails."

"Books and horses? Palomino horses?" Will's steaming mad. "Asher tells you something really personal about his dad, and you say you like horses? How is that better?"

"Oh God," I say. "I get it now." I'm shaking. *My hands. My voice.* I get it, and it makes me sad. *So sad.* I try not to cry, but I feel my lip quivering. *Just like Chloe's does.* Just like that time I told her she couldn't have chocolate pudding.

Will looks at Henry and asks if anyone has sunscreen as Sloane nods her head. "Do it, Asher. Say something."

I shake my head. Whisper, "I can't." Lip quiver is getting worse. Like, tears-about-to-sprout-from-lids worse.

Will says, "Henry's turning red."

The cop drives by again. Henry waves.

"Try," Sloane says softly. She takes my hand. Pulls me back in. *She doesn't want me to drift away.*

"Just something small," she says.

I want her to tell me that it's okay. That I don't have to say any- thing if I don't want to. That we can just get back in the car and drive. But she doesn't. She just holds my hand and looks at me expectantly. I want to say, *My mom died thirteen months five days six hours and twelve minutes ago*, but I know that's wrong. I want to say, *A drunk driver killed her*, but I know that's wrong too. *I have to do this right*. I eat an M&M.

It comes out as a whisper. "I . . ."

Sloane puts her other hand on my arm. Squeezes it gently.

"Keep going," she encourages.

Will looks completely baffled.

"I . . . used to like to play the guitar."

Sloane nods her head and then wipes away her own tears. Henry is looking dazed and confused. Lost somewhere in his own head. Will just looks flat-out befuddled. Mouth hanging open like we told him that a spaceship just landed in the parking lot and now he's standing there wondering why he can't see it.

Sloane eats an M&M and whispers, "On Fridays after school me and my two best friends used to get our nails done at the mall."

I whisper, "I like In-N-Out Burger, but they don't have any near where we live."

Sloane starts to smile. A wet-cheeks, half-sad, half-happy smile. "I want to paint my room yellow," she says.

I follow that with "I kissed a girl and I liked it."

Sloane says, "I kissed a boy and I liked it too."

I smile.

Will yells, "What the fuck is going on here?" His fingers are covered in melting M&M's because he's now got his bag of candy open like he's trying to play, *wants to play*, but he doesn't get it, and he's afraid he's missing out on a life-changing existential revelation.

I wipe away more tears, then try to explain. "That day, Peter Pan was trying to get us to tell each other something about ourselves that wasn't about losing the person we lost."

Will asks, "Who the hell is Peter Pan?"

Henry pops in with a starry-eyed look and says, "Evelyn loves Peter Pan and the whole Darling family."

"*What???*" Will asks.

Sloane says, "He means the woman who runs the bereavement group," even though I never told her that's what I call her. "She kind of looks like Peter Pan." Sloane continues, "She was trying to teach us that we're more than our loss. And none of us could do it. Asher and you said nothing, and I said ten things about my dad. It's like we don't exist outside of their deaths. She was trying to remind us that we do."

Will has that *I'm processing this slowly* look on his face.

Sloane sits down on the sidewalk and eats the rest of her M&M's. "We were people in our own right before this terrible thing that happened to us happened to us, and we're people now—even if it doesn't feel that way. That's what the M&M's were supposed to teach us. It hit me when I started thinking about how much fun we had playing the best-movie-kiss game, like, shit! I used to *watch movies*. Then I realized, shit! I used to *like* movies."

Will eats an M&M, sits down next to Sloane on the curb, puts his elbows on his knees and his head in hands, and says, "I used to be on swim team. I held the school record for the butterfly."

Sloane smiles and hands Will another M&M from his bag. The cop drives by a third time and slowly eyes us again. Henry is a few steps away now. He's taken Evelyn out of the car, and he's clutching her in her box. Will's sitting there on the curb all hunched over, counting his M&M's. "I played soccer for a bit, but swimming was more my thing," he says to no one in particular, and then he eats another candy.

The cop pulls up next to us, rolls down his window, and asks, "Is everything okay here?"

Henry says, "Yes, officer. We're just taking my wife to meet Elvis."

The cop eyes him. Then he looks at Sloane, the most obvious candidate for Henry's wife.

Sloane smiles at the cop and then helps Henry back into the car.

I stand up and offer Will my hand. I pull him up, but it's like trying to lift something that's too heavy for me.

"Hey, that thing earlier about Simon and Bram?" I ask. "Does that mean that . . . you know . . . ?"

"I'm gay?" he asks.

I nod. "I just thought with all the M&M-eating and soul-baring, I'd ask."

He looks at me for a minute but doesn't answer.

"I mean, you don't have to tell me. I was just . . ."

He asks, "Are you a dog?"

"What?"

"You're saying that if I thought the gay kiss was memorable and romantic, I must be gay, so I'm thinking that if you think the *Lady and the Tramp* kiss was memorable and romantic, you must be a dog."

I say, "This is what I get for making friends with a philosophy student," and he says, "You're right about that, but no. I'm not gay."

"Why didn't you just say that?"

"More fun to give you shit. And, as long as you asked, I have an on-again, off-again girlfriend, so you don't have to worry about me liking Sloane and us getting into a fight because you kissed her in the snack aisle at the rest stop."

"So you saw."

"I see everything, my friend."

I smile.

"Why are you smiling?" he asks.

"Because that means that I don't have any competition for Sloane, which is all I really wanted to know anyway."

Will seems to think about that. "In the car."

I look at him, questioning, and he clarifies.

"I'm just saying that there are plenty of guys who would be interested in Sloane, so it's just that you don't have any competition for Sloane *in the car*."

I give that some thought. "I don't know. I think Henry could give me a run for my money."

We both look over at Henry and watch him fuss over Evelyn as he gets her tucked into her spot next to him on the floor of the front seat.

"Yeah, but Sloane would have to pry Evelyn from his heart first, and I don't see that happening," Will says.

"Plus, Evelyn is hot," I add.

We're both still watching him. Will laughs. "So, very, very hot."

When we walk back to the car together, I realize that I truly, truly have a friend. And that I'm one small step closer to somewhere better than where I've been—and it's not just me. All of us are. Then, before we climb back into the car, I say to Will, "I'm driving. You haven't slept." He tosses me the keys and I tell him, "You know, Michael was lucky to have you as a brother," and Will gives me a hug. A sweaty, chocolaty hug.

Then I grab Sloane's hand and ask, "How do you feel?"

She says, "Unstuck," and smiles. "How do you feel?"

I say, "A bit like a dandelion that just found a crack in the concrete," and Sloane gives my hand a squeeze and smiles that funny half smile of hers before she climbs back into the car. And I swear, it's like she knows *exactly* what that means.

31

We're just outside the city limits, cruising into Memphis, when I look over at Henry and say, "I'm thinking that we'll go to Graceland tomorrow. I want to go to a hotel to get ready. . . ."

He looks at me expectantly. I don't finish the sentence.

"Get ready for what?" Sloane asks.

I glance back at her in the rearview mirror and say, "Okay. Here's the thing."

Will mutters, "Oh, shit."

I look back at him and ask, "Oh, shit, *what*?" Challenge him for calling me out, wondering if he knows something, or if he's just bluffing. But he doesn't add anything; he just slumps down in the seat a bit and looks straight ahead, eyes focused on the back of Henry's seat as the whole car gets quiet.

A few minutes later I pull over to the side of the road and ask Sloane to get out of the car to talk to me.

Will says, "Why'd you pull over?" Then he looks around the car. "This is weird. Does anyone else think this is weird?" But Henry is the only other anyone, and he's talking to Evelyn and apparently not listening.

As soon as I open my door, Will looks over, peeks out from

behind his hair, and says, "Oh, shit, *this*, Asher." But I ignore him.

Once we're out of the car, I tell Sloane that I have to take this girl I don't know to her prom tonight. I kind of have to yell because trucks are whizzing by us at high speed in both directions. She pulls her dad's motorcycle jacket in close and has her arms crossed, circling her chest steaming-mad tight. I want to say that I'm sorry, so sorry, but I don't, and she just stands there for a minute looking at me before she asks, "What girl?" Her face is blank and vulnerable and open as I think about how much I don't want to hurt her and what I came here to do and how much those two things are on a collision course.

And then I do what I do best. I tell her a BIG LIE I make up on the fly. I just let my mouth take a wild improv run up and down the keyboard. I'm Bud Powell on a concert grand. Or Louis Armstrong with my horn wailing, just Asher and that mouth of his, winging it.

And it's a train wreck.

"Just some girl," I say.

"Some girl? You're taking *some girl* who lives in Tennessee to her prom? Tonight?"

I nod. "She's my cousin twice removed and we've never actually met in real life and I hate her."

"Why?"

"Why what?"

She shrugs. "Why do you hate her?"

"It's complicated. But in a nutshell, it's because she likes Ed Sheeran."

Sloane rolls her eyes and says, "Asher, everyone in the world loves Ed Sheeran." So I say, "My dad is making me to do it," and Sloane asks, "Your dad is making you do *what* exactly?" and I say, "He's making me take this girl to the prom," but Sloane doesn't look like she's buying it, so I whisper, "Look, if I don't take her to the prom, my dad said he'll . . ." Sloane gets this look like, *He'll what?* And I can't think of anything. Then she just says, "Asher," and the way she says it breaks my heart because Sloane has this sad, worried, disappointed-mom look on her face, and then she just gets back into the car without even challenging me, so I slide into the driver's seat, start the engine, and pull out and try to act like nothing just happened, and when Will asks, "What's going on?" I say, "Nothing." He says, "Okay, then."

But it's not okay then. Not with him, and not with Sloane. They're both pissed, but for a different set of reasons.

I know that underpinning both of those reasons is the fact that I'm lying. Will knows it. Sloane knows it. Shit, *Evelyn probably knows it.* The way I figure it, the only person who believes anything I say is Henry, and he talks to dead people. I glance over at him, and he's reading an old brochure from a million years ago about Graceland. The pamphlet's all pawed over and dog-eared, and he's studying a picture of Elvis's plane that he has circled in orange Magic Marker.

I turn back to the road, thinking, *Henry's chasing a dream, and I'm chasing a nightmare*, and Sloane and Will just want some version of the truth—one that I can't seem to deliver.

Then Will leans forward from the back seat and drops my phone into the cup holder. "You left it here," he says, with this *watch out I snooped* tone and his eyebrows raised up like a couple of foul-weather flags.

I'm thinking, *Oh, shit!* but it's more like, *OH, SHIT!!* and that's when I start talking about Elvis Presley working undercover with the FBI.

"Okay," I start, "so here's a theory. Elvis didn't die; he was put into witness protection because he was working undercover to help the FBI nail some mob guys."

Henry looks up and smiles, and Will says, "Bullshit!"

I'm thinking that it might have been a general *bullshit* not related to Elvis at all, but either way I say, "No, I swear! It's true. Some mob guys who were in an organization called 'The Fraternity' were interested in buying Elvis's plane, so the FBI reached out to him and asked him to wear a wire and record them. So he invited them onto the plane and got them talking and saying incriminating shit."

"About what?" Will asks.

"How the hell do I know?" I say. "Maybe the whereabouts of Jimmy Hoffa."

"Who's Jimmy Hoffa?" Sloane asks, her voice all icy.

"The head of the Teamsters Union who kind of disappeared in a *cement shoes on the bottom of a river* kind of way," Will tells her.

Sloane's still pissed and ignoring me, but she's now leaning forward and looking at the brochure Henry is holding.

"Then when the mob hit men found out that the King was working undercover, the FBI decided to fake his death and put him in witness protection," I add.

"Evelyn thinks that they buried Jimmy Hoffa in Elvis's grave," Henry announces.

I glance over at him. "I see that Evelyn's familiar with the theory, then."

Henry beams.

"And you believe all that?" Will asks him.

Henry just keeps smiling.

Will takes out his phone, then reports, "Only four percent of Americans think Elvis is still alive."

"Yeah, but four percent of the US population is what?" I ask, glancing back at him in the rearview mirror.

Will pulls the calculator on his phone up and says, "Over thirteen million people."

I nod. "Which is nothing to cough at."

Sloane has her phone out too, and she says, "Half of the people in Iceland believe in fairies."

I catch her eye in the rearview mirror and say, "But no one lives in Iceland," and she says, "I wasn't talking to you."

Then Will looks up from his phone and says, "Holy shit! Almost half of Americans believe in ghosts! That's more than 150 million people, so the whole Elvis thing and the whole Iceland thing aren't that weird."

I look at Henry and think, *And the whole Evelyn thing.* Plus, I'm thinking, Chloe talks to all sorts of people who aren't real, like her stuffed animals, and THEY TALK BACK and it makes her happy, so who fucking cares who believes in fairies or ghosts or dead Elvis? Then I look over at Henry and think, *Or dead Evelyn.* But I don't say any of that. My whole goal was to change the subject away from ASHER AND GRACE AND THE PROM AND THE BIG LIE, and I did that.

"By any chance," I call out, trying to sound casual, "does anyone know where to get one of those wrist things?"

I catch Sloane's eye in the rearview mirror again, and then she quickly looks away and starts flipping through one of her motorcycle magazines, and she's back to wearing her signature *I'm completely toppled* look. Then she says, "You mean a *corsage*?"

I think about saying, *I thought you weren't talking to me*, but smarten up and don't. Instead I say, "Yeah, a corsage. That's it."

She doesn't answer and Will just stares at me. He's pissed again too. But Henry's bent down, showing Evelyn a picture of Elvis's plane, so at least they're not mad at me.

Three blocks later I put my directional on and pull off the road and into the parking lot of a small shopping center. If I don't count the two stores on the far end that are boarded up, there are three options. There's Leroy's Discount Liquor Barn. The Ammo Alley Gun Shop. And the Mess of Blues Florist.

Will asks, "Why are we stopping?"

I say, "I need to pick something up."

He looks around. "What? Like a gun?"

I get out of the car without answering him, and Sloane follows me. There's a motorcycle parked out in front of the gun shop, and she walks by it slowly. I stop to wait for her.

"Like it?" I ask.

"No," she says. "Too small."

"Too small for what?" I ask.

"Beale Street."

I want to ask what that means, but she's mad, so I don't.

There's a bell on the door of the shop, and the lady behind the counter looks up as we enter. She calls out, "How can I help you folks?"

I call over, "I need a corsage." She eyes me, then Sloane. "For the prom tonight?"

Sloane is glaring at me as I say, "Yes, ma'am."

The sales clerk steps out from behind the counter and smiles, like me and Sloane are such a cute couple. "Collegiate?" she asks, beaming away.

It takes me a minute to figure out that Collegiate must be the name of a local high school.

"Don't know which school, actually," I respond.

She's probably wondering how it is that we have no idea where we're going, but she heads over to a refrigerator full of flowers anyway and looks back over at Sloane and asks, "What color is your dress, honey?"

I'm thinking, *Oh, shit!* and Sloane calls out, "It's not for me, but I believe it's purple." And then she leans in close and asks sarcastically, "What color is her dress, Asher?" and I mumble, "What's the opposite of purple?" to nobody in particular. The saleslady picks up on the tension and says, "We can always go with white," as she pulls out a couple of boxed wrist corsages from the flower fridge.

I look at them and ask, "Do you have black? Or maybe black and orange?"

Sloane makes a noise like a snort, and the saleslady looks startled, then kind of flinches. I ask a defensive *"What?"* because they're acting like I ushered in a cold wind, maybe like when Edward walks into a room in *Twilight*. Then I shrug and say, "I guess no one ever asked for ugly flowers before."

The saleslady looks down and says, "No black and orange. I have yellow and pale pink, if you don't like white."

"How will these look with purple?" I ask, looking at what she selected.

"Any of them would be great," she says.

I say, "Then I don't want any of them."

Sloane whispers, "Asher," and then the lady pulls out two more boxed corsages from the fridge and says something about baby's breath and tea roses and yellow being popular this year, and then she adds, "This is all I have unless you want something custom."

I pick up one of the boxes sitting on the counter and take out my wallet. "I'll take this one."

The lady says, "I don't suppose you want a nice bag to carry it in?" and I say, "Absolutely not."

"Something else you want to tell me?" Sloane asks as we make our way back to the car and she eyes the too-small-for-Beale-Street motorcycle.

"No," I say. "Not really."

"Anything *you* want to run by *me*?" I ask as I eye the bike, still wondering what she meant by Beale Street.

"No. Not really," she says.

Then I toss the corsage into the back of the Jeep where I figure, in this heat, all those tea roses and baby's breath will surely wilt.

When we get in the car, Will's got my phone again. I grab it back from him, pissed, and say, "Not cool, dude."

He doesn't respond. He just gives me a look of disbelief with his eyebrows raised.

"How are you opening it, anyway?" I ask.

He says, "Your passcode is one-one-one-one-one-one," then turns to stare out the window.

I say, "Shit." Then, "Not anymore," and change it. Then I try to see what he was looking at, but he's already shut any open apps.

When I start the engine, Sloane's still pouting, but she calls out, "Let's go to the Memphis Zoo to see the pandas."

Will sighs. "I thought we were going to Graceland or a hotel. No one ever said anything about going to the zoo," and I'm starting to feel things begin to unravel fast in the back seat.

"Who doesn't like the zoo?" Sloane asks, and Will calls out an aggressive "Me."

"Why?" she pushes, and he tells her that he doesn't like animals. I figure, *Sloane's up for a fight with anyone who'll take the bait, and right now that anyone is Will.*

She doesn't prove me wrong. And neither does he.

"Everybody likes animals," she challenges as I pull out of the parking lot and back onto the road.

"Not everyone," Will snaps back.

I don't know why Will's being weird about the zoo, but it's pretty obvious that Sloane's being mean to him because she's mad at me. And I don't know what Will saw on my phone, but he's obviously mad at me too. Henry is just staring out the window not saying anything. I ask Sloane to GPS the directions, and twenty minutes later when we pull into the parking lot of the Memphis Zoo, things heat up even more because Will refuses to get out of the car. He's practically curled up in the fetal position on the back seat.

Sloane looks at him, then at me, and says, "I guess you two will just have to wait in the car with Evelyn." I figure by *you two*, she means me and Will, and that I was just officially uninvited. She climbs out and then helps Henry out of the front seat, and the two of them head for the entrance with Henry slowly walkering along-side her. I'm stuck sitting there in the car with Will and Evelyn as the air rapidly heats up to a broil. If I squint, I can almost see grill marks on my skin even though we've got the windows cranked wide open. Will gets out and sits down on the curb, and I hop up, then plop down next to him and ask, "What now?" figuring he's going to have a whole lot of questions about what he saw on my phone, but he doesn't.

He just ducks behind his hair and looks at his feet, and the two of us just sit there for a while until he finally says, "We took Michael to Memphis after he was diagnosed. Right before he got really sick. To St. Jude's hospital for a second opinion."

I freeze.

"After, we came here to the zoo."

It takes me a minute to process. I'm afraid that I might say the wrong thing or *not say the right thing*, but I end up asking the thing I'm most afraid of hearing the answer to because I can't just let this conversation hang there in the air.

"*After?*"

I'm terrified that *after* means *after Michael died*, but I can't *not ask* since he put it out there.

"*After* the doctors and the hospital and the tests and the diagnosis of terminal," he clarifies.

"Jesus, Will. I'm sorry."

He's picking away at the soft melting tar of the parking lot with a small rock when I whisper, "You should have said something. Sloane never would have been so . . ."

"Fucking awful?" Will asks, and I say, "Yeah, that's the phrase I was looking for."

He's now using a bigger rock he found to chip away at the tar. "Look," I say, "don't take it personally. She's mad at me."

"For?"

We exchange a look. "Stuff."

He looks down and I stand up, pull the car keys from my pocket, and glance around the parking lot. There are families everywhere climbing in and out of cars—moms and dads. Little kids. Old people like Henry. Babies. Teens. And they're all having a great time. I look down at Will sitting there pulling apart the parking lot, looking defeated and lost, and say, "Let's go. We don't have to tell Sloane any of this if you don't want to. We can just leave her here with Henry for a while. We'll pick them up later."

Will looks up at me. "Can we just sit here, please?"

"Sure." I say, and then I sit back down next to him.

"I did this," he adds, as we both look over at a family climbing into the car across from us. "I said yes to coming to Memphis, and I knew what Memphis would do to me. Shit, I *jumped at the chance to come here.* I didn't even think about it. It's like I wanted to reopen the wound."

We watch the mom buckle the last kid into a car seat before I announce, "Sometimes I think about driving to the spot of my mom's accident. You know, just to see it."

"What is that?" Will asks.

"It's like we fucking *want to hurt*," I say.

"My therapist said revisiting places can help, or it could be a form of self-harm, like cutting yourself."

I turn to him. "You have a therapist?"

He looks at me, eyebrows hiked up like, *Don't I look like I have a therapist?*

I ask, "So which is it? Helping or hurting?" and he says, "Don't know yet." Then we both stare at our feet for a while.

"We brought Michael here to see the giant pandas," Will says, breaking the silence. "That was three years ago." He takes out his phone and shows me pictures. I scroll through them. Will looks pretty much the same, just skinnier. His mom and dad look like ghosts. Pale and almost see-through. *Translucent*, like Henry. Their faces pulled taut, their smiles forced like they've been stretched to the limit. But Michael looks great. He's wearing a baseball cap and smiling and standing at the rail, looking at the pandas eating.

Will's looking over my shoulder as I scroll. "Le Le and Ya Ya," he says. "Double-fisting bamboo."

I scroll to the next picture.

"Michael didn't know he was sick yet. This was the last time we did something as a family before my parents told him."

I hand him back the phone. "That's why you wanted to come here."

"What do you mean?"

"It was the moment before everything changed, and you want it back." I start chipping away at the tar, thinking, *We want it back and we can't get it back*. Then I say, "When my mom died, she was driving home from the mall."

Will looks up.

"She went there to buy me new soccer cleats." I look away. "Mine were stolen from my gym locker, and I had a game the next day. So . . ." My voice trails off.

"Asher . . . ," Will starts. "I'm . . ." But he doesn't finish. He just leans back and wipes the sweat from his forehead with the back of his arm.

"My first day back at school after the accident, Coach handed me the cleats. The ones that were stolen from my gym locker."

I look over at Will and watch his face fall and practically tumble into his chest.

"Coach told me that the janitor pulled them out of one of the trash bins in the locker room. He knew right away that they were mine. I mean, no one else at school had the lime green Nike Superflys.

"When he gave them to me, I saw this flash of white light, you know, like the kind of *rage* that could blind you. I'd been making up all these stories in my head. Hero stories that made me feel better. Like the kid who stole my cleats *needed cleats* to get a soccer scholarship because he had to work two jobs just to pay for his grandma's heart medicine. Or he was going to sell them so he could buy food for his six little sisters. Shit like that. But Coach just pulled the rug out from under those fantasies when he handed those cleats back to me because it was clear that the kid who took them *did it as a fucking joke*. Probably a hoot for him and his ass-hole friends.

Will says, "Asher . . ." Just my name. I mean, *I get it.*

"That's why my mom died. Because someone stole my cleats. Coach said, 'You're lucky someone found them and you got them back.' I thought, yeah, I'm lucky. Then I quit the team. Just said, 'I'm not playing soccer anymore,' and he got that blank, big-face-no-words look, you know, the one that adults get when you drop a bomb on them. For a minute it looked like he might say something else, but he didn't. And I just left. On my way out of the locker room, I stuffed the cleats back into the trash bin. I didn't want to look at them or hold them or wear them. Coach was standing in the doorway to his office watching me. I could almost see his head shaking back and forth as he was probably thinking, 'Asher is headed nowhere good.' He was right."

I kick at the pebbles at my feet.

I look over as a kid walks by us with his mom. He's holding a balloon in one hand and one of those giant rainbow swirled lollipops in the other. Me and Will watch as he gets into the car with his mom. Neither one of us says anything.

I don't tell Will that the day Coach handed me those cleats was the day before I smashed seventeen gym lockers with a baseball bat.

Or that I'm still spiraling down and headed nowhere good.

That it's *game over* and even I know it.

Will just chips away at the tar at our feet, then says, "I wasn't always nice to Michael."

I look over at him and think about saying, *Oh, shit.*

Or *Try not to think about it.*

Or *I'm sorry.*

Or *It doesn't matter.*

Or *That's normal.*

Or *That sucks.*

But I don't.

I just sit next to Will on the curb, sweating in the Memphis heat and chipping away at the hot tar as we both bleed.

34

It's almost an hour before Sloane and Henry come back. Henry's wearing a Memphis Zoo hat and has hot-pink zinc oxide on his nose and cheeks, and Sloane seems to be in a better mood. Henry looks all big-eyed and button-busting when he says, "So we have a plan?" and Sloane winks at him, then hops into the back seat.

I look at Henry and ask, "What's going on?" but he just smiles, then fusses over Evelyn, and Sloane's sitting in the back of the car looking smug.

We drive to a store called Miss Cordelia's in Harbor Town on Mud Island because Will says he's hungry and that's where he wants to go.

"Miss Cordelia's is a food store?" I ask.

He nods his head.

"And it's not going to upset you?"

He says, "No."

I say, "You're lying," and he laughs and says, "Maybe a little."

"What are you guys talking about?" Sloane asks, but when neither of us answers, she just starts gushing about the pandas, and then she tries to get Will to eat an M&M from a bag she bought at the concession stand.

He refuses, saying, "That's a trap I'm not falling into ever again." I'm thinking, *At least everyone seems to be in a better mood.*

"Fine," Sloane says. "Be secretive." And then she eats all the candy herself.

I look at her in the rearview mirror and ask, "How many did you eat?"

Her face brightens. "Only one."

"You're lying," I say.

"Prove it," she challenges, and I say, "I don't have to. One will do."

"What do you want to know?" she asks.

"Do you have a boyfriend?"

A smile flickers across her face. "I'm not entirely sure."

"What does that mean?" I ask, catching her eye in the mirror again.

"I thought I did, but it turns out that he might be dating someone else."

"Not possible," I say. "Must be a misunderstanding," and she turns away and looks out the window.

We head over the bridge from the mainland to Mud Island, park the car, and walk into Miss Cordelia's. It's a cute little market with expensive-looking food. Sloane buys Vitaminwater and an apple, and I eye the Pepperidge Farm variety pack. Henry buys iced tea and says it's for Evelyn, then drinks it himself. Will buys everything. Lorna Doones, whoopie pies, snickerdoodles, and a family-sized bag of Kettle Brand Honey Dijon potato chips. I end up ordering a ham and cheese sandwich on a bulky roll with mustard and mayo from the guy behind the deli counter. While I wait for him to make the sandwich, I stare slack-jawed at a jar of Dolores cooked and pickled pigs' feet, wondering how hungry I'd have to be before I ate something like that.

The sandwich guy eyes me, then says, "Hogs only have two toes because they're what they call 'even-toed ungulates.'" It's like he thinks my shock has more to do with the number of toes pigs have than with the fact that people eat their feet. Then he says, "The ham on your sandwich came from the same animal," as if he finally caught on and decided to give me shit for judging, but I'm weirded out because I don't know what that means exactly. I'm wondering if he means *the same exact pig*, like somehow he *knew the pig* or *slaughtered the pig himself* because how else could *my ham have had those feet*? Then to knock me down another notch he says, "But the meat on your sandwich came from the ass."

I take the sandwich from him, not sure if I still want to eat it, but I pay for it anyway and then turn and walk toward the exit where Sloane is waiting for me by the door, which I take as a good sign. I dump the sandwich in the trash bin and step outside. Sloane hurries out after me and asks, "Why'd you do that?"

"Do what?" I ask as I head toward the car.

"Throw a perfectly good sandwich into the trash?"

"I've decided to become a vegetarian."

She has to jog to keep pace with me. "Vegetarian, vegan, lacto-ovo, or pescatarian?" she asks, and I look at her like, *What?*

Then I say, "Nothing pink and cut into circles. And nothing with feet."

"That's not a thing, Asher."

I tell her it should be a thing and pull open the rear hatch of the Jeep.

Sloane peers in and sees the corsage sitting there all wilted, and then she moves some stuff over and spots the tuxedo. I'm thinking, *Here it comes*, so I look away and stare at a poster that someone pinned to a telephone pole advertising something called the Royal

Flush, which, according to the slogan, is the premier porta-potty and VIP toilet trailer rental company in the South, and which, from the look on Sloane's face, is exactly what I am about to get.

She's staring at the tuxedo and not saying anything.

Then my phone pings with a text from Grace asking, ETA??

I mumble, "Oh, shit," then type, Late but not too late, as Sloane slams the trunk closed.

Then something else catches my eye, and I turn away from one mess to look at another.

35

Will's standing statue-still, looking dumbstruck and freeze-framed on a grassy area near the parking lot of Miss Cordelia's holding a Yoo-hoo and a big bag of snickerdoodles. There are already empty cookie boxes and plastic junk food wrappers scattered at his feet.

I follow his line of sight over to a little boy sitting on a bench, then slam the trunk shut and mumble, "Oh, shit," again.

Sloane looks over at Will and says, "I know. He's going to be sick if he doesn't stop eating."

"No. That's not it."

"What, then?" she asks.

"Follow his gaze."

The little boy he's looking at is sitting on a bench next to a nurse in a uniform. His little head is bald. Not buzz-cut, blond-kid bald. *Smooth, chemo bald.* And he's very pale. Ghost-white, sick pale. And skinny. *Sick skinny. Can't-eat skinny. Gonna-die-soon skinny.*

I look up and around, my eyes scanning the area. And *now* I see it. There are doctors and nurses in scrubs everywhere. *In the parking lot. At the picnic tables. Talking on the phone. Walking dogs near the apartment buildings.*

And cancer patients.

Too many cancer patients for it to be random.

And they're kids. Little kids. Sick kids. *Sick, skinny kids. With no hair.*

I whisper, "Google St. Jude's hospital."

Sloane says, "Oh, no!" then takes out her phone. "It's just over the bridge," she mumbles.

"Michael was treated there," I tell her, and Sloane looks back over at Will and says, "Oh, shit." But it's more like, *OH, SHIT!* even though it's a whisper.

"Should I . . . ?" Sloane asks.

"No," I say. "Let me."

She stays by the car, and I hurry over to Will. He's still staring at the little boy, but he's got his hair in front of his eyes like he wants to SEE but not be SEEN.

He's trying to hide but . . . *He. Can't. Not. Look.*

I put my hand on his arm. "Will, don't."

He doesn't say anything or move.

"Look, we should go," I try.

Nothing. He's just laser focused on the kid.

"I know what you just told me at the zoo, but before that I didn't know that Michael saw doctors here in Memphis." My voice is a little breathless in the heat. I'm thinking, *I'm a bad friend. I should have known. I should have figured it out.* When I'd asked him to come on the trip, he'd said yes right away. I should have known that there was a reason.

And that reason is sitting right over there on that bench.

Will says, "I did. *I* knew the hospital was here. I wanted to . . . remember, I guess."

"Shit, man, I'm sorry." But I know it's not enough, or okay. Not even a little bit. I don't know what to do, so I just stand there with him for a few minutes.

"That kid over there?" he finally says. "He has a chance."

The boy's smiling, laughing as he plays some game with the nurse.

"How can you tell?" I ask.

"Do you know what the survival rate is for neuroblastoma?"

I feel like I should lie. *I always lie.* But this time I tell the truth. "It's over eighty percent."

Will looks at me. Does a double take—then turns back to the kid.

I try to pretend that the little boy isn't sick. That he's just sitting on a bench with his mom, not some nurse, and they're playing this game Chloe likes.

I spy.

I spy a tree. I spy a yellow bird. . . .

I want to scream. *My turn! I spy a healthy kid! I spy recovery. I spy tomorrow!*

Then I try to pretend that he's on a swing, holding on tight. His small sneakers reaching for the clouds. His mom laughing and calling out, *Tell me when your feet have touched the sky!* But Will looks like he's still waiting for me to explain how I knew what the survival rate for neuroblastoma is, so I say, "When you told us what Michael had that first night in Room 212, I Googled it."

He lifts up his right pant leg and exposes his lower leg. I look down. There's a small tattoo above the ankle. It says *80%.* "Michael had an eight in ten chance of *not dying.* And he died."

"How do you know the boy over there has the same thing?" I ask.

"I don't," Will says. "I just know that it's cancer, and the overall survival rate for childhood cancer is over eighty percent. So whatever he has, he has a really good chance."

168

I nod my head, feeling a little better.

"We held on to that good chance and lost."

I spy a broken heart.

I spy a broken friend.

"What else do you know?" Will asks.

"What do you mean?" I ask.

He turns to me. "What else do you know about Michael?"

I almost whisper. "That the year before he got sick, his T-ball team, the Franklin Lakes All-Star Ninjas, won the six-year-old league championships when the final game went into extra innings with Michael on first base."

Will looks at me in disbelief.

"*Bergen County Gazette*," I explain.

Will smiles, then turns away, watches the boy for another minute.

"And . . . ," I whisper, "I also know that Michael died on April seventh of last year."

Will lifts up his other pant leg.

I look down.

He has 4-7 tattooed above his ankle next to a small heart and a baseball bat. Will's face says, *I spy a real friend.* I try to smile, but it comes out crooked and wet since a tear or two has already raced down my cheeks.

The two of us watch the little boy for a few more minutes. The nurse sees us and nods her head. It's like *she knows.* Not something specific, not about Will or Michael or neuroblastoma, just *something.*

I can almost hear her say, *I spy someone who's walked in this family's shoes.*

Will says, "Let's go."

I ask, "Are you okay?"

He says, "Yeah. Surprisingly, I think I am."

I start picking up the empty junk food packages spread around his feet. "No stomachache? Intestinal problems? Nothing like that?" I ask, and he smirks.

"Stomach's good. Just heartache. But no more than usual."

I put my arm around his shoulder, and we head toward the parking lot. When we get to the car, Will goes to collect Henry, and Sloane whispers, "Is everything okay?"

I say, "As okay as it can be." Then I ask, "Why are you here?"

Her face is open. That question was unexpected. "What do you mean?" she asks.

"Why did you say yes when I asked you to come to Memphis?"

"Just because," she tries.

"You're not being honest," I say, and she raises her eyebrows like, *So what?*

"And *you* are being honest, Mr. *I have a tuxedo in the trunk*? And I'm going to the prom with my"—she does air quotes—"cousin?"

"Spill," I challenge.

She shrugs. Looks down. "The hog convention."

"What??"

She takes her tough-girl, biker-chick stance. "I'm here for the Tennessee State Hog Rally."

"Hogs like *ham-sandwich-pigs-feet-in-vinegar* hogs?"

She looks down. "No. Hogs as in Harleys. A motorcycle rally. My dad always wanted to ride his bike down Beale Street. So I'm going to do it for him."

"When?"

"Tonight."

"Tonight? The hog convention is tonight?"

"Yeah, tonight. When, you know, you take another girl to the prom."

"I don't get it. You don't have a motorcycle."

"I don't get it either. I thought we had something going."

"We do," I say.

She looks at me like, *So?* But I can't explain about Jack Daniels and Grace and the catfishing and Sam Hunt, so I just stand there.

Her hand is on her hip when she says, "We're going to steal one."

"Steal one, as in *steal a motorcycle*?"

She nods.

I glance around the parking lot and finally say, "When you say 'we,' I suppose you mean . . ." I'm about to say *me*, but she jumps in front of that and says, "Me and Henry."

I almost laugh. "*Henry?* You and Henry are going to steal a Harley-Davidson motorcycle?"

"We have it all worked out."

"You talked to him about this?"

"Kind of."

"Kind of?"

"When we were at the zoo, he told me that he had a motorcycle when he was young, so . . ."

"You do know that was in another century, right? Like, when he could *walk and think clearly*?"

"I can ride," she defends. "Not well, but *well enough*. I told Henry I was going to *borrow* a bike—something big and bad with loud pipes."

"Borrow?"

She shrugs.

"Big and bad and with loud pipes?" I question.

"I want to make an entrance. You know, *roar*. But don't worry about the details. I'll figure something out on the fly. You have your . . . thing tonight. And Henry said he'd help."

We both scan the parking lot, looking. I'm looking for Henry, but I suspect Sloane is shopping for a bike she can steal.

"Just look at him," I say when I spot him with Will across the way. "Are you really going to involve him in a *crime*?"

"He's perfect," Sloane says. "He'll never get in trouble. No one will send Henry to jail. We'll just say he's old and senile. The cops will probably give him a lollipop."

"We? *We'll just say?*"

"Well, supposedly he's your grandpa, so maybe you could back me up on the old-and-senile thing."

"So that's the plan?"

"Pretty much."

Henry's walking along the edge of the parking lot picking flowers—weeds, actually—undoubtedly for Evelyn.

"Fuck," I say, and Sloane asks, "*Fuck* as in, *fuck no*? Or *fuck* as in, *fuck yes, I'm in if you need me, Sloane*?"

"I thought you didn't need any help."

She kind of shrugs again. Then I kiss her, and she has my answer.

"Why do you keep doing that?" she asks, smiling when the kiss ends.

"Do you want me to stop?" I ask.

"No. I want you to *not* take another girl to the prom."

"I want you to not steal a motorcycle."

"I see where this is headed," she says.

"Really? Where's that?" I ask.

"Nowhere," she says, but she's still smiling and I'm still smiling, and then I ask her how she feels about living in Ecuador.

She doesn't answer right away, but before she walks over to collect Henry, she says, "So that's your plan? You're going to do whatever it is that you're going to do with some girl you apparently hate, and whatever it is will be so bad that you're going to have to hightail it to Ecuador?"

I don't confirm or deny.

But she doesn't actually sound that surprised, or that upset.

Then as Sloane walks away to tell Will and Henry we have to hit the road, I open the trunk and take my mom's letter out of my bag.

It took me *thirteen months, five days, nine hours, and nine minutes* to lift the single piece of powder-blue paper folded in three out of that envelope and actually start to read it, but I finally do it, right here in Memphis in Miss Cordelia's parking lot.

There are nine perfect, neat letters standing like brave soldiers on invisible straight lines. They say, *Dear Asher.*

And just like on the envelope, there's a fancy loop to the *A*, and the *r* swoops up at the end.

I don't have to muster up the strength and courage to read what comes next. It's almost like it just *happens*, like some kind of force takes over and moves my eyes down a line. I mean, I swore I wasn't going to look, but *I look*. It's like when you drive by an accident and you say to yourself, *Here it comes! Don't look!* But you LOOK anyway. And it's not like you look *a little*; you don't *sneak a peek*; you fucking slow down and crane your neck and stare at it with your eyes wide open like you have to see the bodies and the blood and every fucking detail of the broken chassis and crushed steel and splintered glass and shattered lives. I mean, you *think you don't want to*, but you do.

So here it is. The next thing my mom said to me after *Dear Asher. Today is the most important day of your life, and mine.*

As I read those words, tears spill from my eyes and slide down my cheeks, then cascade onto the ground without even making the tiniest effort to hold on. I swipe away the next set of tears, and then the next and the next as I look down with blurred vision and a broken heart at what she wrote, then back across the parking lot at Henry and Will and Sloane.

Then I think about Grace and Jack Daniels.

About Chloe and my dad.

And I think to myself . . . *My mom's right. It is.*

Today is the most important day of my life. What I do next will define me.

And somehow she knew that, even back then, when we hardly knew each other.

36

Sloane shows up at the car with Henry and Will, and I'm about to tell Will that I should drive, but he pops into the driver's seat when I get distracted by a kid walking by.

The kid's wearing his soccer uniform—knee socks, shin guards, nylon shorts, game shirt. And beneath all that, *cleats*.

They're not the Nike Superflys. And they're not lime green . . . but they're *green*.

I watch him walk into Miss Cordelia's, and then I turn and look in through the car window at Will. I'm about to challenge him and tell him that I should drive, but he says, "I just feel like driving," and I get this weird feeling like I'm a little kid and I'm scared, but I don't know why.

I end up saying, "Fine," and climb into the back seat with Sloane.

The weeds Henry picked are sticking up out of Evelyn's box and already wilting. I'm thinking about my mom's letter, about this being the most important day of my life, and about tonight and Grace and Jack Daniels and Sloane stealing a bike and Henry going to jail and ME BEING ARRESTED FOR MURDER, and I start to get this sick, scared feeling as two more kids in soccer uniforms walk into Miss Cordelia's.

Then this random thought flashes through my head. It cuts in out of nowhere, like a jolt of electricity. It's just this image.

Of a shoe. Lying by the side of the road. And it's shredded.

Will pulls out, heads back toward the bridge, and then *another flash*. Another random image.

The shoe again. But now I can see that it's a soccer cleat—a lime-green Nike Superfly.

And it's not shredded. It's brand new. A tag hangs from the laces.

I sit bolt upright. Sloane asks, "What's wrong?"

I mumble, "I wasn't sleeping."

Sloane's distracted, looking at her phone and calling out directions to Will. "Turn right up ahead onto Harbortown Circle."

Henry asks, "Where are we going? Evelyn is tired."

Still reading from her phone, Sloane reaches forward and pats Henry's shoulder.

Another flash.

I see the black Land Rover. My mom's car with the dent in the left rear panel and the New Jersey Devils bumper sticker just sitting in the mall parking lot. The sun is beating down.

I look at Sloane and say, "I'm awake."

She makes a face like, *So what?* Then she calls out, "At the traffic circle, take the second exit onto A. W. Willis Ave."

Another flash. And another.

And then . . .

37

I remember . . . *my mom.* We're talking. I have to turn my head to the left to see her.

I'm in a car. *Her car. In the front passenger seat.*

I remember . . . that day. *The mall. The crowds. Trying on cleats. Foot Locker.*

Then I'm in the car again. My mom is sitting next to me. *She's in the driver's seat glancing in the rearview mirror.* I'm looking straight ahead at the waves of heat rising from the hot tar of the pavement in front of us. I hear a horn. Look back over my shoulder. I catch a glimpse of the shiny grille of a tractor trailer glinting in the sunlight before it passes, then cuts in front of us. *Too fast. Too close.*

My mom brakes so we don't hit it. Says something I can't remember.

Another flash.

The truck slows down. My mom changes lanes, passes him. I look over at the driver.

Lil Durk is blasting on the radio.

Just like in my nightmares.

I glance at Sloane. I'm confused.

Then another vivid image.

I'm in the car. My mom is driving. I remember the shirt I was wearing. *Pale blue button-down.*

But this *isn't* like the nightmares. *This is different.*

Sometimes in the nightmares I'm driving, and sometimes my dad is driving and sometimes Chloe is driving and my mom is sitting in the back seat. But this time . . .

I blurt out, "I'm. Not. Sleeping."

Sloane looks worried. "Why do you keep saying that?"

I turn away. Close my eyes. Mumble, "You can't have a nightmare when you're awake."

Then another flash.

The truck is behind us again.

I remember a bright, burning light. So bright that I had to cover my eyes. And *heat.* I remember it being *hot.*

It's not the sun. *It's fire.*

I lean forward, cover my eyes. Yell, "No!"

Sloane puts her phone down, asks, "*What? Asher, what?*"

Then there's another flash as I remember even more. I hear the cry of tires screeching. Feel the impact as my mom's Land Rover is hit, in s-l-o-w motion just like in my nightmares. Then the music stops in the same spot as in my dreams. With Lil Durk rapping, "Dis ain't what you want. Dis ain't what you want. . . ."

"*Oh God!*"

"Asher, *what?*" Sloane repeats.

Then I see and feel and hear the airbags of my mom's car as they explode in a loud, face-slamming *Pfffffttttt! Baaaammmm!* And I feel, actually *feel*, the impact as the back of my head hits the backrest. *Hard.* I fly forward. *Hard.*

Then I hear glass shattering.

My head's spinning—I remember that *we were spinning*—the whole car was spinning.

Not *this* car! Not my dad's car. *That* car! *My mom's car!*

Another flash and it's rolling over. The Land Rover is rolling over . . . and over.

And then I remember that *the song didn't end. It's just that I couldn't hear it anymore because of the screams. My screams.*

There were no mom screams.

She couldn't scream because . . . Another flash and I remember and see . . .

Oh God!

Everything.

In the nightmares this is where the world goes black—there's nothing at all, just dead, blank, vacant silence for a long time. And then the sirens in the distance. At this point my foot's usually slammed down hard on the imaginary brake pedal or I'm trying to pull my mom out through the window of the imaginary car, but her head isn't connected to her body, or it is connected to her body but when I pull on her arms, her head comes off, just falls and rolls like it isn't attached. This is usually when I wake up, and this is when the real horror begins because *I remember that my mom is dead.*

But this time it's not a dream. This time I'm awake and *I remember.* And it's different. Different from what my dad told me happened.

Because I was in the car. I wasn't driving, but I was *there.*

And I remember.

Because of some kid wearing green soccer cleats in Memphis.

I remember everything.

I scream, "No!" Will swerves, then corrects.

I tell myself that I can't possibly *remember* the accident because

I.

Wasn't.

There.

I look at Sloane and say, "I was there."

"Asher, where? You were *where*?"

"In the car, with my mom."

Her face is blank.

I say. "I was there that day.

I.

Could.

Have.

Saved.

My.

Mom.

And.

I.

Didn't."

39

Sloane has her hand on my back. Cars are flying by in all directions. Sloane's yelling, "Will, pull over!"

I close my eyes. More flashes. Out of order. Jumbled . . .

The brand new cleats again, lying on the pavement next to the Land Rover. *I remember tripping over them when I stumbled out of the car.* Then a cop car, the lights hitting my face. The sirens in the distance. The back of an ambulance, the clerk in the shoe store, his shirt, *black and white stripes.* The soda I bought at the mall. *Orange Crush.* Then the car keys in my mom's hand, me begging to drive. Her saying, *No. It's rush hour. Besides, I feel like driving.* Me, annoyed, fiddling with the radio as she accelerates up the entrance ramp to Route 287.

Then entire coherent sections come back.

Me teasing my mom as she pulls into the flow of traffic. *I could have done this!*

Her saying, *It's rush hour, Ash. Lots of trucks.*

Her glancing in the mirrors, changing lanes.

Me looking down at my feet. Brand new soccer cleats sitting in a bag on the floor.

"Big game tomorrow," I tell her with a smile.

Lil Durk's pounding from the car speakers.

My mom saying, *Turn it down.* Her voice taut. I can hear her stress.

Me pleading, "I love this song."

A flash of her face as she tightens her fingers on the wheel.

Then we're talking.

Talking about tomorrow's game. Banter back and forth, random comments . . . about Coach Melvin, dinner, Chloe's teacher, music . . .

All's good.

She reaches for the radio. I tease, "I'll do that. You drive."

I remember how I felt. I remember sinking into the seat and feeling the excitement over my new cleats. The promise of new shoes. The game tomorrow.

How I closed my eyes, then opened them as I felt the car slow down.

How I glanced at my mom, then over my shoulder. *That truck again.* The one with the shiny grille. My mom's eyes darting from the front windshield to the side mirror to the rearview.

I recall again in a vivid flash when I first saw the tractor trailer appear behind us. How he passed us, slowed up, then ended up behind us again just a few minutes later. *A game of cat and mouse.* How I checked again a moment later and was surprised that he was closer.

A lot closer.

How I thought, *That was fast—too fast! Too close!*

Riding our bumper.

How my hands started to sweat, my mom looking in the mirror saying, "I'm just going to let him pass us again."

How I glanced back over my shoulder at the truck. A big rig. How I caught a shimmy to his front end that didn't look right, the way he swerved into the middle lane.

"Mom . . . that truck. He's . . ."

Her eyes are checking the mirrors again.

She hears the horn.

He's *leaning* on the horn. Truck horn. *Big rig, truck horn.* Even over the radio we both hear Jack Daniels leaning on the horn.

I remember the worry on her face this time.

Too late, though.

It was only a fraction of a second before impact.

I remember the car spinning around and around, but this time, there *are* mom screams. *Loud mom screams.* Then metal against metal and other NOISES. *LOTS OF NOISES.*

The airbags exploding and the face-slamming *Pfffffttttt! Baaaammmm!*

A car crash is loud.

Then I remember being still. Not moving. *Quiet. Scary quiet.*

I blink a few times, and I'm in my dad's car. In Memphis. Sitting next to Sloane. *Remembering.*

Sloane says, "Asher, you're scaring me!"

Will asks, "What's happening?"

I close my eyes. Relive every detail. *Again.* Run through all of it in my head, over and over.

Out of order, it's a visual mess. I feel the impact as the back of my head hits the backrest. *Hard.* I hear the glass shattering. Then I'm standing next to the car. *Don't know how I got there.* I'm okay—I can walk, but my head . . . I reach up, and there's blood running down. *Lots of blood.* My cheek. *A bump.* My eye! Hurts! *Blurry. Can't see.*

Then his face. I blink. Squint. *Dizzy.*

I can see his eyes, lips moving; he stumbles.

I take a step toward him. Stop. He's walking toward me. *The driver of the truck.* But my mom . . . She's . . . I turn, confused. . . .

The Land Rover . . . It's burning. . . .

I see smoke. Orange flames licking the black paint. My brand new lime-green soccer cleat sitting on the side of the road, spilled out of the box. I turn back to the truck. The grille glaring at me. Voices . . . Dizzy again . . .

I turn back to the car. *The flames!* I cry out . . . *Mom! MOM!*

And then everything fades to BLACK.

Darkness. For the longest time.

The coma.

It wasn't from hitting my head on the coffee table like my dad said. It was from the accident.

In real time it happened *fast.*

Remembering comes in slow motion. And out of order. Like the pieces of a puzzle tossed and scattered onto the floor.

Lucky me. My brain decided to play back every detail jumbled and in S-L-O-W M-O.

Sloane is shaking me. I look up. "I saw a kid . . . back there. With green cleats. Then Will said, 'I feel like driving. . . .' That's what my mom said . . . and I remembered, Sloane. I remember everything."

We're pulled over on the side of North Danny Thomas Boulevard in Memphis when I tell Sloane, tell Will, tell Henry, tell *me*, "I was in the car. I was there. I could have done something, seen something, said something. I could have saved my mom!"

And just like in all my nightmares, Lil Durk is screaming in my head. . . . "Dis ain't what you want, Asher. Dis ain't what you want."

40

I was there. I was there. I was there.

I'm sure of it.

It's not like it is in the nightmares I've been having, with all the messed-up parts about Chloe driving and my mom's head coming off. This feels real and different because I'm *remembering*, not dreaming.

And I remember every detail. Stuff my dad and the lawyers didn't tell me. Stuff I *couldn't know* if I wasn't there. And the memory of that day doesn't come back bit by bit. It comes back intact and *with force*. All at once. Crystal clear and certain.

The doctors said it wouldn't happen until I was ready.

I look out the car window.

I'm not ready. Nobody could ever be ready for this.

They said that my brain would know when I was ready to handle it.

They're wrong!

I'd asked, *Handle what?* The doctors said, *The stress of what happened.*

But they didn't tell me what that would look like.

Or when it would happen.

Or how hard it would hit.

Or that it could be triggered by something small.

Something like a complete stranger wearing green soccer cleats. Or Will saying, "I feel like driving."

I look around at Will. At Sloane. At Henry. At Evelyn, even.

My legs hurt, back hurts, eyes hurt. . . . I punch the back of the seat.

Sloane whispers, "Maybe you're wrong. Maybe . . ."

Will says, "Asher, call your dad. Sloane's right. Maybe you're wrong."

I shake my head. "I'll call my dad, but I know what he's going to say."

I know it in my heart.

Then I bang my forehead against the window glass over and over, thinking, *Nobody ever told me that the truth can be like fire. That it can suck all the air out of your entire world and suffocate you.* And nobody ever told me that sometimes we hold on to our lies, both the lies we tell and the lies that are told to us, just so we can breathe.

41

Forehead pressed against the window glass, I hear the loud blare of a truck horn and jump.

Sloane has her arms around me, her face pressed against my back.

My chest is heaving. Tears fall. Full-on panic. Raw emotion. I don't know what to do with it. *There's so much!*

The stages of grief hit fast and hard in rapid-fire succession. Like machine-gun bullet hits. *Shock and denial, pain and guilt. Anger and bargaining. Depression, reflection, loneliness.* But no *upward turn.* No *reconstruction and working through.* No *acceptance* and no *hope.* Just profound LOSS. *Soul-crushing loss.* And more anger and guilt than can fit inside one person.

Sloane tries to console me. "Maybe it's just another nightmare. Maybe you—"

I stop her there. "*No! I was there.* It's not a nightmare. *I remember.*"

It's the truth.

The truth I didn't want to hear.

The truth that I didn't want to hear so badly that I completely blocked it from my memory for—I look at my phone—thirteen months five days nine hours and nineteen minutes. And it's worse than an eighteen-wheel tractor trailer hurtling down the highway at high speed driven by Jack Daniels.

BECAUSE I WAS THERE. I could have done something, seen something, said something. I could have done something differently and saved my mom.

And I didn't.

42

We just sit in the breakdown lane. No one talks.

I pick my phone back up. Call my dad. My hands shake.

He doesn't pick up.

I text him as tears fall onto the screen. Please call me! I remember everything. I remember the day of the accident.

A minute goes by. *It feels like forever.*

Nothing.

Two minutes. Five minutes. *Eternity.*

Still nothing.

So I type, You should have told me. And then I wait.

Seven minutes later my phone rings.

I jump. Answer it.

My dad says, "Let me explain."

I say, "Later. Please explain later. I can't listen now. Just tell me the truth. Yes or no. Was I with her?" My voice sounds abrupt, like my words are clipped and have sharp edges.

But there's silence.

Then rage rushes in and I scream, "Tell me! The day mom died, was I in the car?"

There's just more silence on the other end.

I have my answer.

I hang up and slip the phone back into my pocket and stumble out of the car and onto the side of the road.

Cars fly by. My feet burn on the hot tar.

Sloane and Will and Henry climb out after me. I step away, tell them to give me space.

My phone rings. I don't pick up.

It pings.

I take it out of my pocket and look down.

My dad wrote, You have to hear what I have to say. We told you what we told you because you blocked it out and the doctors said you couldn't survive the truth. Not until you were ready. And then they told me that when you were strong enough, you'd remember.

I choke back sobs, then type, I SENT HER TO THE MALL FOR CLEATS AND THEN I DIDN'T SAVE HER!

It's a statement of fact. Not a question.

NO! he writes. IT'S NOT YOUR FAULT! A drunk driver killed your mom. You did nothing wrong. And you did try to save her. You ran over to try to pull her from the car, Asher. You were a hero. You were lucky to survive. Chloe and I almost lost you. You could have died that day too!

Sloane is leaning against the car, crying. Will looks stunned. Henry is clutching Evelyn.

I hate my dad for doing this. *For lying to me.*

I text Peter Pan and ask, Did you know that I was there? Did you know I was in the car with my mom?

She doesn't write, *Who is this?* She writes, No. I didn't know that. I only knew that you couldn't remember anything about the day that your mom died. That's all I was told.

I stare at the three dots blinking on the screen. She's typing. Then this pops up:

Are you sure you were in the car? How do you know that?

I type, I remember.

Then I explain everything about what happened and about what I was told and about dissociative amnesia, and that everyone has been lying to me. It's a mess—typos, information out of order, almost incoherent. . . .

But Peter Pan gets it. She types, I can only imagine how hard this must be for you. And how hard it must have been on your dad to lose his wife and almost lose you and then have to lie to try to protect you.

I type, I hate him.

She writes, Remember what I told you about the people around us. This is new for them, too. They're trying, but they don't always know what is best, or how to help.

I want to be mad. I want to *hate.*

I want to hate my dad for this. For all of it.

But deep down I know that I can't.

Sloane comes over. Will comes over. Henry comes over. They surround me in a hug. Evelyn is in the middle. I tell them what my dad did. What everyone did to me. The doctors, the lawyers . . .

Sloane says, "Asher, they were just trying to save you."

I know she's right.

They simply smashed my bike. Then strapped a life jacket over my clothes, put a helmet on my head, and covered my hands with aluminum foil and hoped that was enough.

I call my dad back and say, "Just tell me everything. This time, the truth."

44

My dad explains everything. How I went to the mall with my mom to buy cleats that day. How she sent him a text saying we were about to leave and she was going to drive. How we were hit by the drunk driver in the tractor trailer. That I was seen trying to pull my mom from the car. That I was badly hurt in the accident and when I got to the hospital, I had to be put into a coma. That when they woke me up two weeks later, I had no recall of what happened, or of being in the car. How the psychiatrists evaluated me and how they tried to tell me what happened, but I pushed back. They said that *I wasn't ready to hear the truth*. They told my dad that it was better to let the memory come back on its own.

Then my dad says, "I want you to call Fran Cooper."

I wipe the tears from my face. "I don't know who that is."

"The woman from the hospital who leads the bereavement groups."

Peter Pan.

"You *know* her?" I ask, shocked. "How do you . . . ?" It feels like such a betrayal. *Another betrayal.* "Do you, *what?* Talk about me?"

"No! It's not like that. I called the hospital and asked for her after you took the car, just to see if she knew anything, or had any idea where you were, or who you were with. I called her for advice."

"What'd she say?"

"She said to tell you that you could call her anytime and that she hopes to see you next week for the Monday-Wednesday and Tuesday-Thursday groups."

"Do you hear yourself?" I scream. "Mom died . . ." I want to say thirteen months five days nine hours and like thirty-two minutes ago—but I know that freaks people out, so I just say, ". . . more than a year ago, and I'm going to bereavement groups four days a week!" I glance at Sloane. "It's like I'm *stuck*. And I'm not getting better. And I didn't know why. And now I do. This whole time my brain has been fighting the truth."

"Please just come home. We need to talk and get you help with this. Maybe your doctors have given me the wrong advice. I want to try a different route."

"What do you mean, *try a different route*? I didn't know we were on a route at all!"

"Asher, please!"

I feel cold all over. Hot on the inside, cold on the outside, and breathless. I say, "I'll call Fran Cooper." Then I hang up the phone.

45

She picks up on the second ring. I don't say anything, not even hello.

Peter Pan says, "I'm glad you called."

Then silence. Just me breathing. And cars whizzing by.

"No matter how bad this seems now, Asher, it's going to be okay." Her voice is calm, almost a whisper. *Mom-calming-a-little-kid whisper.*

"You don't know that," I manage to say.

"Yes, I do. So you need to trust me."

"I can't."

"You can if you want to."

"You act like I have a choice here!"

"I know a lot of things happened to you that were beyond your control. And I can't imagine how scary that must feel. But you do have a choice in the way you handle it from here. It may not feel that way, but you do. Please remember that."

More breathing. I'm trying to hold back tears. I don't know why I called her.

"Can I tell you a story?" she asks.

"No!" I almost yell. "I can't hear a sad story like the Zachary story. I don't want to be told to suck it up because someone else has bigger problems than I do."

"I would never say that. And that's not what I wanted you to take away from that story. I just wanted you to know that bad stuff happens to other people too. Sometimes when we're in pain, we forget that. And this story is different, anyway. It's about hope."

I don't say anything, so she keeps talking.

I like the sound of her voice.

"Remember the boys from Thailand who were trapped in a cave a few years ago? They were soccer players just like you—there were twelve of them, just little kids."

"No."

"Sure you do. *Think.* They went into the cave to explore with their coach, and then it rained and the cave got flooded and they couldn't get out?"

"Okay, yeah. I remember a little."

"They were over a mile from the entrance. They sat there in the dark for days. When their families realized that they were missing, they sent out search parties and found their bikes at the cave entrance and figured out what must have happened. The cave was full of water. Expert cave rescue divers arrived from around the world with special equipment to try to locate them. They brought sniffer dogs and drones and robots. By the time the rescuers found them, they'd been trapped for nine days, and a rescue seemed all but impossible."

"What does this have to do with me?"

"You know what those boys were doing all that time?"

I don't answer. A truck flies by and leans on the horn and startles me.

"They were waiting. Hoping. Believing. Taking care of one another. And *digging*."

Sloane comes over and puts her hand on my back.

"Think about that, Asher. They had hope, and they tried to save themselves."

Sloane starts rubbing her hand up and down my back. Peter Pan keeps talking. I don't want them to stop.

"They were wet and cold and scared. They had very little food, and they still believed, and they still dug with whatever they had. The rescuers were the best cave divers in the world, and even they had trouble reaching the kids. They feared that they couldn't get them out. They brought the boys food and supplies. They brought in engineers and drilling equipment, pumps and experts in hydraulics."

Her voice is soft like a whisper. Hard to hear with the traffic.

"They removed tens of thousands of gallons of water. They tried drilling down from the surface. Ten thousand people were involved in the rescue. Government agencies, soldiers, scientists, geologists. Some of the boys couldn't even swim."

"I remember."

"Those twelve kids had to do only one thing. *They had to trust the people who came to rescue them.* And that's what I want you to do here. There are a lot of people working to help you get better. I want you to close your eyes as you sit in the dark and trust us."

I don't say anything for a long time. My head is spinning. Rage and sorrow and guilt and self-pity and anger have formed a current of destruction. A riptide in my head. But I'm tired. *So tired of being mad.*

Peter Pan eventually asks, "Are you still there?"

I manage to say yes, but it comes out sounding weak and wet.

Sloane still has her hand on my back.

"You're supposed to ask me what happened to those soccer players."

"What happened to them?"

"They got them all out safely. Every one of them."

"What does this have to do with me?"

"There are a whole lot of cave divers here for you, Asher. Not just me and your doctors, but your dad and Chloe and Will and Sloane and Henry. You need to trust us. You need to close your eyes and trust us even though it may seem impossible that you'll get to the other side.

"And there's one more thing." She pauses. "I'm going to ask you to dig a little too."

Then I say something I never thought I would say.

I say, "Okay."

I have no choice. *I'm trapped in a cave under the ground with no way out.*

"So, you trust us?" she asks.

I close my eyes and whisper, "I trust you."

46

After we hang up, I think to myself that there's one thing that I remember about that cave rescue in Thailand that Peter Pan didn't mention.

One of the Thai Navy SEALs died when he was trying to save those soccer players.

Standing on the side of the road outside Memphis with Sloane and Will and Henry and Evelyn as constant reminders of just how big love is, I know that I don't want anyone to die trying to rescue me.

Not me. Not my dad. Not Chloe. *Not anyone.*

But Peter Pan just asked me to trust her and trust all the other rescuers, and that's fine. *Maybe I can do that.*

But she also asked me to *dig.*

And I'm looking around for something to dig with, and I don't see a fucking thing.

47

We get back in the car.

Will starts driving. I haven't said a word. No one has.

I'm just slumped down in the back seat thinking about what I said to Peter Pan.

I trust you.

I'm wondering if it's true when Will pulls over in front of a motel and says, "Let's stay here. In a real hotel. In real beds. And take showers and . . ."

I feel like he wants to say *recover*, but he just leaves the "and" hanging there for us to fill in with anything we want to on our own.

Sloane looks out the window and says, "I can't stay anywhere creepy." Her voice is soft.

"What do you mean by *creepy*?" Will asks, almost whispering.

Sloane points up at the perfectly normal-looking motel sitting in front of us. "Creepy," she states.

Will looks at it and says, "Shit."

Sloane announces, "I'll pick a hotel," and Henry says, "Evelyn prefers Days Inn or Motel Six," and I try to disappear into the seat.

Sloane rolls her eyes and takes out her phone. Then she says, "Peabody."

Will is annoyed and asks, "What does that mean?"

"The Peabody Hotel. Downtown Memphis. Start driving. I'll GPS it."

"Sounds expensive, Asher," Will calls back to me, but I'm numb. *I want them to stop talking.*

As he pulls the car away from the curb, I say, "I don't care. Whatever Sloane wants. Book two rooms. My dad's paying." It comes out all monotone, like the words are heavy and dead. Sloane reaches for my hand. I pull it away.

Henry is skeptical because Evelyn likes Days Inn or Motel 6, but Sloane tells him not to worry, that if Evelyn likes Motel 6, she's going to love the Peabody, and a few minutes later when we drive by the front of the hotel and pull into the parking garage, Henry announces that Evelyn is very happy.

When we enter the lobby, it's super formal and old-school elegant, and as I approach the front desk, I keep thinking, *I was in the car! How could I not have remembered that?*

As I look around, I feel self-conscious and completely out of place. It's not just because I've been wearing the same clothes for more than twenty-four hours and Sloane's wearing boots and a jacket that don't fit and Henry's carrying his wife around in a cardboard box. And it's not because my face is red and swollen from crying, and it's not even that the lobby is crowded and this place is fancy—Southern fancy, where women wear church hats in the middle of the day like it's Easter Sunday. It's because *I'm not like everyone else. I was in the car. I was in the car and I could have done something, seen something, said something. I could have saved my mom and I didn't. So that means . . .*

I.

Killed.

Her.

"May I help you?" the clerk asks with the biggest smile I've ever seen.

I reach into my pocket, then hand over my dad's credit card. She keeps lighting up the room.

I decide that I hate happy people.

"We made a reservation online," I mumble, and she starts typing.

"You have two adjoining rooms. Is the fourth floor okay?" She's glowing like the sun.

I nod. Then I glance over at Sloane. She and Will and Henry are watching me and whispering. Sloane sees me looking at her and quickly picks up a magazine called *Garden & Gun.* I ask the lady behind the counter, "Why are you so happy?" She doesn't look startled by the question; she just looks pleased, like that was a compliment.

"Here in the South, we add sugar to everything sour," she confides. Then she leans forward and adds, "Especially if it's a bad day."

Her lips are bright red, her teeth so white that I decide I might need sunglasses if I want to keep looking at her. I take mine out. Put them on. *I'm hiding.*

Then she asks me if I would like to upgrade to the *You Don't Know Jack Package.* She keeps talking and smiling. "You'll receive a commemorative bottle of Peabody select Jack Daniel's single barrel Tennessee whiskey, a Jack Daniel's cocktail, an appetizer in the Peabody Corner Bar, and . . ."

This isn't happening. Can't be happening. Did she just say "Jack Daniel's"?

The rage comes surging back.

I was in the car.

I could have done something, seen something, said something. I could have saved my mom, *maybe. But he killed her! Jack Daniels killed my mom. Not me!*

I don't hear anything else the hotel clerk is saying even though she keeps talking and I keep standing there. Then she points behind her to a poster advertising the Jack Daniel's Special.

I flash back to what Peter Pan said about the kids in Thailand in the cave and how I'm supposed to trust the people coming to rescue me and that I'm supposed to dig my way out of this pain and anger that's got me trapped so far underground that rescue seems impossible. Then the hotel clerk says, "The Jack Daniel's Special also includes free internet access and self-parking in the Peabody garage," and I manage to mumble, "Free parking?" like that'll clinch the deal.

She nods her head like that's really special. Luckily, Will walks over and asks, "Are you okay?" probably because the blood has left my face and the whole lobby is spinning. The hotel clerk just keeps smiling and lighting up the entire place, probably thinking, *How do I handle the weird customer who won't talk?* And then the air vibrates with the sound of a trumpet—a brass horn—and it feels like that story from the Bible, the one that says some angel—Gabriel, I think—will announce the end of time with a trumpet call that'll raise the dead.

I start thinking either the world *is* ending or I'm having a brain aneurism or a stroke because there can't be a trumpet because it's too weird and Little Miss Southern Sunshine standing behind the desk selling Southern hospitality and free parking can't have just said *Jack Daniel's—would you like the Jack Daniel's Special?* And then all of a sudden I feel sick—sick like I might throw up right here on the counter.

I turn around in slow motion, and the lobby seems to have filled up with more people than there were even a few minutes earlier when we walked in. It's now overflowing with people, and my head is overflowing with thoughts, and none of them are good. Then I see a man wearing a red uniform with brass buttons and white fringe holding a brass trumpet and I think, *Oh, okay. There is a trumpet.* But then I notice all these little kids, girls mostly, with bows in their hair and fancy dresses and ankle socks and patent leather shoes, and they're sitting along the edge of a red carpet, and I can't make sense of what is happening, and the lady behind the counter with the red lips and the world's biggest smile is still waiting for me to answer about the Jack Daniel's Special when Sloane grabs my arm and asks if I'm okay and then points because there are mallard ducks waddling in a line through the hotel lobby. That's when I decide that I have to leave. As I make my way through the crowd and out the front door, where it is enormously hot—Southern muggy hot—and stand next to the doorman and concentrate on breathing, I'm convinced that I'm losing my mind. *Lost my mind.* But then the doorman says, "If you don't go back inside, you'll miss the ducks," and I figure he's either on board with the crazy, or there really are ducks. I take some deep breaths to collect myself, walk back inside, and sure enough, there are ducks exiting stage left in a perfect line like they're little kids going into the lunchroom in a military school, and as I look around, everyone in the crowd is happy and laughing, and they're now serving tea and cookies, which seems so pleasant and respectable, but I'm still having trouble processing what's happening in the lobby and inside my head.

I walk back over to the desk and say no to the Jack Daniel's Special. Then I ask the clerk if I can borrow a pen and a piece of paper so I can draw a picture. She doesn't even act like that's a weird request, probably because here in the South they add sugar to anything sour, even if that thing that is sour is me. Her job is to smile no matter what, like even if a guest says, *I would like ten bottles of vodka, a stripper, and a llama brought to my room*, she would say, *Right away, sir*, as she smiles. So of course she says, "Right away, Mr. Hunting," not to the vodka and stripper and llama but to the writing implements, and she calls me Mr. Hunting because I paid for the rooms with my dad's credit card and she thinks I'm someone I'm not. When she hands me the paper and pen, she is of course smiling wide and white even though in her head she's probably thinking, *Why the fuck does this weirdo want to draw a picture right at this moment?* But I step to the side and draw a picture of a Jack Daniel's Single Barrel Tennessee Whiskey bottle that swallowed a family. *My family.*

I copy the shape of the whiskey bottle from the poster for the Jack Daniel's Special hanging on the wall behind the clerk. I draw an empty bottle lying on its side, and I can see all of our faces— mine, my mom's, Chole's, and my dad's—in silhouette peering out at the world from where the whiskey would have been IF SOMEONE HADN'T ALREADY DRUNK THE WHOLE THING. When I'm done, I hold the picture up to look at it and decide that at first glance it might look like a cricket bat, but if you squint your eyes and use your imagination, it could look like a boa constrictor that swallowed an elephant—or a hat—or even an eighteen-wheel tractor trailer that swallowed a family after it slammed into something like a 2018 black Land Rover. I take a picture of what I drew and text it to Peter Pan, and just so there is no confusion, I type, You might think this is just a picture of a hat, or you might think it's a boa constrictor that swallowed an elephant, but it's really a picture of the Jack Daniel's bottle that swallowed my entire family.

Peter Pan responds almost immediately, and she says that it doesn't look anything like a hat or a boa constrictor that swallowed an elephant, and she can see very clearly that it's a picture of the whiskey bottle that swallowed my family.

That makes me feel a little better, but I'm not sure why.

Then I think that maybe it's because it sums up what happened and maybe it's because it's my way of telling Peter Pan that I read the book she gave me and saying, *Thank you, it might have helped a little, and just so you know, you asked me to, so I am trying.*

When I look up from my phone, the clerk behind the counter is pretending that I'm not weird, and she's just smiling away trying to turn everything in the room that is sour into sweet, even if that sour thing is me having a breakdown. She doesn't even ask to see what I drew—maybe she thinks that I'm an engineer or architect and I just had a brilliant design idea that I sketched and sent to a colleague. I mean, there's no way she'd ever think that I drew a whiskey bottle that swallowed a family because there's no way she'd ever know that asking someone about the Jack Daniel's Special could have that effect on them.

So I don't say anything about the Jack Daniel's Special, even though what I want to tell Little-Miss-Southern-Sunshine-we-add-sugar-to-everything-sour is that I ALREADY GOT THE JACK DANIEL'S SPECIAL and I don't say anything bad about the mallard ducks mainly because I know Chloe would love them; I just keep my mouth shut about everything, even though I can't believe any of this is happening when there are horrible things going on in the world like EIGHTEEN-WHEEL TRACTOR TRAILERS WITH DRUNK DRIVERS BEHIND THE WHEEL AND EIGHT-YEAR-OLDS AND DADS WITH CANCER AND KIDS LIKE ME WHO CAN'T SAVE THEIR MOMS. I just shove the picture into my pocket and make my way through the crowd to Will and Sloane, who are loading up on cookies, and Henry, who is having tea with Evelyn on his lap, and they're all still looking at me weird, like I might die any minute, and they're talking about the duck parade to try to change the subject because they're just trying their best to act normal. Sloane says that they have the duck parade twice a day in the Grand Lobby, and Will asks, "Why?" And she says, "Just because, I guess." But I'm thinking that confirms that the ducks are real and it actually happened and it wasn't me having a seizure or a brain aneurism.

When Sloane is reading information on her phone about the Peabody Ducks out loud to anyone who will listen—stuff that nobody wants to hear except maybe Evelyn, like the fact that when they are off duty, the ducks live in a ROYAL DUCK PALACE on the roof that is made out of marble and glass—we head upstairs to our rooms, and on the way to the elevator we almost lose Henry, who stopped to chat it up with a bunch of old people drinking tea. I go back to retrieve him because I'm worried that he might tell them who's in the box or that I'm the kid who didn't save his mom from burning up in a fiery car crash and cause a scene.

In the elevator the three of them argue about whether it would be more appropriate for me and Will and Henry and Evelyn to share a room and Sloane to have her own, or if it would be better for Henry and Evelyn to have their own room and for me and Will to share with Sloane. Then Sloane settles the argument when she takes the box from Henry and says that she and Evelyn should share a room because they need to get to know each other better, and that's a hard argument to even reply to, let alone counter. Besides, it makes Henry really happy, so no one objects. Then Sloane smiles at me, and I don't know what it means, but I figure I now have to share a bed with either Henry or Will, but it hardly matters because I

SENT MY MOM TO THE MALL TO BUY ME CLEATS AND THEN I DIDN'T EVEN SAVE HER WHEN WE CRASHED. I mean, sharing a room and a bed with Henry and Will has no pros and is basically all cons, whereas sharing a room with Sloane would have been all pros, no cons, but she apparently would rather share her room with a dead person than with me, and knowing what I know about me, I can't blame her. Even so, I try not to look for too much meaning in that, even though I am tempted to remind her that if she lets go of my hand for too long, I might drift away, especially now when the current is pulling me so hard in a dangerous direction.

48

When we get to the rooms, Sloane pulls me aside in the hallway and asks, "Asher, are you okay?"

And I lie and say, "Yes."

Then she puts Evelyn on the floor and picks up my hand and starts slowly tracing the outline of my fingers as she breathes in and out, and I don't stop her, but when she's done, I pull my hand away and we both look at our feet.

She whispers, "I'm worried about you." Then "It's not your fault."

I don't say anything back or trace her fingers; I just stand there, and then she asks, "Who's this girl you're taking to the prom, and why do you hate her so much? For real this time."

I don't answer because it's basically a whole complicated mess that got even more complicated now that I know that I was in the car with my mom when she died because now I know that I can't save anyone who is about to burn up. Not my mom, not Sloane, not me, not anyone. Plus, Sloane's hurt, what with the hand-holding in the back seat and the kissing and then finding out that I'M TAKING ANOTHER GIRL TO THE PROM, so I just say, "I have to take a shower," and head into the room.

After my shower, Henry's napping on one bed and I'm sitting

on the other one wearing my old dirty clothes because I left my backpack in the car. I'm watching a video on my phone of the scene from the Quentin Tarantino film *Inglourious Basterds* where the character called the Bear Jew walks out of the tunnel with a baseball bat that's covered with the carved names of Jewish people in danger from the Nazis, and then he beats a Nazi soldier to death with the bat. He shatters the Nazi soldier's skull and all the bones in his face, killing him in the most violent and disturbing way you could imagine as a way to get even with him for all the Jews who are being killed by the other Nazis.

Will comes out of the bathroom with a towel wrapped around his waist and looks over my shoulder, looking alarmed when he asks, "What are you watching?"

I don't say a Quentin Tarantino film or *Inglourious Basterds* or a psychopathic killer. I say, "Batting practice," then click out of the video. Then he stares at me like he wants more, so I just get up and say, "I'm going to take a walk," and then I leave the hotel room.

He calls down the hall after me. "Asher, are you okay?" Then "Should I come with you?" And finally "Hold on! Sloane told me you have a prom to go to!" But I just keep walking toward the elevator without answering him, thinking about how confused I am, how much I want someone to blame and to pay for what happened to my family, and how fucked up it is that I'm not sure if that person should be Jack Daniels or me or the kid who stole my cleats or Nike or Mia Hamm or the governor of New Jersey and the guy who built the mall, or the whole f-ing lot of us.

I walk out the front entrance, stop to text Grace a line from an Ed Sheeran song—something about the sins of the father weighing down in the soul—and tell her I'm running late but will be there soon, and then I storm around the block before I head to the parking garage, where I take my mom's letter out of the bag I left in the trunk of my dad's Jeep. I lift it out of the envelope with the broken blue heart and then stare at the single sheet of powder-blue paper with the loopy *A* and the swoopy *r* and read that second line again.

The one that comes after *Dear Asher.*

The one that says, *Today is the most important day of your life, and mine.*

Then I make what the shrinks would call *real progress* and read the next line:

It says, *I don't even know you, Asher. But I know that you are perfect.*

It makes me cry. *That even for a minute my mom could think that I was perfect.*

But then I figure she could only think that because she didn't know that one day I was going to lose my soccer cleats and she would die trying to buy me a new pair. And she could only say that I was perfect because she didn't know that thirteen months five days and a whole bunch of hours and minutes and seconds *after* she died trying to buy me those cleats, I was going to drive to Memphis under the guise of taking some heartbroken old guy who carries his dead wife around in a box somewhere he never got to go as a giant excuse to maybe or maybe not kill Jack Daniels and in the process break the heart of my dad and sister and Sloane and Grace—two girls—three if I count Chloe—who never did anything to me.

I mean, when my mom wrote that me-being-perfect thing, it was only day one of an entirely new life. So she didn't know *anything* about me yet. And I hadn't done anything wrong yet. So basically it's not her fault that she was so off about me.

I mean, when she wrote that, she didn't know how the Asher show was going to end.

49

Thirty minutes later me and Will and Henry are parked out in front of 114 Culvert Street. Henry's sleeping in the front passenger seat, and me and Will are standing outside the car. Will's on the driver's side, and I'm standing across from him on the passenger's side. We both have our doors open so Henry doesn't suffocate, and me and Will are looking at each other over the roof when he says, "Sloane's gonna be really pissed when she finds out we took off when she was in the shower and we brought Henry with us."

Sloane is back at the Peabody probably trying to scheme how to steal a Harley from the hotel garage, so I say, "I had to stop her from stealing a motorcycle," and Will kind of nods like, *Good luck with that*. I'm about to add, *I'm not really sure Henry would have been much of a help*, but he looks up at the house we're parked in front of and asks, "Are you really going to take this girl to the prom?"

And I get it. I mean, after everything that happened today, plus I've been procrastinating and now I'm a couple of hours late and I'm not dressed yet and don't even appear to be in a rush. I look up toward the door to the house, then back at Will, and then down at my feet.

He asks, "When are we going to hit fly balls, Asher?" and I look up, and he has a stern, no-bullshit look on his face, like he's Vladimir Putin or maybe Anderson Cooper on *Anderson Cooper 360*, and now I know why he insisted on coming with me. *He knows something.*

I quickly glance back down at the street, trying to calculate how much Will's figured out, and then, just like that, he says, "I don't want you to do it."

As I'm trying to decide what he means and what he knows, he adds, "I know this wasn't the easiest day for you, but I'm going to ask you to do something for me anyway, which I'm hoping will make it better."

I look at him with big, clownlike question-mark eyes, and he says, "Leave the gun. Take the cannoli."

I keep staring at him, blinking and thinking that this is just like the ducks in the hotel lobby and the brass horn and the Jack Daniel's Special and I'm once again losing my mind wondering why people keep saying and doing things that don't make any sense, and then I ask, "What the fuck is that supposed to mean?"

Will just stares back at me with a look that says, *Don't make me explain everything*, and I figure that it's been a hard day for both of us so maybe I should cut him some slack, so I ask, "Who said that? Kierkegaard?" and he laughs, which makes me feel better, which is good because I can't handle any more stress than I already have, and then Will says, "Shit, no. I doubt there were cannolis in Denmark back then."

"Who, then?" I ask.

"A mob guy in *The Godfather*. I don't remember which one."

"You don't remember which mob guy, or which *Godfather*?"

Will kind of smiles. The corner of his upper lip turns up just slightly on the left side of his face. "Does it matter?" he asks.

I shrug as I keep watching him. He's tense, and I can tell that *he knows. I didn't tell him, but somehow he knows.* Maybe not *exactly* and not *every detail,* but he knows something is wrong, and about to be even *more wrong,* like maybe he can feel that a storm is brewing. I look around, and even though the weather has been absolutely perfect, it feels like the wind just picked up and the sky is about to open and crack with thunder and dump torrents of rain down on top of us. Both of our car doors are still hanging open, and my hands are on the roof as I look up and away from him because I don't really want to see his face or defend myself or justify what I'm about to do, or get talked out of it, or be judged, and I don't want to talk about anything. I know that I have to move and pull the trigger and get this *done.* I can't figure out if me knowing that I was in the car makes me want to kill Jack Daniels more or kill him less because the threads of blame are getting harder to pull apart. I've started to think that maybe it is all on him, that maybe it's like my dad said and I'm not responsible, or maybe it's partially on me *and* him. I've always blamed him and me and the guy who invented tar and Mia Hamm for making me love soccer and definitely the kid who stole my cleats and Nike for making them in lime green and the governor of New Jersey for allowing people to drive and a whole bunch of other people, but I can't sort through these thoughts right now because they're like a bag full of poisonous snakes that have taken up residence in my head.

I look up at Jack Daniels's house, thinking, *Shit, it's late.* Way too late to pick up your date for the prom. We already missed the important stuff like pictures and all the pregame festivities and the grand entrance and all the *You look so amazing* bullshit. I was supposed to pick Grace up almost three hours ago, and back at the hotel Sloane told me that being this late was cruel and passive-aggressive, even though I explained that I had texted Grace three times to update the pickup time. Then I said, "If you think about it, it's actually cruel and aggressive-aggressive," and then Sloane got a worried look on her face, like WHAT IS REALLY GOING ON HERE?

I glance quickly back over at Will, and he shrugs and says, "*What?* It's exceptionally good advice."

I almost forgot what we were talking about, but then I say, "You think the leave-the-gun-bring-the-cannoli thing is exceptionally good advice?"

He says, "Yeah. I do."

I lean down, use my hands to shield my eyes, and pretend to look into the car. "Do we even *have* a cannoli?" I ask. "I mean, I'm looking, and I don't see any cannolis, Will."

"It's a metaphor, Asher."

"Meaning?"

"Jesus, a metaphor is a—"

"I know what a metaphor is! I meant *what does leave-the-gun-bring-the-cannoli mean*? In English."

He shrugs again. "It means when you're headed off to do something that you think is so important, it's actually *more* important to remember what's *really* important."

I think about that. "So, you're saying that in this case, the nonexistent metaphorical cannoli is important, not the nonexistent metaphorical gun."

He nods. "Yeah, but by *gun*, I mean the very real, nonmetaphorical *baseball bat* sitting on the floor in the back of the car. Metaphorically speaking."

The hair prickles on the back of my neck. *He knows. . . .*

"And by *cannoli* you mean . . ."

"Anything, Asher. Fucking anything. Bring *anything* up to that house except the baseball bat. Fuck it. Bring Henry. It'll be a hoot."

My heart beats faster for a few minutes, and then I ask him flat out. "So you know . . . *what*, exactly?"

"Pretty much everything," he says.

"So you know where we are?"

"114 Culvert Street in Memphis."

"And you know whose house this is?"

He nods.

We both look up at the house for a minute, and then I take a few pacing steps away from the car, and that's when I see it. *The big rig parked in the back.* No trailer attached, just the cab. And behind it, the garage with the doors open, shit spilling out—a tractor, a kid's bike, lawn furniture, an ATV, and an old broken-down-looking motorcycle with the tires missing. I look back at the truck, at the glint of the steel. The monstrous teeth of the shiny grille.

I turn back to Will. "And you know that I'm not here just to take some girl to the prom?"

He nods again.

And then my mouth does that spontaneous propulsive thing where it spits out words that I never intended to say. "And you don't want me to kill him? You don't want me to kill Jack Daniels?"

Will's mouth drops open. I look at my feet, then back at the tractor trailer with the shiny grille that's tucked behind the house.

I look right at the big rig that killed my mom.

50

When I look back over at Will, he has a pained, drawn expression, like the Nazi did when he saw the Bear Jew coming toward him with the baseball bat—or worse, even. At first that Nazi looked smug, but Will actually looks like I just hit *him* with the baseball bat. But then he exhales slowly and looks up at the sky. "Jesus, Asher. I didn't know you call him Jack Daniels, and I never thought you were actually going to *kill him*. I just thought you wanted to *scare him* or *maybe hurt him*. And I didn't think you were actually *serious*."

"Even after what my dad told me today? And even after you saw what I was watching on that video? That's what you thought? I came all this way to *scare* him?"

"Yeah, Ash, even then."

I raise my eyebrows and turn away.

Will says, "You know, there's no way that I can let you do this. I can't."

He keeps talking but I stop listening. I just stare at my feet. The truth is, I wasn't one-hundred-percent sure that I was actually going to kill Jack Daniels either. Even before I remembered that I was in the car and even before my dad told me what he told me. And now the fact that I was in the car confuses everything, which gets me thinking about how everything is interconnected, and *that* gets me thinking about bagels and pancakes and locust infestations in Latin America and delivery guys in Bangkok catching on fire.

Then I remind myself *that I could have done something, seen something, said something.* I could have saved her. *Maybe.* And that means *I Killed My Mom* too. Me and JACK DANIELS, we did this together. I mean, the more I think about it, it's like I thought. It was a whole group effort.

My dad says the "me" part's not true, but I'm not sure he isn't lying.

I hear my dad. I hear Sloane and Will saying, *He was drunk. He was wrong. He should be in jail. You're a victim. You could have died too.* But I can't help thinking, *Maybe . . .*

Maybe . . .

Maybe if I had . . .

I turn back to Will, thinking, *I can't admit that I'm wavering.* That I'm not even sure at this last minute that I really want Jack Daniels dead. That maybe I just want *to see him.* Look him in the eye—*confront him. Scare him,* like Will said. Or that maybe I might be about to make a mistake—a tragic mistake. That just maybe I'm about to drive a big rig fueled with rage and hate at high speed into a stone wall.

I can't admit that. Not to Will. Not even to me. At least not *now.* And I can't back out.

I feel trapped.

I think about my mom's letter. The second line—*Today is the most important day of your life, and mine.*

I kick the side of the car. The hinge creaks and the door slams shut. Henry's in the front seat. He startles like he was hit with a jolt of electricity, but somehow he stays asleep.

That's when I look up and ask Will, "How'd you figure it out?"

51

"I Googled some stuff," Will says.

"About my mom?"

He nods.

"And the accident?" I ask, as anger starts its slow climb up from my gut to my head.

Will nods his head again. "And then I put two and two together. The video you were watching earlier from the Tarantino film kind of put your anger and the baseball bat into perspective."

"It'd be impossible for you to have come to the conclusion you did without more information. So you, *what*? Looked through my phone, right?"

He doesn't deny.

"Read my text messages?"

He shrugs.

"Those two times I caught you?"

He looks uncomfortable. "A whole bunch of times more than that."

"You had no right to do any of that!" I yell. "I thought you were my friend, Will."

"I'm trying to be your friend, Asher."

The front light comes on up at the house. I look over my shoulder, then turn back to Will.

"Asher, I'm trying to help."

I just stare at him. "Shit, Will. Don't take this from me. I *need this*. I need to *fix this*. Especially *now. Especially with what I know now.*"

"You can't fix it, Asher. Not here. Not like this. You can only make it worse."

I don't want to listen to him. I cover my ears. I like being *mad*. Mad at *someone specific*. *Mad with a plan*. Mad at someone who's not me. "You should leave me alone. Walk away. Leave. Right now. Bring Henry and Sloane with you and take a bus back home."

"You want revenge," he states.

"Of course I want revenge!"

"Okay, so what's the plan? You know, exactly? Maybe I can help."

"I thought you said I shouldn't do it?"

"I did."

"So how can you help if I'm not going to do it?"

"By, kind of, redirecting your efforts. Tweaking the plan."

I glance at the baseball bat lying there on floor in the back seat of the car.

Will tracks with me. "That's the plan? The baseball bat? That's it?"

I shrug.

He says, "I thought there'd be more."

I don't say a thing, and I refuse to look at him.

"Might want to rethink the plan, then," he suggests.

I glance up at the house again. Then in the direction of the big rig sitting behind the house by the garage. *The big rig that killed my mom.* "*Now* might not be the right time to rethink," I tell him.

"*Now* is *exactly* the right time."

I search his face for an answer. "Why? Tell me *why*, and I won't do it."

"Because revenge is a really, *really* short game. It feels good for, like, a few *seconds. Maybe.* It's not worth it."

"According to who?"

"Me." He pauses, then adds, "What's your plan for after?"

"After?"

"*After.* You know, it takes, *what?* Maybe a minute, maybe five minutes on the outside to kill an old drunk guy with a baseball bat? And then you're standing there in his house with the dead body lying there all bloody on the floor, and the rest of his family's hysterical and crying and cowering in the corner looking at you, wondering if you're going to kill them, too. Or maybe they shoot you. Truck driver in the South—I'm guessing he has a gun. And now he's dead and maybe you're dead and the sirens are screaming in the background because in all the commotion and horror *someone* called 911. Maybe his wife or kids. Maybe a neighbor. Maybe even *me*, Asher. *Maybe I called 911.* And then the cops are coming, and me and Henry and Evelyn are out here and Sloane's back at the hotel more messed up than before because you just messed with her head, and your dad and sister are back home praying to God that things will somehow, someday, maybe go back to some kind of normal, and you're either lying on the floor in a puddle of blood or you're just standing there in the house over a dead drunk guy trying to figure out why the fuck you just turned into him. *Then* you have an epiphany. By your own doing you are now just a slightly different iteration of the monster you hate so much, and then you see it. You have one of those *What the fuck just happened and what the fuck did I just do and I wish I could take it back* moments when all of a sudden you can see into the future, and the next eighty years are sitting there laid out in front of you, and they're not looking so good. In fact, you're seeing bars on your cell and just maybe the death penalty and a trip to a gas chamber or an encounter with a lethal injection. And you know who got hurt the most? *Chloe and your dad. And Sloane. And Henry. And me.* So yeah, since we're all in this together, I'm just suggesting that you reconsider your plan and take into account what you have planned for *after*."

"Shit, Will, don't ask me that."

"Too late. I just did. So, what's the plan, Asher?"

And that's when everything comes tumbling down.

"Well?" he demands.

I whisper, "Ecuador."

Will says, "I can't hear you."

"Ecuador," I almost yell. I'm mad at Will for Googling stuff about my mom and for reading my text messages and for asking the *after* question because I'm on a path to self-destruct and for some sick reason *I'm enjoying it* and *I'm stuck in it* and yet because I'm not *entirely stupid*, I know how lame my answer sounds.

"Shit, Asher. Do you really want to spend the rest of your life dead? Or on the run? Or in some jail for fucking *murder*? I mean, is that what you want for your dad and for Chloe? Instead of . . . oh, I don't know?" And then he kind of screams, *"Just about anything else?"*

Will's holding his hands up and waving them around, like all the good stuff I'm going to miss out on in life when I'm standing over Jack Daniels's dead body or I'm six feet under or filling up an urn or in prison riding the slow track to the death penalty—or maybe if I'm really lucky, hiding out in Ecuador—is floating around right there above our heads, ripe for the picking.

"Instead of *what*, Will?" I wave my hands around too. "This life I've been living? *This pain?*"

"Say to yourself, 'I should be sad if sad feels right—even massively sad—just not self-destruct sad. Never self-destruct sad.'"

I don't say anything and he's quiet for a minute, and then he asks, "You know who said that?"

"Of course I know who said that!" I snap as I think about Peter Pan standing in Room 212.

"If you do this, then it means that the accident took your life too, Asher."

A few more lights turn on at the house, and my phone pings.

I kick the side of the car again. *Henry still sleeps through it.* "So you don't think I should kill him, then?" I ask.

"No. I do not."

We both stand there.

"So what do I do? I have to do *something*. He killed my mom, Will!" I take a few steps away and glance again at the truck sitting behind the house. *The big rig that I see in my nightmares. The big rig that killed my mom and almost killed me. The big rig I can now remember.*

Will leans up against the car and says, "'I don't believe in yesterday.' Do you know who said that?"

"No. Who?"

"John Lennon."

"John Lennon. The guy who wrote 'Yesterday' doesn't believe in yesterday?"

"Honest-to-God truth. And it's good advice."

"What is?"

"You know, *let it go*. Step over the past. Drop *yesterday* and think about *tomorrow*."

"I can't do it."

"Do what?"

"Get past this. Or let it go. Or step over it. I don't know *how*."

Will looks exasperated. Lost. Pissed off. Sympathetic. All at once. "I'll help you."

"So, help me. Tell me what to do."

"Now?" he asks.

"Now would be good, Will."

He looks around, then sighs. "Did you read *Fear and Trembling*?"

I look at him, frustrated, and throw my hands up.

"Kierkegaard's *Fear and Trembling*," he says, "where he explains the story of Abraham's struggle to follow God's command that he kill his own son and how Abraham has to take a leap of faith and trust God, and how that type of faith is necessary to reach the third sphere of existence?"

"Shit, *no*. I didn't get that far," I say snidely.

"Okay, I'll make it simple for you," he says. "Bats always turn left when leaving a cave."

"*What??*"

"When they fly out of a cave, bats always turn to the left, even if left is the wrong way to go. Even if it means they'll crash into a stone wall and die. It's some kind of instinct."

"So fucking *what*?"

"So, I'm just asking you to turn right," Will says.

"Turn right? Like God asked Abraham to do?"

"Exactly."

"So you're God in this story?"

"No. I'm Will in this story."

"Very funny."

"What I mean, Asher, is that I just want you to take a Kierkegaardian leap of faith and do the opposite of what every bone in your body is telling you to do so you don't slam into a wall and die."

"So, just go the other way?"

"Yeah. Go against your instinct. So, tonight, just *turn right.* Take Grace to the stupid prom and then walk away."

"You know her name."

"I read all your texts, Asher."

"So, just take her to the prom and then walk away? *That's* what you want me to do?"

"Yes. Just, you know . . . be a half-decent date and then walk away. Live your life. Turn your wounds into wisdom."

"Shit, Will! Really? I'm about to go kill a guy, and you just keep dishing out Biblical philosophy and quotes of the day?"

He throws his hands up again, but this time he doesn't wave them around; he just holds them up there like he's Atlas and I'm the whole world.

"Who said *that*?" I ask, and his lip turns up again in that sunny-day way of his. Then Henry snorts so loudly that he jolts awake and scares all three of us.

And then I make the decision to turn right. *Just like that.* Whether I kill Jack Daniels or I don't kill Jack Daniels is my choice. And yet until now, it never felt like it was my choice at all.

And then I laugh. Everything suddenly feels more ridiculous and ironic—more Tim Burton than Quentin Tarantino.

"*The Godfather*?" I ask.

"What?" Will asks, genuinely confused, his arms finally back at his sides.

"That saying? *Turn your wounds into wisdom*? Is it from *The Godfather*?"

Will smiles. "Hell no, Asher. Does *turn your wounds into wisdom* sound like something a hit man for the mob would say?"

"Kierkegaard, then?" I try as Henry looks up at me with a confused, old-person, I-might-burst-into-tears look on his face as he blurts out, "Where am I?"

I pat Henry's shoulder and say, "Nowhere."

Will just looks embarrassed at the whole mess we're in and shakes his head.

"John Lennon, then?" I ask as I keep my hand on Henry's shoulder through the open window to comfort him.

Will starts to laugh. "Worse."

"What do you mean, *worse*?"

"You don't want to know, *worse*."

"Try me."

"Oprah. It was fucking *Oprah*," Will says.

I start to laugh.

Henry pipes in and says, "My Evelyn loves Oprah," in a wistful way.

Now I've got tears streaming down my face, and not a single one of them is trying to hold on. I'm laughing so hard that my back begins to spasm. I can't see or stand. I crumble to the sidewalk. I mean, I'm standing here with Will and Henry and Evelyn next to my dad's stolen car, and I'm trying to decide if I'm going to kill Jack Daniels, and Henry's trying to figure out where the fuck he is, and Will's quoting *The Godfather* and John Lennon and Oprah while Sloane is back at the hotel plotting to steal a Harley and probably still trying to calm her mom down about some lie she told about a litter of fabricated premature orphaned gerbil/hamsters to make her more comfortable with the fact that she ran away to Graceland with an octogenarian and two weird kids from her bereavement group—one of whom might be full-on deranged and about to commit a felony.

"Oprah?" I ask.

"What, man? *Turn your wounds into wisdom* is fucking good advice," he defends.

He had me there. *It was good.*

Henry opens the door and climbs out of the car, cradling Evelyn in her cardboard box. He whispers, "My lovely needs some air," and then he takes a few steps away from us. Me and Will watch him, and I swear to God he's waltzing, doing the foxtrot or the box step or something. *One-two-three, one-two-three.* Then he starts slow dancing as he sings the Elvis song, "Are You Lonesome Tonight?"

As Henry's clutching Evelyn, he spins and turns counterclockwise until he's almost to the front door of Jack Daniels's house. He stops on the lawn just short of the door next to a pair of pink flamingos where it's all dark and shadowy. We're both watching Henry when Will asks, "Do you think it's sad, or, you know, kind of nice?"

I continue to watch as Henry clutches Evelyn so lovingly. Not like she's some burden to struggle with, like a bag of groceries or a box he's moving into the attic. It's like she's precious.

"Kind of nice," I say. "Definitely kind of nice."

"Do you think we should tell him?"

I give Will a once-over. "Tell him what, exactly?"

"You know, that Evelyn's . . ." Will looks at me with his eyebrows raised a half mile above his eyes. He doesn't want to say it—none of us wants to say it—so I ask him, "What did she have for dinner last night?"

He looks startled. "Who?"

"Evelyn."

"The chicken Caesar salad, like always."

"There you go."

"There you go, *what*?"

"There you go, if she had the chicken Caesar salad, then she's not, you know . . ." I raise my eyebrows, just not nearly as high as Will can raise his.

He looks shocked. "Asher . . . you don't actually buy into the whole *Evelyn thing*? Do you?"

I watch Henry with her for a minute as he dances back toward the car and then say, "Hell yes, I do."

"You know," Will says as Henry starts whispering to Evelyn, "if that's the case, we should get him a new box."

"Is that a metaphor?" I ask.

"No, man. I'm serious. I worry that the cardboard will rip and Evelyn will . . . spill out."

I can't believe how the conversation has turned. I can't believe how completely different I feel now than I did just a few minutes ago. And that scares me. I mean, it's like that thing I said before about how everything is interconnected and how if you get the bagel instead of the pancakes, that can cause some far-fetched, seemingly unconnected disaster like global warming or a locust infestation in Latin America or make a pizza delivery guy in Bangkok burst into flames, and that makes it impossible to function or make even the simplest decision.

"Will," I say, "you should be one of those negotiators. On a SWAT team or something. Talk people down off ledges. Show them the light. Take their weapons and whisk away their bad intentions. Arm them with sappy words of wisdom from dead philosophers. That kind of shit." I'm nudging the curb with my foot, watching as Henry sidesteps and swirls farther away from us, waltzing in the direction of Grace's front door again. I feel so confused and over-whelmed, *but lighter.*

"Just for the record, Oprah's not dead, dude," Will says.

"Right," I concede.

We stand there for a minute watching Henry and looking up at the darkening sky. I'm not sure if I say thank you, or if I just *think it*, but somehow in that moment I decide *for certain* not to kill Jack Daniels, and the thank-you is right there sitting between me and Will.

And then he says, "Put it in the vault."

"Put what in what vault?"

"The thank-you you were just about to say. Stick it away for later."

"What do you mean?"

"You were just about to thank me for saving your ass, and I'm saying to put the thank-you in a metaphorical vault, because sometime I might want to get repaid."

"Repaid?"

"For saving you from self-destructing."

"How would I do that?"

"By saving me."

"Okay," I agree, wiping away a few surprise tears. "I'll put the unsaid thank-you in the vault, and I'll leave the gun in the car and bring the cannoli. But just for the record, all that good stuff in life you're asking me to reach for isn't exactly low-hanging fruit."

Will looks more serious than I've ever seen him when he says, "No one said it would be. So, you're just gonna have to reach higher, Asher."

I strip my clothes off and put the tuxedo on right here on the side of the road outside the house of the man who killed my mom. I yank the pants up and button the shirt. Then I tie the laces on my soccer cleats. The old ones from two years ago that are too small and have holes in the big toes and gum on the bottom and nubs that are worn down to almost nothing.

I smooth my hair and stuff the front of the rented shirt into the pants but leave the shirttails hanging out in the back, which I think would look kind of cool under more normal circumstances. Then I toss the jacket over my arm, thinking that it might look like Asher is so cool that he doesn't care about things like tucking in his shirt because he has more important things on his mind. Or it could just look like he's a crazy mess, and that makes sense because CRAZY LUNATICS WHO COME THIS CLOSE TO MURDERING THEIR DATE'S FATHER don't bother to tuck in their shirts or put the jacket of their tux on, even if they are planning to go to the prom.

"How do I look?" I ask Will.

He says, "Barely passable. They'll think you're drunk." Then he smiles.

The irony of that kills me. I mean, *really kills me*. If Jack Daniels thinks I'm drunk, it will just explode the sun or burst a blood vessel in my brain or something. But I run with the cosmic injustice of it.

I take the baseball bat from the floor of the rear seat, hold it up for Will to see, nod my head, and put it in the trunk. Will's watching me carefully when he asks, "Did you even bring a baseball?"

I say, "No." Then I add nervously, "Just so you know, Grace thinks my name is Sam Hunt."

Will nods. "I figured that out." And then he explains, "Your phone. I saw it on your phone."

We both stand there for a minute before I go up to the house.

"Are you sure you're okay?" he asks. "Because we could just bolt and get out of here. Stand her up. It would suck, but it wouldn't be the end of the world. Plus, the dance already started."

"No," I say, looking at the time on my phone. "It *just* started, and I have to do this. See him, you know?"

Will nods. "What are you going to tell her? Jesus, you're hours late and you look like shit and you've got some pretty fucking big baggage and . . ."

I say, "I have no idea," and then I pick up the corsage that I left to wilt in the trunk.

It's a white gardenia surrounded by tiny yellow roses with baby's breath all tied together in a big bow with a blue ribbon, and it's seriously wilted.

Will smiles and asks, "Does that monkey suit have any pockets?"

I slam the trunk closed, then look down and pat my pants. He tosses me a bag of M&M's. I stuff it in one of the pockets, then say, "Here goes," and turn and walk past Henry, who's still on Jack Daniels's front lawn dancing under the darkening sky with Evelyn as

I head up the stone path to knock on the front door of 114 Culvert Street to confront the man who killed my mom.

The monster who apparently I am now *not going to kill* even a little bit.

On my way up the walk my phone pings, and I stop to take it out of my pocket.

It's Sloane. She wrote, The hog rally is going to be over and how am I supposed to steal a motorcycle without Henry?

I type, Do you know how many people die in motorcycle accidents each year?

She writes, 5,246.

Then she types, Don't be a dick, I don't care if you hate her.

I put the phone away and step onto Jack Daniels's front porch.

The door flies open before I even get a chance to knock. Since I'm hours late, I'm guessing that they must have been watching for me out the window.

It's him. He's standing there.

Flannel shirt.

Gray, unkempt beard.

Massive stomach.

Jack Daniels in the flesh.

And he's drunk.

I don't know why that possibility never crossed my mind, but it didn't. Every time I thought about how this would unfold, him being drunk never fit into the equation. Poetic justice, after all. *I continue to be blind and stupid, and he continues to drink.*

And not tipsy. Not inebriated. *Fucking hammered.*

He's fermenting.

And he reeks. The whole house must reek because the smell of alcohol is wafting out the front door.

His mouth is draped open. His eyes have a glazed, wet look, like whoever's in there is lost behind the drink. Then a sneer appears across his face. He stumbles. Almost tips over backward. I don't make a move to catch him. I just stand there and wait. He's wheezing. Breathing heavy like he's a human smokestack with charred chimneys for lungs.

I'm just standing there with my broken heart and screwed-up head with my shirt untucked holding my tuxedo jacket and a wilted corsage. I glance back over my shoulder, and Henry's still waltzing on the lawn with Evelyn, and Will's still standing by the side of my dad's car looking his best in his role as chauffeur.

I manage to say, "I'm here to pick up Grace," but I don't extend my hand.

He looks me up and down. Wipes his hand across his mouth. "What are you, a soccer player?" he asks. It comes out slurred and sloppy. His tongue thick. He's staring at my feet.

I'm thinking, *You don't recognize me from the day of the accident?* Then I'm thinking, *Which means that I'm a perfect stranger from out of state here to pick up your seventeen-year-old daughter, I'm three hours late, I showed up with a motley crew, looking questionable at best, and that's all you've got? A comment about my shoes?* But I don't say any of that; I just turn my eyes away, look down, and wiggle my big toes—the ones that stick out of the holes in the leather. I thought I would be filled with rage, but I'm not. I feel more calm than I have in thirteen months, five days, eleven hours, and—I look at my phone—thirty-five minutes.

When I don't answer, Jack Daniels yells, "Gracie," and I hear footsteps and muffled voices on the stairs and then in the hallway behind him.

Jack Daniels doesn't invite me in, or say anything else, so I just stand there on the stoop thinking about everything Will said. I think about how short-lived the upside of getting revenge would be, and I think about *after, the short game and the long game*. But mostly I think about Chloe and my dad and all the stuff floating around above my head, all the high-hanging fruit that I couldn't even see before. All the possibilities for *after*. And for the first time in a long time, all those possibilities don't feel impossible to reach or unlivable—or nonexistent. And they don't feel like a death sentence—or Ecuador.

They feel oddly positive. And possible.

There are more muffled voices coming from inside the house, but Grace doesn't appear, so I put the corsage down on the front step, then take the bag of M&M's Will gave me out of my pocket and rip it open. Then I hold it up and offer one to Jack Daniels.

He kind of grunts and shrugs, then holds his hand out. It's shaking. I pour some M&M's into his open palm, and he pops them into his mouth. I reach into the bag and take one out and slowly eat it as a gray cat slinks between Jack Daniels's legs and along the doorframe and then bolts outside. He doesn't stop the cat or even seem to notice. He just keeps staring at me in a stupor, sizing me up. He swallows the candy, then glances over at Henry and Evelyn on the lawn, then at Will standing next to the curb by the car.

I decide to tell Jack Daniels something about myself.

"I am a soccer player," I say. "And I was going to wear a pair of new cleats tonight. The Nike Superflys in lime green in a size eleven and a half. But the day my mom bought them for me, they burned up in a fatal car accident between the signposts on 287 West when she was hit by a drunk driver hauling frozen shrimp and Jack Daniel's in a big rig. She burned to death that day, so this is what I've got."

I point at my feet. Wiggle my toes. Swipe at a tear.

Jack Daniels cocks his head to the side, and I see shock and then fear flash in his eyes.

I take another M&M from the bag and eat it. "I was in the car that day too. In the passenger's seat. I survived. But I guess you knew that. This," I say, doing a dramatic allover body point, "is what's left."

I hold my arms up for him to inspect me. The messy hair and heart, the untucked shirt, the wrong shoes, the wilted flowers and crushed soul, all right here on his front porch for him to examine. Then the knife comes down sharp and decisive.

"So, you see, I had to wear these cleats tonight because you killed my mom thirteen months, five days, eleven hours, and"—I look at my phone again—"exactly forty minutes ago."

54

Before Jack Daniels can respond or even process what I just said, Grace appears behind him in the front hall in her purple prom dress.

She's trying to smile—to make sweet the sour—but she's been crying, so it's a sad smile and bittersweet.

I reach for her hand. "Sam Hunt, Grace. It's nice to meet you in person."

She wipes away a tear, and she is Chloe and my mom all wrapped into one, and I realize that I don't want to hurt her. *I want him to suffer*, but I don't want his family to suffer the way mine did.

Jack Daniels is on high alert, trying to figure out how to process the information I just gave him and what to do about it, but his brain won't work. He doesn't know what's going on *exactly*, but he knows it's not good. And he can't *think*. He looks at me and then at Grace and says, "Gracie, you can't go. This guy isn't who he says he is."

I thought that whatever he said, whenever he managed to say it, would come out as a roar, a belligerent, self-righteous roar, but it's more of a whimper. His words slurred and sloppy, like his tongue is too big for his mouth and his lips are numb.

He almost tips over again, and it's clear that the words that came out of his mouth broke his daughter's heart. I can see that. Every single syllable broke her heart. I want to stop him from breaking hearts. Grace looks at him with hurt—*real hurt*. Not because he killed my mom—there's no way that she knows that. There's no way *I want her to know that. She doesn't have to hurt any more than she hurts already.*

I look at him and wish that he knew what he's done, what he's *doing*, to my family and to his. And I wish he could stop, but because he's drunk, he half falls into the doorframe, unable to do a thing.

I spent so much time envisioning this moment, thinking about hurting her to hurt him, hoping to get revenge to heal my hurt and criticizing her in my head for how she looks and what music she likes and resenting her happiness, and now I don't care what she looks like or which artists she listens to because *I don't see hair and skin or flesh.* I see *heart.*

Hers, not mine.

And hers *is shattered.*

Maybe not as much or the same as mine, but it still hurts and it's unbearable to see. When I look at her now, I can practically see her heart bleeding through her dress.

As I live this moment, the moment that I thought would feel so good, I realize that it doesn't feel good because I hurt her and she didn't do anything to me.

And I hurt her on purpose.

I glance back over my shoulder at Will and think, *I will fix this. I can't fix what her father did, but I will fix what I did.*

Grace's mother shows up at the door with a smile. "Hello," she says with her hand extended. "You must be Sam."

She looks nice. Normal-mom nice. I'm glad that Grace has her. I've hated Grace for having a mom, and now when I see Jack Daniels in the flesh, I'm glad that she does.

He doesn't know what's happening, or what I'll do, but I think he knows that Grace is going with me, and he's scared.

As bad as I feel about so many things right now, I still want him to feel that. I want him to hurt.

When I look at him, I see that he is *nothing. Nothing* to me.

Everything to Grace, maybe—or at least he could be—but for me, he is *over.* I can't let him ruin any more of my life. Not another single second. Will's voice is in my head. Peter Pan's voice is in my head. And they are both saying, *You can't be self-destruct sad.* Then I remember Sloane looking so vulnerable in her motorcycle boots and leather jacket sitting in group, standing on the street corner when I picked her up, leaning against the wall in the lobby of the rest stop, and I take out my phone and send her a text. I write, Don't worry. I won't be a dick and I'll find a way to take you to Beale Street.

Then I pick up the corsage I had placed on the stoop and strap it to Grace's wrist.

She says, "It's beautiful," even though it's all wilted.

I kiss her cheek and then say, "You look perfect."

She turns to her mom, smiling.

I say, "Let me take a picture to send to my mom."

The blood drains from Jack Daniels's face.

Grace smiles. And poses. I snap a few photos that I wish my mom could see.

Henry waltzes to the door, *one-two-three, one-two-three.*

I say, "Grace, this is Henry."

His arms are wrapped around Evelyn. He says, "I took Evelyn to the prom. June seventeenth, 1957." His face is beaming.

"And Henry is . . . ?" Grace's mom asks, looking confused. Worried a little, but mostly just confused.

I don't blame her. Henry is clutching a cardboard box, his fly is down, and he's now waltzing across the lawn again. *One-two-three.*

"He's my grandpa, and we're taking him to Graceland tomorrow." Grace's mom kind of nods.

This is the South, where they take everything sour and make it sweet.

I have no idea if anyone can put two and two together. My two and two, Henry's two and two. Or Jack Daniels's two and two. But at least I realize now that Grace didn't deserve this either.

Connor shows up at the door. He squeezes his head out between his parents. He's littler than I thought he would be. Smaller than Chloe. *I even hated him.*

I announce, "My friend Will is going to drive us tonight, and Henry's wife, Evelyn, won't go over thirty-nine miles per hour, so there's nothing for you to worry about."

Grace's mom looks around as if she's searching for Evelyn. Then she asks if she can take a picture of me and Grace together.

I take Grace's hand, and we follow her mom to the patio on the side of the house where there are lights on. I see the big rig up close. My heart speeds up.

The sheer size of it. The steel grille . . .

Grace's mom takes our picture. Jack Daniels waits on the front steps. After a few minutes Grace gives her mom a hug, and we start walking toward the car. When we pass him, I see fear, real fear, but Jack Daniels doesn't say a thing.

Halfway to the street we hear a rumble.

I turn back to look toward the house.

A motorcycle has appeared on the driveway. It came from the back, from the direction of the garage.

Jack Daniels is still standing on the front steps, leaning against the side of the house. He's looking over at the bike too.

Will calls to me from the car, "Where's Henry?" then runs across the front lawn to join us.

I quickly scan the yard and don't see him.

Grace asks, "What's your grandpa doing riding my dad's Harley?"

I say, "Oh, shit!" followed by "That's not my grandpa . . . ," meaning, *That's not Henry.* CAN'T POSSIBLY BE HENRY.

Will says, "Oh, yes, it is!"

Someone flips on some more outdoor lights. I glance around the yard, thinking, *There's got to be another explanation. That can't be Henry straddling that bike!*

But aluminum-walker-sweet-pea-growing-whale-watching-slow-driving Henry is nowhere to be seen. There's just some scary-looking dude with a black, visored helmet straddling a hog. And not the old, crappy bike that was lying with wheels off on the driveway either. *A badass cherry-red Harley.*

Will says, "It looks like Tom Cruise on the Kawasaki Ninja in *Top Gun*."

"Or Christian Bale on the Batpod in *The Dark Knight*," I add.

And then I see the cardboard box strapped onto the seat with what looks like two bungee cords.

I say, "Look behind him. On the seat."

Will whispers, "Evelyn."

Grace says, "What's going on here?"

I whisper, "Oh shit, oh shit, oh shit."

Then Henry revs the engine of the bike and we hear it roar.

I look up at the house again, and Jack Daniels is looking over at the bike and simultaneously waving his hands around in animated conversation with Grace's mom. She's holding on to his arm, preventing him from going anywhere—or falling.

"Someone better tell me what's going on here," Grace demands.

I turn to her and say, "I'm not who you think I am."

She looks alarmed. Not draw-your-weapon, tar-pit alarmed, but alarmed enough that Will says, "Asher, careful."

Grace looks from me to Will, then back again. "Your name is Asher?" The blood drains from her face.

"Let me explain."

She steps back. "You're not Sam Hunt?"

She recedes again. *One, two, three steps.* She glances over at the house and then back at me.

"Who are you?" But it's more like, *WHO THE FUCK ARE YOU?*

"Asher Hunting."

It takes a minute, but then there's a flash of recognition on her face. "You're Asher Hunting?"

I step toward her, wondering how much she knows. She steps back. Her mom calls out, "Grace?" Grace holds her hand up to say, *Give me a minute, Mom.*

I say, "I know how this looks. . . ."

She stares at me. "What are you . . . ?" She stops. Resets. "So you're . . . *what*?" she asks as she glances back at the house again.

Her parents are still there, arguing now. Her dad stumbles.

I say, "I'm not going to hurt you," which somehow feels like it just makes things worse because when Grace turns back to me, she looks more scared than before. "So . . . you WHAT? *Stalked* me?"

I don't move. Will makes a sound like a whimper.

"You made me think that you liked me? Sent me pictures? Conned me like a fucking psychopath for almost a whole year? Agreed to take me to the prom just to ruin it for me?"

"I . . . was . . . just . . ."

"A complete asshole?"

Will mumbles, "She has a point."

I whisper, "Shut up," and he shrugs.

"I can't believe this. I can't believe *you*! What the hell is wrong with you? Why did you even come? Why—" She pauses and then goes from looking really pissed off to really scared and asks, "Why are you here?"

My face is blank. I still don't know how much she knows. *And what can I say anyway? I mean, even if she knows everything? That I lied and strung her along so I could hurt her? Then I drove here to kill her father? Or I just came here to mess with her head?* All of a sudden what I thought I wanted to do makes no sense to me. I hear Peter Pan saying, *You think that you don't have choices, Asher, but you do. You have choices.*

I mumble, "I'm sorry. And I swear . . . I'm not going to . . . you know, hurt you or . . . hurt . . ." I look up at the house. "Anyone."

Neither one of us says anything for a minute as we both watch Henry. "For real?" she asks, turning back to look at me.

I nod my head. "For real. And . . . about the prom . . . I'm sorry."

She drops her eyes to her feet. Then she says, "I hate him," and looks up. "For the drinking. For doing this to us. And for what he did to you and your family."

I say, "Oh, shit, you know?" But it comes out like, OH, SHIT! YOU KNOW!

Will says, "Oh, boy . . ."

Grace nods her head. "Not everything. Not all of it. But enough. I overheard my parents talking—*a lot*. I recognize your name." She glances at the house again. "I know it doesn't mean anything or fix anything, but, God, I'm so sorry about your mom."

My voice is quiet when I say, "I didn't think you knew anything about what happened. You never said anything about an accident, or problems at home, or anything about your dad all those times we talked. . . ."

"Yeah, well, he's not exactly my favorite subject."

Seeing her standing here looking so sad and small in her purple dress that actually looks really nice on her makes me realize just how big of an asshole I've been. "Just so you know, I hate me right now, and I didn't mean to . . ." But I don't get to finish because the Harley roars again and we all look over as Henry revs the engine and lurches a few yards forward, then wobbles and swerves and almost tips over.

Will says, "Oh, shit! Evelyn!"

Grace's mom calls over again. "Gracie?"

Grace calls back, "I've got this, Mom," then looks at Will and asks, "Does he have a gun?"

Will shakes his head and says, "Just a cannoli."

Grace looks at him like, *What the fuck?* Then she looks at me, and I hold my hands up and say, "Like I said, I'm not gonna hurt anyone. I swear. But we might need to steal your dad's bike. You know, just for . . . *a thing.*"

"*A thing?*"

I shrug.

She kind of nods, looks in the direction of Henry, and says, "I don't know what kind of *a thing* you've got in mind, or what your plan is here, but unless you or your grandpa or maybe your friend have a Class D motorcycle license and experience on a piece of machinery like the one your grandpa just jacked from my dad's garage, then I'm pretty sure I should drive the bike."

Will looks at me. I look at Grace. She pulls some pins from her hair, and it tumbles to her shoulders. "Don't be so surprised that I'm willing to help you," she says. "I'm pretty pissed at you right now, Asher Hunting, but in some messed-up, weird way, *I get it.* So I'm totally down with stealing my dad's bike. Burning it, crashing it . . . Selling it, if you'd like. Right now, I hate him just as much as you do. He did this, too. He ruined the prom, along with a whole bunch of other stuff."

"Didn't see that coming," Will mumbles.

"What do you have planned?" she asks. "Reenacting a scene from *Hell Ride*? Or *She-Devils on Wheels*, maybe?"

I whisper to Will, "What's she talking about?"

He whispers, "Motorcycle movies. She's naming motorcycle movies."

"Or maybe you just want to go for a spin?" Grace offers.

I can't think. Have no fucking clue what to say.

Then Grace asks, "Do you have a sweatshirt I can borrow?"

Before I can answer, she slips her dress off and drops it onto the lawn.

Her mom calls, "Grace?"

She yells back, "I've got this."

Grace is now wearing bike shorts and a tank top with her purple high heels.

"What?" she asks defensively as me and Will gawk at her. "Bike shorts and a cami are just as good as Spanx."

I whisper, "What are Spanx?"

Will mumbles, "I have no fucking idea."

I open the car door and rummage through the pile of clothes on the back seat and pull out Sloane's pink sweater and hold it up. Grace eyes it and says snidely, "Let me guess. Your girlfriend's?"

I nod.

She shakes her head and takes the sweater from me.

"You're not mad at me?" I ask as she puts it on.

"For stalking me? For catfishing me? Yeah, I'm pretty fucking mad. But I'm pretty sure my dad killed your mom and got away with it, so . . . here we are. The question is, *Where do we go next?*"

I look at her in disbelief.

"Look," she adds, "I had a really hard time with this in the beginning. My dad's drinking is bad enough to deal with, but then when I overheard bits and pieces of the accident and your mom and what happened in court, I started to think about what he did to your family." She looks down. "I hated my life. I hated him. For a long time. But then I went to this group. . . ."

"You go to a group?"

"A group at the hospital. For kids affected by a family member who's an alcoholic."

Will leans in close to me and says, "Bet you didn't see that one coming either."

"And it helped me understand that my dad's drinking isn't on me. That I can't control him. Or it. That he's sick and *he* has to decide that he wants to get better, not me. My job is to *survive*. And to take care of my mom and brother. Plus, my mom isn't letting him drive anymore—not even a car. Definitely not the Harley. Nothing with wheels. Not until he stops."

I look over in the direction of the truck sitting in the back. *The shiny grille grinning like teeth, the chrome stacks.* "So . . . the truck . . ."

Grace follows my gaze. "It just sits there. He has a job on the loading dock now." Then she takes out her phone and sends a text. She looks up at me and says, "Just letting my mom know."

"Know what?" I ask.

"That my plans changed. That I'm okay and you're not going to kill me." She looks up. "You're not gonna kill me, right?"

"Right."

Then she puts her phone away and starts moving toward the bike. "You coming?" she calls over her shoulder.

Will looks at me and shrugs. Then I see his face shift, and he has this look like, *How hot is she?*

"I thought you had a sort of on-and-off girlfriend back home."

"I totally made that up."

"But you're still not gay?"

"Jesus! That's not how it works, Asher! I just said I had a girlfriend so you'd know that I wasn't interested in Sloane."

"Then go for it," I tell him as I watch Grace head over toward Henry. "Just don't do anything to mess this up until *after* we take Sloane and her dad on a spin down Beale Street on that flaming-red Harley-Davidson CVO Street Glide Milwaukee-Eight Screamin' Eagle."

"What the hell? You know what kind of bike that is?"

"Been doing some research."

"Since when?"

"Since I figured out that I might have to steal a hog."

We both look over at the bike.

"It delivers one hundred sixty-six newton meters of torque," I say.

"What does that mean?"

"No fucking clue."

Will smiles.

Then I text Sloane that we got her a bike and tell her to meet us on Beale Street. She writes back, How will I find you?

I type, Look for the biggest, baddest cherry-red hog, and me and Grace will be on it.

She writes, I'm guessing that Grace is the girl you were supposed to take to the prom?

I type, No. You're the girl I was supposed to take to the prom.

She sends me back a heart emoji and three motorcycles.

Will's looking over my shoulder as I type, so I tell him to stop reading my texts.

"Nervous habit," he says. "Full disclosure. I've been texting with your dad, too."

I let that sink in. "*What?? When?*"

"This whole time. Your dad was worried. And with Shirley. I've been texting Shirley."

"Who's Shirley?"

"Sloane's mom. Oh, and I've been texting with Anna and Claire, too."

"*Why?*"

"I miss Michael, so I kind of like having fake adoptive sisters," he says. "Three of them."

I think about that. "I could use the help with Chloe," I say. "And Anna and Claire are a mess."

Will smiles. "You have to get Chloe a phone, then. You know, so we can text without your dad."

"Jesus, Will. She's four."

He shrugs.

Grace, from the look of things, has convinced Henry to climb off the bike. I call over to her, "You can't drive a motorcycle in those shoes."

She yells back, "The hell I can't!" and then just to prove that I'm wrong, she straddles the hog with her heels on.

She looks intimidating in her bike shorts and Sloane's pink sweater and her purple strappy heels.

"Is she real?" Will asks.

"Like *real*, real?" I ask as we watch Henry hand Grace the helmet and then unstrap Evelyn from the back of the hog. "Or real like . . . Evelyn?"

"Right now I'm thinking real like Ms. Marvel from the Avengers," Will says. "Or maybe Elektra or She-Hulk."

I tell him that I don't know what real is anymore. Or if it matters.

"Is she a villain or a hero?" he asks.

"Hero," I respond.

"Cyborg or human?" he asks with a smirk.

"Not entirely sure," I say.

"Do you think she has superpowers?"

Grace revs the engine of the bike.

I say, "Probably."

Will says, "I'm in love."

I tell him to collect Henry and Evelyn, take the Jeep, and meet us on Beale Street. Then I run over to Grace, and she hands me a helmet, and I climb onto the back of the bike, put the helmet on, drop the visor, and slip my arms around her. She revs the throttle. The hog roars. Then she asks, "You ready to make some noise, Asher Hunting?" Her voice is crystal clear coming through the speakers in the helmet. Jack Daniels is yelling and waving his arms, but we can't hear him; we can just see his face animated with anger and his arms flailing. Grace's mom is holding him back. I'm guessing Jack Daniels told her who I am. I'm also guessing she trusts Grace's instincts because when Grace looks over at her, her mom waves.

"Where to?" Grace asks.

"The hog rally on Beale Street," I say.

"And after?" she asks.

It feels really good knowing that there's going to be an after because just a few minutes ago, I wasn't so sure.

Grace revs the throttle again.

"After," I say, "we take Henry and Evelyn to Graceland."

"Evelyn is *who*, exactly?"

"Long story," I say, and then the sky rumbles with thunder and a few drops of rain start to fall as I cling to the daughter of the man who killed my mom and we peel out of 114 Culvert Street at high speed on a cherry-red Harley-Davidson Screamin' Eagle.

56

The rain comes down hard and heavy as we wind along the Mississippi River making our way into downtown Memphis, then slows to a light drizzle by the time I point to Sloane standing with Will and Henry and Evelyn on the corner of Beale Street and South Danny Thomas Boulevard. Grace surprised me and blasted Sailcat's "Motorcycle Mama" and Steppenwolf's "Born to Be Wild" and Mötley Crüe and Hendrix. Pure old-school, hard-core rock 'n' roll the whole way, not a single Ed Sheeran song in the mix. We rode hard and fast and loud, leaning into the corners and hugging the wet roads, weaving through traffic, tearing up the streets, me tucked in against her back, holding on tight.

"How'd they beat us here?" I ask through the headset, more than a little awestruck and breathless, after we come to a stop.

"We took the scenic route," Grace tells me. "The way I figure it, you owed me at least one dance tonight, and that was it."

I say, "I'm really sorry."

She says, "It's okay, really."

I ask, "Why?" and she surprises me and says, "I needed this too."

So I say, "Didn't see that coming."

And she says, "Me neither."

When Grace hops the bike up onto the sidewalk next to Sloane, we're soaked to the skin, and the streets are slick and shimmering with light; Beale Street's flashing neon and leather and hip-deep in bikes. Henry's got Evelyn covered in a plastic bag, and there's music and smoke and people spilling out onto the sidewalks and streets, and all this energy that's pumping hard and hot.

Grace sits there on the Harley, visor down, and blips the throttle a couple of times to rev the engine, and heads turn in our direction. Then she shuts the motor down, stands up straddling the bike in her purple heels, pulls her helmet off, and shakes out her hair. Wearing Sloane's pink sweater and those bike shorts, Grace turns every head on the street. Sloane is in awe as she eyes the Harley, not Grace, even as Grace announces to no one in particular that she was here a few weeks ago to hear Snoop Dogg and Cardi B, then looks around and comments that this rally is nothing compared to Wednesday nights.

"What happens Wednesday nights?" Will asks, as big-eyed and in awe of Grace as Sloane is of the Harley.

"Bike night," Grace tells him. "Thousands of bikers descend on Beale Street every Wednesday all summer. You can hear them swarm in and roar out even all the way to my house."

I hop off the bike, remove my helmet, then introduce Grace to Sloane, and even though I explained a little to Grace on the way over about Sloane and her dad and what she wants to do, it's awkward as hell, but then Henry jumps in and introduces Grace to Evelyn. I thought maybe they met back at Grace's house, but apparently not.

That part at least goes better than I thought it might. Henry goes through his rap about going on a whale watch and growing sweet peas and Evelyn being his everything, but he leaves off the part about the chocolate pudding and Evelyn being dead. Grace just eyes the box with the top of the urn peeking out of the plastic bag and listens, and then says, "I have my grandma stored in a similar fashion."

I cringe when she says "stored," but Henry doesn't seem to mind; he's just clutching Evelyn and beaming.

Grace turns to Sloane and yells over the din of the street, "I think I'm wearing your sweater."

Sloane says, "You're also riding my Harley," and Grace takes her in, standing there with her dad-sized leather motorcycle jacket and man boots, and I'm half expecting a fight, but Sloane smiles and Grace smiles back. Then she peels off her leather gloves and hands them to Sloane and gives her a crash course on the dos and don'ts of hog-riding that starts with the basics but quickly morphs into sounding more like a lesson in hog-tying or bullfighting than motorcycle-riding. Grace starts out saying stuff like *Mount from the left, like you would a horse*, but then it escalates to trickier technical shit like *If you want to shed speed, use the rear brakes, never the front*. And *Remember, brake before the curves, turn your head and eyes into the turns, accelerate and decelerate only on the straightaways and . . .*

I'm trying to listen and learn as she spews things out rapid-fire like *Don't tear open the throttle* and *Watch the turning radius*, and then I lean in and ask Sloane if she should be writing this down, but she dismisses me with a wave of her gloved hand. Grace keeps listing all the things to watch out for, and Sloane just looks back at her, starry-eyed, and then Grace does this upside-down peace sign thing with two fingers and tells Sloane that's one hog owner reminding another to keep two wheels on the pavement at all times, and I'm thinking, *Oh, shit!* But it's more like *OH, SHIT!*

as thoughts of me and Sloane doing wheelies up Beale Street and dying flash through my head.

Then Grace steps away from the bike, and Sloane's all big-eyed and red-faced as she slips her leg over the machine. Grace yells over the music, "Remember, all the fancy chrome and flashy tires on this crotch rocket might look cool, but they won't keep you safe. *You* have to do that." Then she hands Sloane her black, visored helmet, adding, "Take her for a rip, but nothing fancy. No pump wheelies or stoppies."

Sloane puts the helmet on, and Grace flips the GoPro mounted to the handlebars on, then steps back. Sloane looks over at me in wild-eyed, cliff-diving, thrill-seeking mode with an ear-to-ear but scared-shit smile on her face, and before she slips her visor down, she asks, "You coming with me?"

I climb onto the back of the bike, put my helmet back on, slip the visor down, and secure my arms around Sloane before I ask, "How many lessons did you take from that creepy guy you found on Craigslist?"

She says, "Not many."

I ask, "How many is *not many*?" and she says, "I'll tell you later."

I mumble, "Oh, shit!" but it's more like, OH, SHIT, WE'RE GONNA DIE! as Sloane starts the engine and we wobble and sputter, then lurch our way over the curb and off the sidewalk and back out onto Beale Street. After a loud and shaky start, Sloane finds her balance, and she gets to ride Jack Daniels's Screamin' Eagle up Neon Row wearing her dad's motorcycle boots and leather jacket, just like she wanted to. I'm sitting behind her, scared to death but not caring, arms wrapped around her waist, me hugging her tight as we roar past the Hard Rock, Wet Willie's, Blues Hall, and Silky O'Sullivan's.

I have to admit, *it's really something.* Then we take a wide turn at the corner of South Fourth Street, almost lay the bike down and spill onto the street because we're going too slow, but Sloane manages to recover with the help of a little extra speed and my extra set of feet on the pavement. Once we're stable, she's revving the throttle . . . *vroom vroom, vroom vroom* . . . as eyes turn in our direction, admiring the bike and the girl, me thinking, *They don't know the half of it.* Then Sloane pops the clutch, peels out, and fishtails, and my heart does a cliff dive as I fear we're gonna crash and skid across the pavement and that'll be how the Asher and Sloane story ends, but we just kind of do a wobble-four-footed-feet-down-try-again kind of lurch-y couple of embarrassing moves forward without actually tipping or spilling or stalling out, then find our balance, which I call a colossal win.

Things smooth out after we take a few runs up and down the street, Sloane getting more confident with each trip. When we finally stop and I'm standing there on Beale Street next to Sloane next to Jack Daniels's Screamin' Eagle, I'm happier than I've been in thirteen months, five days, fourteen hours, and way too many minutes for me to bother to count. I'm happy for Sloane mostly, but happy for me, too. This was her way of saying goodbye to her dad, and I have to admit, Memphis is something else when you ride in on rain-slicked streets at night on the back of a hog. Sloane leans in close to me and says, "My dad just wanted to have ribs and pulled pork and fried catfish and listen to some jazz and R and B on Beale Street."

I put my arm around her shoulder and say, "And here he is, doing just that."

She just smiles and smiles as we stand together on the sidewalk soaking it all in. The bikes parked three deep, the neon flashing, the street wet with summer rain, and Sloane's dad right here with us in our hearts and heads, and just maybe, standing by our side in front of the Blues City Cafe as the music of Earl "The Pearl" Banks floats out on the smoke of dreams and barbecued ribs, me thinking to myself, This is *good*. And this is *after*. A piece of life's high-hanging fruit Will said I'd have to reach high and hard for, and here I am, dangling from a ladder on my tippy-toes, arms reaching for the sun.

57

Two days later we say goodbye to Grace and start the drive back home. We take our time, stop *a lot*.

Linger.

We should have left first thing the morning after the hog rally, but Evelyn still needed to see Graceland. Grace made fast friends with Henry and Evelyn, and that first night when we stopped for something to eat at Applebee's on Union Avenue around midnight, Will looked over at Grace and asked me if she was real or if we'd made her up. And honestly it was hard to believe anything that happened that day was real, but then Grace ordered the chicken Caesar salad, just like the two Evelyns, and I leaned in close to Will and said, "There you go. That proves it. She ordered the chicken Caesar salad. She's real. All of this is real."

Grace even met up with us the next morning. Turns out her cousin works on the grounds of Graceland as a security guard, and she got him to sneak us in, picking us up in his golf cart like we were celebrities who could skip the line at the guest center. We bypassed the tickets and the shuttle bus, and he took us on a personal tour of Elvis's house and airplane—pointing out the white grand piano, the purple bathroom with the poodle wallpaper, all the animal horns, and Elvis's record collection. He showed us the jungle room with the green carpeted floor and ceiling and Elvis's crayon box and seventh-grade report card, and we ended the tour in the Meditation Garden, where he said "Elvis is buried."

"Or not buried," I reminded everyone as Henry smiled.

Grace's cousin even agreed to sneak us in that night, after dark, when Graceland was closed, so Henry could dance with Evelyn under the light of a thousand stars on the front lawn of the King's house.

So that night as the moon shone overhead and Henry swooped and turned, *one-two-three, one-two-three,* holding Evelyn on the front lawn of Graceland, he sang "Love Me Tender," and Grace hummed an Ed Sheeran song—the one that everyone knows about being really old and still in love and dancing under the light of the stars—and Will asked her to dance.

Then Sloane leaned in close to me, her cheek warm against mine as her eyes trailed Henry and Evelyn and they danced across the lawn. "I want that," she whispered.

"Everyone wants that," I whispered back. "It's everything."

Actually saying goodbye to Grace was awkward, partly because it was still weird between her and me, and partly because she and Will kind of had a thing. But unlike on the trip here, this time, on the drive back home, because we didn't want the trip to end, we didn't mind going thirty-nine miles per hour or driving in the breakdown lane.

Sloane and me hold hands in the back, kiss in potato chip aisles, and knock over soup cans in rest stops. We play *Best movie kiss ever* and *If Elvis isn't dead* and talk about where we'll go later this summer, and Henry tells us all the places Evelyn wants to visit with us. Will texts Grace whenever we stop—and when he's not driving—

and Henry holds Evelyn on his lap the whole way. We eat too many Triple Chocolate Meltdowns at too many Applebee's en route from Memphis to home, not self-conscious or feeling like we have to offer anyone an explanation when we ask for a table for eight.

Running out of places to go, and still not wanting to call this journey of ours over, we pull off the highway to stop in some random town in West Virginia so Will can get his hair cut.

Sloane heads into a store, and I wait with Henry in the parking lot because he says, "Evelyn gets her hair done at home, and she's too tired to shop."

"It looks good," I tell Will when he walks out of the Supercuts. "Seriously."

Short on the sides and long on top—not long enough to hang in front of his eyes, though.

I figure maybe that's a good sign—maybe he doesn't need that helmet of his to hide behind anymore.

He looks around the parking lot like he's seeing the world for the first time.

"Do you feel naked?" I tease. "You know, like when they clip a poodle for the first time?"

He laughs and says, "Kind of."

"And that feels . . . ?"

"Liberating."

"I Googled the bat thing," I tell him as we stand next to the Jeep. "You know, when I was waiting for you."

"And?"

"And . . . basically, you lied. Bats don't always turn left when exiting a cave."

He kind of shrugs. Then he smirks. "So?"

"So? You fucking lied to me."

"It worked."

"What do you mean, 'it worked'?"

"I got you to turn right."

He's not wrong about that.

I offer him an M&M. Sloane picked up a giant bag at the last pit stop. He eats it.

"Now you have to tell me something about yourself."

Will smiles. "I have a new friend," he says. "Who has a new life. And it's not in Ecuador."

"Or prison," I comment.

"Or in an urn," he adds.

I hand him another candy, and he eats it.

"How does it turn out?" I ask. "I mean, your new friend's new life?"

"It turns out well," Will says. "Really, really well."

Sloane walks out of the store she was in and over to the car and then holds up her phone for me to see. I take it. It's a picture of Anna and Claire sleeping. "It's from last night," she says. "Do they look like they're breathing?"

I examine the image. Zoom in. *Scrutinize every detail.* "I'd say yes," I tell her. "What do you think?"

"I think so too," she says, looking over my shoulder at the picture.

I hand her the phone back. "What did they have for breakfast today?" I ask, and she sends her mom a text.

"Cheerios," she reports when her mom answers. "Why?"

"That proves it," I say. "If they were alive at breakfast, they were breathing in that picture from last night."

She says, "That's what I was thinking," and then she kisses me, and Henry smiles and says, "No hanky-panky, you two."

Then Sloane holds up another picture on her phone. "I posted this on my dad's Facebook page this morning."

It's a picture that Grace took of me and Sloane standing next to Jack Daniels's motorcycle after we parked it on Beale Street. The pavement is slick with rain; there are hundreds of bikes all around us. Sloane's wearing her dad's too-big motorcycle jacket and man boots, and she's holding the black Darth Vader helmet by her side as she leans against the bike. I have my arm around her. She looks so happy. We both do.

"Wow. It got a lot of likes," I say.

"Yeah, and half of them are from Elvis," she comments.

"*The* Elvis? Elvis, Elvis?" Will asks, looking over our shoulders.

Sloane shrugs.

Then Will pulls up a picture on his phone of Grace wearing her purple heels, pink sweater, and bike shorts and shows it to us, and then he starts singing . . .

"I'm in love, I'm in love, I'm in love, I'm in love. . . ."

Sloane smiles and yells, "Will, stop!"

But he just keeps on singing.

When we cross over the New Jersey border, I announce, "We'll be home in a couple of hours."

I'm driving; Henry's clutching Evelyn on his lap. His eyes are wide and his hair is floating like a halo above his head when I say, "You know, there's one more thing I have to do before we can put a fork in this."

"Put a fork in what?" Will asks.

"This whole journey we went on."

"What's that?" he asks.

"I never finished reading my mom's letter." I catch Will's eye in the rearview mirror.

"What letter?" he asks, and Sloane leans over and whispers something to him as I add, "I think I know a good spot to do it."

58

When we get to the place that's 3.7 miles from the second marker on 287 West where my life got incinerated thirteen
months and too many days and hours and minutes ago to count, I
pull over into the breakdown lane, stop the car, and get out. Will
and Sloane step out of the car too, and I just turn and look back in
the direction of the mall as they help Henry and Evelyn out onto
the pavement.

We all stand there for a few minutes on the side of the highway
as the cars and trucks fly by. Henry's clutching Evelyn and he's got
Sloane's sweater draped over the top of the box as his wisps of hair
fly around his head in the wind.

I thought that standing here, like this, in the exact spot where
it happened, would trigger memories. I thought I would hear the
horn, taste the fear, see the smoke, feel the heat of the fire as the
orange flames licked the black paint and devoured my mom's car.
I thought it would all come tumbling back into my head. But even
as I look down the highway expecting to relive what happened,
expecting to see a flash of chrome, the grille of Jack Daniels's
tractor trailer grinning like death bearing down on me, I just see
a road.

I close my eyes, wait for the screams, the sirens, the voices . . . but they don't come. There's no big rig barreling down the highway, no soccer cleat sitting on the side of the road, spilled out of the box. No Jack Daniels's face, bloated and red, stumbling toward me.

I squeeze my eyes tight. Call forth all those images that have haunted me for the past year. But there are no flashes, no memories from that day.

I open my eyes and see Sloane and Will and Henry and Evelyn and, next to them, the pavement running east and west, and it's just a road, like a thousand others, full of people coming and going.

I turn and look toward the place where the grass meets the trees and think, *We see them sometimes when we drive by, the crosses and flowers—markers where someone died in a crash.* And then we think, *That's sad, I can't believe someone died here, came here and left flowers, dropped tears, planted a cross, left a memorial. . . .*

And here I am. With nothing to leave, nothing to mark the place where my mom's life ended.

And then I remember the baseball bat I'd planned to kill Jack Daniels with.

I take it from the trunk of the car and place it like a monument on the side of the highway where the grass meets the trees and my life almost got incinerated thirteen months ago.

Then I walk back to the car, open the trunk again, and take my mom's letter out.

59

The back of the envelope pops open almost like it has wings. I remove the single sheet of powder-blue paper and unfold it, then stare at the tiny perfect words.

I read the *Dear Asher* part, with the fancy loop of the *A* and the swoop of the *r*, and then read the second line that says, *Today is the most important day of your life, and mine.*

And then I read the part about me being perfect.

Next, I take a breath and close my eyes, and I see flowers. So many flowers that it's like my mom never left. I see sweet peas, the vines climbing, clinging to anything that will hold them up. I see roses with thorns, dandelions poking their heads out of cracks in the concrete. Then I open my eyes and I see Will and Sloane and Henry and Evelyn; and Will's little brother, Michael, playing baseball; Sloane's dad barbecuing; Chloe playing bear picnic; my dad looking happy again. I see Peter Pan and *The Little Prince*, and I see my mom. And she's not burning up; she's living, and I think, *I just needed to move my chair a little in order to see the sun set on the other side of the world.*

I blink away tears. Look down at the pale blue sheet of paper again. The very first and the very last thing my mom ever said to me.

I can't bring myself to read the middle.

It's too much to handle. At least right now.

I tell myself that I'll just read the end. Peek at the last couple of lines like Sloane said she does when she reads a book.

Baby steps, I remind myself. *Recovery is about baby steps.* I walk back toward Sloane and Will and Henry and Evelyn and clear my throat. "Ready?" I ask.

They nod.

"I read the beginning already, and I'm skipping the middle."

Sloane whispers, "That's okay."

"Here it is, then. Last couple of lines." I clear my throat and start reading.

"Growing up, Asher, you're going to make mistakes."

My voice quakes. I blink away more tears.

"Lots of them. And so am I."

My shoulders heave. I take a breath, then continue.

"I just want to say, right here at the very beginning of our life together, before either of us has screwed anything up, that I forgive you, and I hope you'll always forgive me. For everything and anything. Big and small."

She signed it:

"Love, Mom"

The *L* has a fancy loop at the bottom, and both *m*s swoop up at the end.

I drop the letter to my side. Sloane takes my other hand into hers. Will says, "Now you have to do the hardest thing in the entire universe."

"What's that?" I ask through my tears.

"Listen to your mom," he says, "and forgive yourself. For everything and anything. Real or imagined. Big and small."

I look up at Will, and he has this *look* like he's gonna say something else. I say, "Don't. Quote. Kierkegaard."

He smiles and says, "Accept that life can only be understood backward; and yet it must be lived forward."

"That sounds like Kierkegaard. I told you not to quote Kierkegaard."

"It means that we all have to accept what we can't change or control, and move forward, even when we're afraid."

It's quiet for a minute. Then Will says, "You're gonna get mad. I have one more Will-ism."

"Just say it." I sigh.

"The best revenge is living your best life."

"Oh, shit, you didn't!" I say.

"Didn't what?" Will asks.

"Quote Oprah, again." I'm covering my ears, half laughing, half giving him shit, and totally listening.

Then Henry says, "My Evelyn loves Oprah," and everyone laughs.

After Will gets Henry strapped in the front seat with Evelyn tucked in on his lap, I wipe my eyes and face with the back of my arm and then carefully fold my mom's letter up, slip it into the envelope, and place it back into my bag in the back of the Jeep. Then I hand Sloane the book. The one with the white cover that has a picture of a little blond kid standing on a barren planet looking up at the stars, and I say, "You should really read this because sometimes when you're an elephant that gets swallowed by a boa constrictor and you draw a picture of it, the rest of the world just sees a hat."

She takes the book from me and says, "And sometimes you only have to move your chair a little, and you can see the sun set all the way on the other side of the world."

Will chimes in with "And sometimes a crate is just a crate, but other times it's a crate that holds everything that is important to you."

I look over at both of them in disbelief as cars and trucks whiz by. "So you guys have read *The Little Prince*?"

They nod.

"Both of you?" I ask, weirdly annoyed.

"Peter Pan," Sloane says as she hands the book back to me.

Will nods.

I keep looking at both of them. "Shit!"

"We knew her first," Will explains.

I toss the book into the trunk, then scrounge around in my bag for a piece of paper and a pen.

The paper I find is just a scrap—but I don't care. I start writing a letter to Chloe.

I write, *Dear Chloe.*

Nine perfect letters.

The *C* has a fancy loop at the bottom, and the *e* swoops up at the end.

Then I write:

Today is the most important day of your life, and mine.

I don't even know you yet, but I know that you are perfect.

And I just want to say, right here at the very beginning of our life together, before either of us has screwed anything up, that I forgive you, and I hope you'll always forgive me. For everything and anything. Big and small.

Then I sign it:

Love, Asher

The *L* has a fancy loop at the bottom, and the *r* swoops up at the end.

The letter is missing the entire middle, but I figure, *It's something. It's a start.*

Then I fold the paper up, put it into the bag next to the letter that my mom wrote to me, and slam the trunk closed.

60

When we get back in the car, Henry's already asleep. Will looks up from his phone and turns to Sloane and says, "Grace just posted the video from the motorcycle's GoPro on YouTube. I sent you guys the link. She said it's going viral." Then he adds, "You know, Sloane . . . if you do marry Asher . . ."

"Don't get ahead of yourself," she warns.

"I mean in a hundred years. I'm just saying that *if you do*, I can walk you down the aisle."

Sloane's sitting in the back, still wearing her dad's motorcycle boots and his leather jacket, and as she looks at Will with her biker-chick, kick-ass smile, she says, "It's a deal. I mean, you can fucking walk, so why not?"

My phone pings twice. I look at it. It's the YouTube link from Will and a text from my dad. I look up from the phone. "My dad says I have to hurry home because we're out of aluminum foil."

Will asks, "Is that code for something else?"

I say, "It's code for *he's trying*."

Sloane gets this super-serious look and says, "Electromagnetic radiation?"

I smile. Then shrug. Catch her eye in the rearview. "I cover Chloe's hands. Just at night."

Sloane says, "I make Anna and Claire helmets. Just at night."

Will says, "What the fuck???"

Sloane ignores him. "We'll grab some aluminum foil when we get off the highway, Asher. There's a Super Savers near the exit."

Then she Googles something on her phone and calls out, "Hey, there's a brand-new Applebee's off Exit 45. We could be there in eighteen minutes."

Will says, "That's in the wrong direction."

We all smile.

Henry wakes up in time to say, "Evelyn loves Applebee's."

Sloane says, "And I'm starving."

I say, "Applebee's it is, then."

When we arrive, I ask for a table for eight.

The waitress seats us and then says, "When the rest of your party arrives, I'll bring them over."

I say, "That won't be necessary. They're already here."

Then Sloane looks at me with that smile of hers, and she does that upside-down peace sign thing with two fingers that one hog owner does to remind another to keep two wheels on the pavement at all times, and I'm thinking, *Hell yes!* But it's more like *HELL YES!* as thoughts of me and Sloane doing wheelies all summer and not dying even a little bit flash through my head.

Then my phone pings. It's a text from Peter Pan. It says, You guys coming tonight?

Before I pick up the menu to order four entrées plus two grilled chicken Caesar salads for the two Evelyns, the Bourbon Street steak and garlic mashed potatoes for Sloane's dad, the chicken mac and cheese from the kids' menu for Michael, a Coke, two Earl Grey teas, and eight Triple Chocolate Meltdowns, I look over at Sloane and Will and Henry and type . . .

Most definitely.

Acknowledgments

Four for the Road is a work of fiction, which obviously means that it's not based on real events or real people—which obviously means that I completely made it up. But, the truth is, in the process of writing this completely made-up story, the characters became very real to me—like honest-to-God, flesh and blood, real-real. I'm not exactly sure when that happened, but it did.

So, first and foremost, I would like to thank Asher and Henry for allowing me to share their story of love and loss with the outside world. I am grateful to you both for how much you love the people you love. And I hope that when all is said and done, I got your story right, showed respect for your grief, and didn't embarrass you too much. I also sincerely hope that your story will help others struggling with profound loss, because somewhere along the way—many somewheres, in fact—we all face it, and it is so very hard to process and hurts so very much.

I also owe a dept of gratitude to the two Evelyns for playing such important roles in this story. As for Asher's mom, Evelyn, I'm sorry about Jack Daniels and the car crash. *Really sorry.* I know that I could have written you a better outcome. For Henry's Evelyn, I'm sorry that I kept you in an urn/box the entire time. In that regard, you took one for the team. But please know that your very existence is the heart and soul of this story, so perhaps, in time, you can forgive me for the whole urn/box, you-were-dead-when-the-story-started thing. Afterall, I gave you Henry, and he was your everything.

I would also very much like to thank Sloane and Will for being such great friends to Asher. You are the type of friends I hoped you would turn out to be when you first showed up on the page. In fact, you are the type of friends I hope everyone gets to have when they are growing up. Friends who chew up our bad thoughts when we can't, and who save us from ourselves when we don't know how to save ourselves. Friends like you should be a birthright; friends who hold our hands so we won't drift away and who teach us to breathe slowly and to trust love again when it has betrayed us—even when the voices in our heads are telling us that we can't. But more than that, you, Will and Sloane, are the type of friends who make sure that we leave the gun and take the cannoli when we are about to do something that will destroy our lives, so I thank you for that.

I would also be remiss if I didn't thank Asher's dad for putting up with him and thank Chloe for sleeping in a bike helmet and life preserver—in both cases, that was way beyond the call of duty. But it was very clear to me that in addition to great friends, Asher needed a dad with tremendous emotional stamina and an adorable younger sister who plays bear picnic and refuses to eat pepperoni—or any other orange meat cut into circles—simply to remind him of what is important.

I am also grateful to Peter Pan for not ripping up her therapist license and taking a job as a pillow tester or cookie baker. The world needs supportive people like you, people with soft voices and freckles, just the right smile, and large bags of M&M's; caregivers who have super hearts and superpowers, and who do the hard work of helping us pick up the pieces when we fall apart.

But honestly, of all the characters in *Four for the Road*, I owe the largest debt of gratitude to Grace. Let's face it, the whole catfishing and driving-to-Memphis-to-kill-your-dad thing could have gone south in a thousand different ways. So, for starters, I need to thank you, Grace, for not reporting Asher to the FBI cyber-crimes unit for violating Section 2261 of the Interstate Anti-Stalking Punishment and Prevention Act. I also have enormous gratitude that you can ride a Harley in heels and shamelessly rock bike shorts under evening attire. The fact is, the world needs more girls like you. The strong, brave type who don't topple easily—and who never topple because a love interest does them wrong. Clear-thinking, independent girls with fair, just hearts who love both Ed Sheeran and Jimmy Hendrix, and who don't let others define them; girls who willingly wear confidence and integrity in place of a prom dress when the situation calls for it; girls who know to lean into the turns, and who can still find a way to dance when the roads are slick and the ground threatens to fall out from underneath them.

But . . . as you might suspect, *Four for the Road* wouldn't be possible without the help of some actual living, breathing, hard-working, talented *real people*, too—some actual book people I didn't make up in my head, and I am so very grateful for all of their support and hard work as well.

At the tippy-top of this real-people list is Alex Borbolla, the editor at Atheneum who fell in love with Asher and Henry's story and then managed to convince her co-workers to buy a book about dead people who eat at Applebee's—that could not have been easy—so, thank you for that, Alex! And thank you for reading and rereading the manuscript, for providing such clear and insightful editorial notes, and for shepherding this project the enormous distance from words on a page to book on a shelf. Your eye for pacing and your love of character and voice and language—along with your enthusiasm and big heart—give you great creative sensibility and editorial insight, while your gentle and supportive bedside manner made the whole process of tightening and polishing and—Oh, Dear God—cutting and deleting, practically painless, if not an absolute delight.

I would also like to thank the rest of the talented Atheneum team for doing the hard work of the business of book publishing; for packaging this story up so beautifully and sending it off into the world polished and pretty. Thank you to Karyn Lee for designing such a striking and pitch-perfect cover, and heartfelt thanks to Guy Shield for the beautiful artwork and artistic vision—and thank you for adding the sweet peas! I am grateful to Rebecca Vitkus and Clare McGlade for the meticulous copyedit, and your restraint and understanding regarding the "comma problem," and for your deft handling of Asher's rambling inner monologues. Thank you to Tatyana Rosalia in production, Tara Shanahan in publicity, and everyone else involved in the technical and laborious behind-the-scenes work of making this book the best it could be. I greatly appreciate your collective knowledge and professionalism, and your ability to be such good cheerleaders throughout the entire process.

As for my agent, Molly O'Neill, and the rest of the crew at Root Literary, an enormous THANK YOU!! I have tremendous respect and gratitude for your talent and expertise. Molly, as I have told you too many times to count, you are the absolute best. A force and shining star in every way. You know more about books and publishing than seems possible. Your love for the art and the craft of writing makes your contribution to every project invaluable. I also know that dealing with writers (read, *me*) is not always easy. And I know that I probably annoy you more than most, but you are nice enough to pretend that I don't. I thank you for that, and for so much more. You are a brilliant literary agent, and I don't know how anyone can be as smart as you are or know so much about books, what makes them shine, and how to sell them, so all I can say is thank you again, and lucky me! ☺

I also owe a debt of gratitude to reviewers, librarians, booksellers, and readers. You are the whole reason books are written—without you, writers would simply be felling trees alone in the forest with no one hearing a sound, so thank you for taking the time to read and comment and cherish books.

To my family: Yes, it is finally true. I have finished this book. So, a huge thank-you to my husband, Tom, and my daughter, Kate, for reading and rereading early drafts and late drafts—and every draft in between—and for loving Asher and Henry perhaps even more than I do. Thank you both for your unrelenting support and endless patience and for sharing my love of writing. Also, thank you to J.M. for giving me boy-think and soccer; to Kenzie for sharing my love of flowers and for playing bear picnic and for taking the no-orange-meat-cut-in-circles rule all the way to no-meat-ever for both of us. And a huge thank-you to River Flynn for reminding me how much I love books with pictures in them, and for teaching me the Daniel Tiger song. And, yes, since you've all asked at one point or another, I actually did buy a pair of lime green Nike Superflys in men's size 11½. And yes, I have been driving around with them in my car. And no, it's not *that* weird, so don't worry. And one final thought: As for the whole carrying-a-deceased-loved-one-around-in-an-urn/box—no worries there either. That's strictly a Henry and Evelyn thing. I promise. ☺